the
wish

Born in New Zealand, Heather Morris is passionate about stories of survival, resilience and hope. In 2003, while working in a large public hospital in Melbourne, Heather was introduced to an elderly gentleman who 'might just have a story worth telling'. The day she met Lale Sokolov changed both their lives. Lale's story formed the basis for *The Tattooist of Auschwitz* and the follow-up novel, *Cilka's Journey*. In 2021 she published the phenomenal conclusion to the Tattooist trilogy, *Three Sisters*, after being asked to tell the story of three Holocaust survivors who knew Lale from their time in Auschwitz-Birkenau. *Sisters Under the Rising Sun*, a heart-wrenching novel based upon the experiences of women in Japanese POW camps, was published in 2023 to great acclaim. Together, her novels have sold more than 19 million copies worldwide. *The Wish* is Heather's first contemporary novel.

Also by Heather Morris
The Tattooist of Auschwitz
Cilka's Journey
Three Sisters

Sisters under the Rising Sun

Stories of Hope

the
wish

Some stories live forever

HEATHER
MORRIS

ZAFFRE

First published in the UK in 2025 by
ZAFFRE
An imprint of Bonnier Books UK
5th Floor, HYLO, 105 Bunhill Row,
London, EC1Y 8LZ

A CIP catalogue record for this book is available from the British Library.

Hardback ISBN: 978-1-78658-216-4
Trade paperback ISBN: 978-1-78658-217-1

Also available as an ebook and an audiobook

1 3 5 7 9 10 8 6 4 2

Typeset by Envy Design Ltd
Printed and bound in Great Britain by Clays Ltd, Elcograf S.p.A.

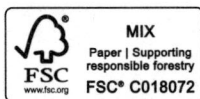

MIX
Paper | Supporting
responsible forestry
FSC
www.fsc.org
FSC® C018072

The authorised representative in the EEA is Bonnier Books UK (Ireland) Limited.
Registered office address: Floor 3, Block 3, Miesian Plaza, Dublin 2, D02 Y754, Ireland
compliance@bonnierbooks.ie
www.bonnierbooks.co.uk

To Toni and Ian who battle and never give up
and
To social workers everywhere – you make a difference

CHAPTER 1

'**H**i, waves, how are you today? Having a rough one? Me too.'

The question is shouted into the wind and the ocean answers, slapping a wave against a rocky outcrop on the beach where fifteen-year-old Jesse sits, dangling her legs above the water. It's late summer, but despite the heat, she wears a long-sleeved T-shirt and shorts, far too big for her, belted tightly around her narrow waist. A large floppy hat in bright neon pink protects her face and neck from the sun. She's very slender and tall, with big brown eyes in a pale face. A gentle spray reaches her knees and she smiles as she watches the water merge back into the body of the ocean.

'You know why I'm here today, don't you? Why we need to talk?'

Another wave crashes into the rock and this time the water sends a salty mist right up to her waist.

'Thank you. So here goes: when Mum went to get Sammy from his friend's place yesterday, I called Kelly, my social worker. She's been there for me ever since it all started – well, you know how long she's been in my life. We had a talk

1

a couple of weeks ago and I told her what I wanted, if the time came. So yesterday I asked her to make it happen.'

The next wave slams into the rock, throwing seawater all over her. She laughs and wipes her face. 'Don't be like that, you knew this was coming.'

When the next wave reaches the bottom of the rock, it breaks in two, swooshing up around the girl, as if trying to embrace her.

'Thank you. But it's going to be fine and, more importantly, my family is going to be fine. But now it's time for me to make sure my wish comes true.'

'Jesse! Come on, honey, it's time to go.'

Jesse doesn't turn around at hearing her name called. She knows it's fanciful to be talking to the waves but she's always felt an affinity with the sea, especially when she sits on this particular spot, looking out at her favourite view in all the world. The spray of an incoming wave hits her in the face, drenching her. She squeezes water from her shorts and in doing so recognises how slack they are around her legs. These legs that had grown too long a few years back for her to continue her passion for gymnastics, and her feet turned into two lefts as she'd continued ballet classes. Wriggling her toes, she smiles. 'But you never slowed me down, did you?' she laughs to herself. Athletics had become her thing, once she'd accepted that she'd never be a prima ballerina. Had things been different, she would have been competing in the under-16s this year, and who knows where she would have gone on to from there?

A gust of wind whips around, lifting her now-soggy floppy hat from her head, but she catches it before it flies away. She rubs her hand over her scalp, enjoying the feeling of the downy regrowth. She'd been delighted to discover it was growing back the colour it had been when she was younger, a soft strawberry-blond, the envy of her friends. When she'd hit puberty, it had turned a mousy brown and she and her mum had expected it to regrow the same.

'Jesse, please, we have to go.'

Jesse sighs, and her smile dissolves. Her mother Mandy is standing below her, beckoning for her to come down. Jesse looks at her mum and her heart aches. Since she was little, everyone said there was no denying that they were mother and daughter. She laughed every time she heard this. To Jesse, her mother is the most beautiful woman in the world, and she does not see that same beauty in herself. A few feet away from her mum, her eight-year-old brother, Sam, plays in the sand. He has the same strawberry-blond hair, bleached lighter by the sun. He, too, seems to be ignoring their mum, filling a bucket with sand only to plonk it haphazardly down, with no interest in creating anything resembling the elaborate castles the two of them have made in the past. Jesse has always felt connected to Sam – a typical protective older sister – and she hates how what's happening to her is affecting his childhood, denying him the puppy he craves, the vacations and outings they once had. She scrambles down the rocks to her mother and hugs her.

'Come on, Sam!' Mandy calls to her son.

Sam acts like he didn't hear her and continues pushing sand into piles.

'Sam!' Mandy calls out louder.

'I'll get him, Mum. You go on, we'll be right behind you,' Jesse tells her mother.

Mandy looks at her daughter, shaking her head. 'I knew you'd be drenched; there's a change of clothes inside the back door.'

Jesse kneels in the sand beside her brother. Gently, she lifts Sam's chin. At first, he resists but then he gives in. Looking into his eyes, Jesse sees how worried he is. She knows that he wants to delay the inevitable, to stay here on the beach that he loves so much, in the hope that perhaps if they don't face it, it will all go away. She knows how he's feeling because she once felt exactly the same way.

'We've got to go, Sam,' Jesse whispers.

'I'm not ready,' Sam bites back.

'I know, I know. I'm not either. But we still have to go.'

Taking his hand, Jesse pulls Sam to his feet and reluctantly he allows her to lead him away from their sanctuary: the beach, the water, the shells, the driftwood that he loves to collect, the smell of the sea. A place of peace. 'Why can't I live here?' she remembers him asking their mother when Jesse first became sick.

They make their way to the gate that separates their property from the beach. As they pass through, Mandy hands them each a towel. Using the outside tap, they rinse their feet and dry them off before putting on the sandals their mother hands them. They walk slowly up the path

4

that connects the beach to their rear deck with its hammock, empty now but once Jesse's favourite spot to read, nap or gaze at the waves beyond. Another thing to leave behind. She follows her mother inside their modest home. There is no comforting smell of dinner cooking or freshly baked cookies cooling down on the bench for Sam to snatch. The table is bare, no places are laid. When Mandy and Sam return home later, Jesse knows that dinner will be taken from the freezer and reheated in the microwave, or it might have to be a sandwich if it's close to Sam's bedtime.

'Get changed, honey, everything else is in the car, we will wait for you there,' their mum says as Sam follows her through the house to the car waiting in the driveway.

Within minutes Jesse joins them outside. Before she gets in the car, she looks back at her home. Her eyes wander up to the window of the bedroom where she has spent more time than a girl her age should.

'I'll be back,' she whispers. She's not sure if it's a promise to the house or to herself.

The dreamcatcher hanging inside the window flutters back at her. She must have left the fan on in her bedroom. She considers telling her mum and going inside to turn it off, but she knows Mandy will go into her room after Sam is asleep anyway. She will sit on Jesse's bed, cuddle one of the soft toys and weep. Just thinking about how this will unfold, knowing there is nothing she can do to make things easier for her mum, causes Jesse to slump against the car. The heat from the car panel sears through her thin clothes and she jumps back. Head down, she takes her place in the front passenger seat.

In the back seat, Sam folds his arms defiantly and stares out the window as Mandy drives out of their quiet street and onto the main beach road, homes and apartments on one side, the grassed foreshore leading to the beach on the other. Outside of the car, bathed in the warm, golden light of early evening, people are going about their normal lives. Couples walk hand in hand, parents chase small children into the shallow waves, dogs run after sticks or balls thrown for them.

Something catches Jesse's eye, and she pushes her hat further back on her head to see better. With that gesture, a memory comes back to her. Her father had bought her this hat six months ago, after she had left her favourite one in the hotel room during their last holiday, despite having been reminded not to leave it behind. Jesse had seen the perfect replacement in a shop, and dragged her tall middle-aged dad in with her, where he'd stood out like a sore thumb amongst all the pastels and neon-coloured clothes. 'What do you reckon?' he had asked the assistant, putting the hat on and modelling it for them before plonking it on Jesse's head with a wink. She remembers the smile on his face; she knew she was forgiven. Always.

My last holiday, she thinks for a moment. *Was that my last ever holiday?* Then, she remembers what it was that had made her push her hat back to get a better look. A brightly coloured hot air balloon hanging low over the water. It is so close that Jesse can see the people inside the basket. They are laughing and hugging each other. She waves to them; they don't wave back – they can't see her.

'I could never go in one of those,' Mandy says, glancing away from the road to see what her daughter is looking at.

'I'd love to. To be flying free like a bird, it must be wonderful. What do you think, Sam?' Jesse asks.

Not even a grunt comes from the back seat. Jesse and her mother exchange a glance, sadness returning to their faces.

'We're here,' Mandy whispers.

Having found a parking spot, Mandy gets the suitcase out of the boot while Jesse opens the rear door and holds her hand out to Sam. He ignores it. Gently she reaches in and undoes his seat belt before coaxing him out of the car. Hand in hand, they follow Mandy into the building. They take the lift, grateful for the stops to their floor that discharge the other passengers. As the doors open and they step out, all three pause and look at the sign in front of them.

PAEDIATRIC ONCOLOGY WARD, 6 EAST

CHAPTER 2

The doors automatically open, inviting them to take the steps that will lead them to the place that has become Jesse's second home.

'Deep breath,' Mandy says, squeezing Jesse's hand.

Jesse, in turn, squeezes Sam's, though he doesn't respond, instead gazes sullenly at his sandals.

Before they have taken two steps inside the ward, the warm greetings of staff, other patients and their family members bring genuine smiles to Mandy's and Jesse's faces. Nobody wants to be here, but everyone is trying to put on as brave a face as they can. The walls are painted in bright, vibrant colours, and light streams in through the windows. The three of them make their way down the corridor, past a mural of an underwater scene, where friendly fish, sharks, octopuses and dolphins wave hello. Mandy and Sam stop at the nurses' station to sign Jesse into hospital as she continues to her usual room. She pauses for a moment in the doorway, watching a girl her own age, cross-legged on a hospital bed, engrossed in her Switch.

'Taking you a while,' Jesse says, and grins as the girl looks up.

'Jesse!' The console is thrown down on the bed just as Jesse lands on it. The two girls hug and laugh. Amy is four months older but Jesse half a foot taller. Amy's Scottish heritage is reflected in her pale complexion dotted with freckles, and her striking green eyes complement what there is of her fiery red hair. Amy flicks Jesse's hat off, revealing her tufts of hair, too short to style. The girls rub each other's downy head playfully.

The two beds are close together, next to each is a bedside locker-cum-table that holds the few precious possessions the girls bring with them, with a water jug and glass on top. Two chairs near each bed are the only other furniture in the room. Either side of the beds, the walls are covered in large pinboards. Photos, posters, letters, dried flowers and drawings separated by creative borders provide a wonderful splash of colour in an otherwise drab room.

'Oh Jesse, why are you back here?' Amy says lovingly. 'You're the last person I wanted to share a room with – if you know what I mean.'

'I missed you. I wanted to be with you, and if this is the only place we can be together, then here I will be. OK?'

'You're such a liar, but I've missed you too. I mean, Ryan and Luke are OK, but they can be such a pain.'

'Mum told me they're back too. Well, let's make the most of it: the dream team are back together, and everyone better beware.'

The girls laugh, and hug again.

'Do they know I'm back?' Jesse asks.

'Yeah, they came in a while ago to annoy me and saw the pictures. Your dad was here earlier today.'

Jesse looks over at the bed she knows is waiting for her. The opposite wall is covered in family photos, her poster of Taylor Swift, along with her other favourite singer, Harry Styles. Her father has been in and put it all back up for her. She smiles. The fact that her favourite possessions and memories are packed into a small case, ready to be taken from her home to a room in a hospital, and that this has long been considered normal, is a joke she and Amy share. 'Doesn't every teenager have such a case packed and ready, aren't they all waiting for the day they'll return to the children's ward?'

'I see you still think Harry is hot,' Amy says jokingly.

'I mean, look at him, and he has the best voice.'

'For a guy, I guess. Did you hear Chappell Roan might do another tour?'

'Might. That would be amazing!'

Amy sees Mandy and Sam cautiously enter the room. 'Hey, Mrs Morgan,' she calls out. 'Hi, Sammy, are you OK?'

'Hello, Amy, how are you doing?' Mandy asks.

'Great!' Amy replies before glancing guiltily at Jesse. 'I mean, you know, OK I guess, Mrs Morgan.'

Sam hasn't responded to Amy's greeting and is still gazing at his feet. Jesse quickly looks from her mother to Sam, then grabs the video game Amy had thrown on the bed.

'What're you playing?'

Before Amy can answer, Jesse switches the game on.

'This is kids' stuff, come on, I'll beat your arse.'

'Jesse. Language,' Mandy says automatically.

'Sorry, Mum.'

'Bring it on,' Amy yells as she knocks the console from Jesse's hands, ending the game Jesse started. 'My turn.'

Mandy places the suitcase on Jesse's bed and begins emptying its contents into the drawers nearby, placing the most recent family photo on top of the bedside table. Sam curls up on Jesse's bed.

'When will Dad be here?' he says sullenly.

'He'll be here soon, he had to go to work,' Mandy tells her son, ruffling his hair.

'He always has to go to work,' Sam snaps back. He snuggles down on the bed, watching the girls playing, his eyes slowly softening and lighting up as they laugh and jostle one another.

CHAPTER 3

'Inspire a Wish.' A hand slaps Alex Daniels on the shoulder with phoney bonhomie.

Alex is hunched over his console at his workstation, screens surrounding him. On each screen are panes of code, animated sequences competing with timelines running at the bottom. To the side are panels of reference documentation and system notes, all needing to be considered, added or deleted. To the untrained eye, what Alex is working on would be incomprehensible. In this windowless room, Alex sits every day with several other men and women, each engaged in the quest to bring a virtual world onto the screens and into the headsets and homes of families across the world.

Alex chooses to ignore the words of his boss and shakes the hand from his shoulder, continuing to stare at his screen. He will turn thirty next birthday but looks much younger. He doesn't know where he got his six-foot-two frame from but he knows it wasn't from his mother: in the handful of photos he has of the two of them together, she appears as a petite woman, slight of frame. Judging by the photos, he did inherit his olive complexion and unruly dark hair from her.

His wavy hair refuses to be groomed and generally stands on end after a day at his desk, as it is now. Alex's vague memories of his mum calling him her Alexander the Great suggests to him that he has a strong link with Greece. Other than that, his origins are a mystery, just like the father he never knew.

'Inspire a Wish, Alex, did you hear me?'

'I wish you would go back into your office and let me get on with what you pay me to do. Inspirational enough for you?'

Ian Williams, the son-in-law of the owner of TriOptic Studios, your basic nepo-baby, swivels Alex's chair around and leans down, his face too close.

'The organisation, stupid. Inspire a Wish, you know? They help sick kids get a trip to Disneyland or meet their favourite footballer, whatever it is that will brighten their day. That's what I'm talking about.'

'OK? But I'm not sure what you're after and I'd better get back to it.' Alex swivels his chair firmly back around. With his mouse, he moves an animated sequence into a live character playing the same game, watching as the timeline stretches on one screen, decreases on the other.

Looking around Alex's workspace, Ian whistles, playing to the others in the room, all of whom are listening intently while pretending not to and continuing to stare at their screens.

'To be honest, Alex, it doesn't surprise me that you don't know about such a worthy institution. Look at you, all wrapped up in yourself. No photos, nothing personal . . . You really are a loner, aren't you? Either that or you have a dark secret . . .'

Losing his concentration, Alex looks around at his colleagues' workspaces. He's been introduced, via photo, to all their partners and children, he's responded appropriately when one of them has proudly shown off the artwork his four-year-old produced at nursery: 'Yeah, for sure another Picasso there, Steve, should put him in art classes.' He contributed generously to the wedding present bought for Sarah when she married Claire a couple of months ago. Alex has no such occasions to mark. He doesn't think people would appreciate buying a gift for his dog – his only companion at home.

Ian knows this – he's needling Alex by pointing it out to the whole team. Alex clenches his fists, his jaw. But he's not going to give Ian the satisfaction of knowing how much he's affected him. Alex breathes deeply, centring himself, before inching his chair forwards as far as he can to put some space between him and his overbearing boss. He could stand and face him eye to eye – in fact, he'd be looking down on Ian's bald head. But he's feeling a bit more generous today, so he makes do with reclaiming some personal space by extending his long legs, causing Ian to take a step back and stumble slightly. He might be the boss, but everyone knows it's only because he married Frank's daughter.

'Ian, what do you want? I'm right in the middle of combining the animated sequences with the live action in the final cut of *Stingrays Rule the Ocean*.'

'I've got a really important job for you. A bit of enthusiasm and appreciation wouldn't hurt.'

'Ian, I told you I'm busy.'

'That's not the attitude, Alex. Regardless of what I ask

you to do I expect "Thank you, Ian, how can I help? Tell me more".'

'OK. Thank you, Ian, how can I help? Tell me more.'

Ian clearly chooses not to notice the sarcasm. 'I need you to go to the Children's Hospital tomorrow at three. You'll meet a social worker there named, um, um . . . what's her name?'

'I don't know, Ian, how could I?'

'Kelly, that's it. Kelly something or other. I'm sure it doesn't matter, there can only be one social worker named Kelly. Anyway, she's got a kid there, a young girl, who wants her own video experience to be customised for her family. Apparently, she's really sick.'

'Whoa, wait up a minute, what are you talking about?'

'You need to listen, enough joking around. Frank, the man who pays your wages—'

'And yours,' Alex throws in.

Alex's words make Ian pause for a second. He hates being reminded that he's the boss's son-in-law, and Alex knows it.

'Frank got a call from a pal of his who knows the head of the local Inspire a Wish Foundation, asking us to help this kid out with a one-off video experience. Well, as you can imagine, Frank sees the chance for some positive PR for a change, instead of all this whining about how we're poisoning the minds of children. I got the word from Frank: make it happen and put your best designer on it. And Frank, not to mention my lovely wife, Cheryl, won't be pleased if we let him down.'

'Ah ha. So obviously you're asking your best designer.

The one with the biggest workload. Ask Steve, he's got kids, he'll be better at this.'

On the other side of the wall that divides their cubicles, Steve instinctively hunches down to make himself invisible. Alex registers this and sighs. It was worth a try.

'Sadly, you and I, as well as every other designer here, know you're the only one with full knowledge of 3D CGI. Frank wants the best; Frank asked for you. I told him that you would grumble every step of the way, but he wouldn't listen. Case closed as far as he's concerned. Three o'clock tomorrow. The Children's Hospital. Social worker. I told you her name.'

'And if I don't do it?'

'If you were bothered to look up occasionally from your millennial bubble, you'll see that business has been tough lately – mess up an opportunity for good PR like this and you're putting all your colleagues' jobs at risk. But yours would probably be the first to go.'

Alex and Ian lock eyes for a moment. Alex breaks contact and looks around the room. One by one his colleagues silently nod at him before looking away. No pressure, mate, they're all thinking. Take this one for the team. Everyone knows TriOptics needs a lucky break right now.

'Three o'clock tomorrow,' Ian repeats. 'Don't be late,' he throws at Alex as he walks away.

Steve gets up slowly and walks around to Alex's cubicle. He's the father of two young children, and Alex is sure that the thought of a very ill young girl at the Children's Hospital fills him with horror.

'Sorry, mate, you know how he is when his father-in-law tells him to do something.'

'Yeah, it's "how high do you want me to jump, Frank, what can I do to please you, Frank".'

'I gotta say, that's a tough gig . . .' Steve shakes his head. 'For a dad, a parent, that's the kind of thing you hope you never have to deal with. Might be easier on you, you know . . .'

Alex sighs. He knows Steve means well, but it's hard not to react to the underlying suggestion that he doesn't have a family to care about.

'We'll all help out if you need it.' Steve calls out to the others in the room, 'Won't we? People? Are you with me? We've got Alex's back?'

The mutterings of support, eyes still firmly on screens, don't fill Alex with confidence.

One by one, Alex's co-workers power down their computers. Around the crowded room screens flicker as slowly, individually and in small groups, they leave for the evening, laughing and chatting, calling out goodnight to Alex and telling him – as they do every night – not to stay late. The last to leave flicks off the main overhead lights, leaving the windowless room in semi-darkness except for the myriad of screens that surround Alex, illuminating him and casting a colourful glow.

Finally, Alex stands, stretches and looks around, realising everyone has left, yet again. He's been distracted all day, his focus gone since his conversation with Ian.

'No point staying here,' he says to himself.

Powering down his machines, he retrieves his motorbike helmet from under his desk, grabs his leather jacket from the back of his chair and struggles into it as he passes the helmet from one hand to the other. His mood is dark, his anger at being given an assignment out of the office hangs over him, and he hates the way that Ian chose to do it in front of everyone, making it impossible for him to say no. He's never been keen on socialising, he likes the work he does, squirrelled away at the end of the long room where he can ignore others and be largely ignored in return.

As Alex leaves the basement car park he is surprised by the strong sunshine outside. He's used to driving home much later, in the dark. His ride takes longer than usual, which doesn't improve his mood as he's driving through peak-hour traffic. Another reason to stay behind.

Turning into his street, a suburban cul-de-sac, his neighbours' kids' bikes and skateboards left outside in front gardens and basketball hoops sagging above garage doors, he slows down, never knowing when a child might run across the street on their way home for dinner after a play date. He arrives at his neat townhouse, the grass perfectly manicured from kerb to building, no flowers or bushes to worry about, the drive leading to the garage, where his ageing car waits for his bike to join it. He hits the remote, entering without needing to stop. His home is Alex's one luxury – that and his motorbike. A Ducati Panigale he spent a year saving for, now his pride and joy.

He is paid very well at TriOptic Studios, something that

leaves him more anxious than satisfied. This is the first time in his entire life that he's had a proper home, a place that's his, safe, where he can't be moved on from at short notice. Everything in his home is as he likes it: minimalist, clean, and all his. Growing up in the foster system, passed from one home to another, drove him to work and save, craving the security of a place of his own. The threat Ian made of him losing his job – and therefore his security – triggered Alex in a way that he doesn't want to acknowledge. Alex's childhood was far from picture-perfect. He was healthy, sure, but he was lonely, finding consolation and companionship in the games he played online, none of his carers pestered him with 'too much screen time', 'you'll get square eyes' comments he'd heard other kids repeat from their parents. He wishes someone had cared about him the way people seem to be caring about this sick kid. That's not her fault, he knows that. Still, it's hard not to feel resentful of other people's supportive families. Leaving his helmet on the bike seat, Alex enters the house from the internal door. Before he can call out, he is greeted by a large golden retriever who jumps up for his usual hug.

'Hey, Max, how was your day, buddy? Same old, same old, huh? Me too. Well, not quite, I'll tell you about it later.'

For the first time today, Alex smiles. Max makes his sadness and anger evaporate. They engage in their homecoming ritual of pats and cuddles before Max brings him his favourite toy to throw down the small hallway. Once they've had a play, Alex changes into shorts, a T-shirt and runners. 'It's early to eat. How about we go for a walk before dinner?'

Max jumps up excitedly at the word 'walk' and Alex attaches a lead to his collar.

Stepping out of the house, Alex and Max set a steady pace to the park at the end of the street. There, he releases Max from his lead to run free. Leaning against a large oak tree, he watches Max as his mind wanders back to the conversation with Ian. A small part of him has always wanted to go it alone, to create his own business, do things his way, rather than TriOptics'. But his fear of losing the stability he's worked so hard to create for himself means he's too scared to become his own boss. One day, maybe.

Alex picks up his pace on the run home; he needs to be in his safe place, his comfort zone. Kicking his shoes off when he enters the kitchen, he fills Max's bowl with dry food and carries it into the hall. Thinking of going to the hospital tomorrow has made him lose his appetite.

'Come on, boy, you can eat in my room.'

Opening the door to his office, Alex flicks on a small lamp before putting Max's bowl down beside one of his many dog beds. In the glow of dimmed light, Alex sits at a large desk and powers up the screen in front of him. One by one, the screens around him come alive, creating a kaleidoscope of colour. Code scrolls across the screens, alongside a host of animated figures, created with the help of artificial intelligence, that blur the line between the real and the imagined. He dreams of creating a way for everyday people to make a film of their lives at a quality beyond anything done today. A combination of homemade videos and what he is an expert at designing: 3D CGI. A way for families to leave recorded legacies of who they were and what they did. Family. The one thing denied him. The one thing he wishes no other child would grow up not knowing. A faint smile plays on his face as he reads the small text watermarked across each image: 'Designed by Alex Daniels, patent pending'.

Having scoffed down his dinner, Max ignores his comfortable bed, picking up a small soft toy. Curling up at Alex's feet, he tucks the toy under his chin and settles down for the evening.

CHAPTER 4

The floodlights of the car park disguise the setting sun. There are more vacant spaces to park in than earlier in the day.

In one car, Dean Morgan sits hunched, looking through the windscreen at the doors opening into the hospital. Dean is tall and rugged, his face lined with a worry that turns quickly to anger, making him look older than his forty years. His tanned skin, light brown hair and brown eyes have no doubt contributed to his stellar rise in the most prestigious law firm in the city. But he's not doing so well right now. The change in his confident, personal approach to colleagues, clients and friends has generally been excused by his daughter's illness – people are sympathetic – but they need to trust their lawyers and Dean is failing to meet expectations. He knows he should try harder but feels powerless to control the anger and pain that surge up in him almost constantly.

His hands grip the steering wheel so tightly his knuckles are white, his expression tight with rage. He watches a couple with two young children leave the building, a boy and a girl holding their parents' hands, all smiles and giggles. Dean hits the steering wheel hard, emitting a primal grunt. Slowly, he gets his breathing under control before getting out of the car. With one more gesture of anger, he slams the door.

Inside the hospital, Dean glances at the bank of lifts, any one of which would take him to his daughter. Instead, he walks down a busy corridor, past the cafeteria where patients well enough to leave their room have gathered with their visitors. Further on, he sees the sign indicating his destination – a place he has been many times before. A place he'd rather avoid. The Social Work Department. A staff member greets him and accompanies him to a private office. Knocking and opening the door, she ushers Dean in, closing it gently behind him.

Looking up from behind the desk where she's seated, Kelly greets him. 'Dean, thank you for coming, I'm sorry to ask you and Mandy to meet me after hours but there is something we need to talk about.'

Kelly Vincent is in her late twenties. She has large round eyes of a piercing blue, which is usually the first thing people notice about her. Her hair is twisted into a messy bun at the back of her head, held in place with a large claw hairclip. It always comes loose as she talks – she's an expressive speaker, waving her hands for added emphasis. She dresses simply, privileging comfort above all else, and wears minimal makeup. Dean likes Kelly and admires the work she does and has often told her how he could never do it. But he also would be happy if he never saw her again. She represents their last two years of living hell.

Dean kisses Mandy quickly on the cheek and collapses into the vacant chair beside his wife.

'We're here now, Kelly, what's this about?' he asks impatiently.

Kelly clears her throat and settles her clear blue eyes on Dean and Mandy. Dean dreads what he's about to hear, and he tries to prepare himself as much as he can, balling his fist up so that his fingernails dig into his palm.

'When you got Jesse's blood results showing her leukaemia had returned, Jesse got in touch with me—'

'What do you mean Jesse got in touch with you? Mandy, did you know about this?'

'No, Dean, Jesse hasn't mentioned anything to me about contacting Kelly.' Mandy's voice is calm and she speaks slowly.

This placatory tone infuriates Dean further. He shifts in his seat, unable to get comfortable.

'Why don't we listen to what Kelly has to say?' Mandy whispers, reaching out to take Dean's hand, a simple gesture she has always used to calm him. He allows her a fleeting touch before pulling his hand away.

'OK, fine, but for the record, Kelly, I'm not happy about this. So, what did Jesse want kept from us?'

'Jesse asked me to contact Inspire a Wish—'

'What?' Dean yells, jumping to his feet.

'This was her idea, Dean. Please sit down and let's talk about it. What did she ask for, Kelly?' Mandy asks, her voice barely above a whisper.

'What the hell does it matter what she asked for!

We're not there yet!' Dean says, his hands clenched into fists.

'We are,' Mandy whispers to him. She attempts to take his hand again, but he pulls away. Dejected, she puts her hands in her lap, looking down.

'No. No, we're not, we can't be,' Dean says quietly, seeing the tears slowly rolling down his wife's cheeks. Fire and water – they used to joke about it. He'd be all blazing thunder when upset, she'd be quieter, weeping, turning inward. But since Jesse was diagnosed, their differing responses to their daughter's illness have driven a wedge between them, Dean's anger getting so out of control to the point where Mandy told him that she could no longer live with him and his fury. He takes his seat again and sighs. Raising his eyes to Kelly's, he says, 'Can we forget all this?'

'I'm sorry, Dean, I can't. Jesse asked for it. It's my job to make sure she gets her wish. Last time she was in, Jesse confided in me what she wanted, which gave me the time to research where I could get the help she needs. I got in touch with Inspire a Wish then and they have already contacted a company who can help.'

Kelly sees on the Morgans' faces the shock she was expecting to see, what she's seen so many times before. The parents have not yet come to the place of acceptance that their child – her patient – has already arrived at. She sits with the silence, knowing that the next words will come from either Dean or Mandy, expecting it to be Dean.

Dean looks between the two women. All his anger, his impotence at failing to protect his family, spikes into rage. He glares at Mandy. 'You've always been too ready to give up. You've got no fight in you, Mandy, you haven't had for a long time.'

Mandy stares down her husband and says with a calm authority that shines through her tears, 'I've fought this for two years, but . . . it's over. We lost, Dean, we lost. I know you don't want to believe it. But all we can do now is let Jesse tell us what she wants and do everything we can to give it to her. This round of treatment is only going to delay the inevitable.'

Kelly knows just how hard it is for Mandy to say the words out loud. She fights to hold back tears – if the parents can hold it together, she must manage also.

'You just want it over with. Is that it? So, you can, what do you call it, move on?'

Devastated at the attack from the man she loves, the father of her children, rage flares up in Mandy. She stands, hovering over Dean.

'How dare you,' she says slowly.

'Mandy, Dean, please,' Kelly says, standing up from behind her desk. 'I know this is hard for both of you but just think how much harder it is for Jesse. It will help her enormously if you can be there for her, support her, get through this together as a family.'

'We haven't been a family in a long time,' Dean hisses, walking out of the room, slamming the door behind him.

The two women sit back down in shocked silence. Kelly has seen this sort of behaviour before, usually in people who are used to being able to fix things, to make things right. Dean is exactly that sort of person, and she recognises that need in herself. It's what drew her to social work, and she knows how it feels when nothing you do is going to change the outcome. Still, she's surprised by just how angry Dean is.

'I'm sorry, Kelly,' Mandy finally says, 'I'm so sorry. He's just so angry.'

'He's hurting, just like you're hurting, and he doesn't know what to do with that pain other than lash out. Would you like me to go after him? I presume he's going to see Jesse.'

'No, let him be. Sam is with Jesse; he won't make a scene in front of the kids. I'm sure I can talk to him later. Thank you, Kelly, this can't have been easy for you.'

'I'm here for Jesse. I'm also here for you, Dean and Sam, you know that.'

Mandy smiles weakly. 'I don't know how we'd have got through the past two years without you. Let's talk tomorrow?'

Mandy and Kelly hug each other tightly before Mandy leaves Kelly's office. Sitting at her desk, Kelly allows a single tear to escape before wiping her eyes.

For what feels like the hundredth time, she asks herself, *why do I keep doing this, putting myself through such painful situations?* Her answer comes quickly, almost reflexively: *I can make a difference. I can help. With each patient, I become a better person, a better worker, even if the change is small.* She scans her office, noticing the stark emptiness. When she first came to the city she lodged with an elderly woman, exchanging free board for a carer role. Her income came from dog walking and pet sitting other elderly neighbours' animals. She thrifted clothes, giving her a lifetime desire for quality over fashion. When it became obvious her arts degree would not guarantee employment, she added a social work degree in her third year and had her placement at the same hospital where she has now worked full-time for the past three years. Her life is small, but it's hers, and she loves it.

She lets out a deep breath and decides to get on with work. There are no family or pet photos on the walls, no childish drawings scattered on her desk, nothing that hints at a life outside the hospital. When the day finally ends, long after her colleagues have left, she'll drive to her modest apartment in an old car, eat a ready meal from a fridge that barely keeps things cold, and sit on a sagging couch, a gift from the elderly woman she lived with during her studies. She knows just which channel will offer the black-and-white movies she's grown to depend on as her only comfort, preferring the steady, measured pace of older films to the frenzied energy of modern ones. It's easier to lose herself in the happy endings of old movies than reflect on her days. And she'll sit there alone, her face illuminated by the flickering light of a screen.

CHAPTER 5

A lex turns his motorbike into the hospital grounds. He's still annoyed with Ian and feels unprepared. What exactly is he supposed to do? Ian has given him no brief, no indication of what actually needs to be done. His bike parked, helmet under his arm, backpack slung casually over his left shoulder, Alex enters the hospital foyer. Retrieving a crumpled-up piece of paper from his pocket, he looks at the words scribbled down as he walks towards the lift bank.

Entering the first doors that open, he barely has time to push the button marked level 6 before he is jostled to the back by adults and children who fill the space, many of whom carry large balloons emblazoned with the words GET WELL SOON and bouquets of flowers, either professionally created or homemade bunches. All too soon the lift stops, and everyone exits as others enter. He catches the closing doors and steps outside. The doors shut, his fellow travellers disappear, and he stands alone.

Scanning the space, Alex's eyes rest on a large sign suspended from the ceiling.

PAEDIATRIC ONCOLOGY WARD, 6 EAST. An arrow points to large double doors.

'What the hell am I doing here?' Alex says to the doors.

Two cautious steps forward trigger the doors as if giving him the answer: *don't ask questions, just go on in there and get the job done.*

Two more steps and Alex has entered the bizarre foreign world of ward 6 East: it looks suddenly like the digital world of a game. He gazes at the brightly painted murals and hears laughter and quiet chatter coming from the rooms around him. Two boys, each wheeling a mobile IV pole with tubes leading into their arms, are caught up in a swordfight with rolled-up newspapers, laughing at each other's attempt to score a hit. Staff, patients and visitors dodge them, seemingly oblivious to the mayhem they're causing. Alex watches, takes a step forward, then a step back. His face registers anxiety and something like wonder.

He's been told to report to the nurses' station and so Alex walks further into the ward, finally seeing a long counter with people behind it dressed in an array of brightly coloured scrubs. A young boy chases a girl behind the counter, and they are both shooed away. Alex finally sees the sign reading NURSES' STATION partly obscured by two women deep in conversation, one dressed in pale blue scrubs, the other in regular clothes. Slowly, Alex makes his way towards them, not wanting to interrupt but finding it impossible not to overhear.

'Kelly, you have to give whoever they send a chance. Stop being such a mother hen,' the nurse is saying affectionately.

'But there's so much riding on this. Jesse's wish is so

important to her,' the other woman replies. Alex notices how her blue eyes flash.

'Dean is so angry about it that it needs to be amazing for him to come around. I just want to make sure that the person who takes this on knows just how important it is.'

'Every wish is important, Kelly, you know that, even though we've never had one for a personalised video or whatever it is Jesse wants.' There's a slight admonishment in the older woman's tone.

'I know. You're right. But who knows what they'll send us – or who.'

'They sent me,' Alex interrupts them, sounding ruder than he meant to.

Kelly and the nurse startle, glancing at each other uncomfortably.

The nurse reacts first, extending her right hand. 'Hello, I'm Sandy, I'm the charge nurse on this ward. Thank you for coming to help Jesse.'

Alex shakes her hand. 'Nice to meet you. I'm not sure what it is you want from me but I'm here anyway.'

'Jesse will tell you what she wants, don't worry about that! If there is anything I can do to help, please find me.'

'Thanks, but I was told to meet a social worker?'

Sandy glances at Kelly who has stood silently by. 'Yes, that would be Kelly,' she says, nudging her arm.

'Ah, the one who wondered who or what was coming?' Alex tries for a jokey tone, but seeing the faces of the two women realises it's fallen flat. He shuffles uncomfortably on the spot, digging his hands into his pockets.

31

'I'll leave you to it,' Sandy says, briskly stepping away.

'Thanks, Sandy,' Kelly answers, turning back to Alex. Holding out her hand, she says, 'I'm sorry. You weren't meant to hear that.'

'Obviously.'

'Let's start again. I'm Kelly Vincent, the paediatric oncology social worker.'

Alex can't help staring at her, momentarily disoriented. She has the bluest eyes he's ever seen. Her hair, tucked behind both ears, highlighting the round shape of her face, is unruly and shiny. She clutches a folder to her chest, and his stomach clenches. The folder, he recognises. Each social worker who passed through his life as a child – uprooting him from one foster home, taking him away from any tentative friendships, depositing him in another one only to uproot him again a few short months later – carried such a folder, detailing his short life. Each one did their job with little compassion or understanding of what it was like for him to be handed from one stranger to another, never knowing how long this placement would last. Now here he is, standing in front of a woman around his age, who bears no resemblance to his memories of the many social workers he's encountered.

'And you are?' Kelly asks.

Alex shakes himself back to the here and now, slowing his breathing, remembering where he is and why.

'Alex Daniels from TriOptics. Look, I don't have much time. How is this going to work?'

Kelly sighs, not bothering to hide her irritation. 'Come

with me, Alex Daniels from TriOptics. First, I'll sign you in, then we need to have a little talk.'

Kelly goes behind the desk, punches something into a computer and gets him to sign a form. She prints off a ticket, which says CONTRACTOR, folds it into a plastic lanyard. 'Wear this,' she says, gathering up her folder and walking to the far end of the ward. Alex follows her, juggling his helmet as he tries to put the strap of the lanyard around his head. Kelly uses a card to open the double doors and walks through, letting them swing back and one knocks into Alex's shoulder. Annoyance starts simmering up in him. Shouldn't this Kelly person be more polite? Isn't TriOptics doing them a favour? He tries to forget about all the other work piling up on his desk right now.

Kelly enters a tiny room and sits behind a table. Alex shrugs off his backpack, places his helmet on the floor beside him, and sits down.

'Alex Daniels from TriOptics. So, you're the one they've sent us.'

'Appears so,' Alex says, rather more tersely than he'd intended.

'I need to be clear with you. You have been brought in to help fulfil a young girl's wish. This is extremely important to her. I have to know that you're on board from the beginning, that you are not going to let her down.'

What? Like I was let down by social worker after social worker? Alex thinks to himself.

'Look, I have been told next to nothing: go to the hospital, fulfil a wish. That's it. How can I promise not to let someone down – someone I haven't even met yet – if I don't know what it is that's wanted from me?'

'I just need to know that whoever takes this on is serious about delivering what they have promised to do.'

'I haven't promised to do anything.' Alex is filled with frustration. 'Again, I was told you would fill me in.'

'The promise TriOptics made.' Kelly sighs again. 'I had a brief chat with someone at your organisation, Ian, I think his name was? He said he would send someone out. But perhaps you should go back and ask him to send someone else.'

Alex looks away. There it is again, that fear of losing his job, his house, Max. Being out on the streets, turning back into that scared little boy with no security, no home.

'I can't do that.'

'Why not?'

'What Ian did say was that whatever this wish is about, it needs someone who can work with 3D CGI. That's me, I'm the only one in the company who has that skill.' Alex looks down at his hands, then clears his throat. 'Look, if this isn't going to work, I'll send the kid our latest game she can play on her tablet. It hasn't been released yet.'

'This isn't going to work, your attitude's all wrong.'

'My attitude? You're the one with the attitude! How about you find me someone who can tell me what the kid wants, why I'm here?'

Kelly takes a deep breath and seems to be considering.

'OK, OK,' she says at last. 'I see we have got off on the wrong foot. Why don't we speak to Jesse, and she can decide what she tells you. How's that?'

CHAPTER 6

Two girls are sitting together on a single bed. Dressed in identical T-shirts bearing the face of Taylor Swift, they are each playing on Switches. They spend more time watching the other's screen, laughing and nudging, trying to put each other off their play.

Alex comes to stand next to Kelly in the doorway. She smells like fresh laundry. He can't help but notice the contrast in the way she looks at the two girls, soft and warm and full of affection, with the way she looks at him, harder, judging him and not liking what she finds. The girls are obviously undergoing chemotherapy, but the way they're joking together gives Alex the impression that their treatment and diagnoses are the furthest things from their mind right now.

'Can we help you?' one of them, the taller one, asks playfully, her eyes large and dark.

The other one giggles, her hand over her mouth, her freckled face blushing.

Caught off guard, Alex looks from one girl to the other before looking to Kelly. She walks over to the bed and ruffles the taller girl's spiky hair.

'OK, Jesse – you know your wish? I've found someone who might be able to help, but we have to put him through his paces first.' She grins.

'Jesse, meet Alex. Alex, this is Jesse. And this is Amy, her roommate.'

'Hello, girls.' He gives a forced smile.

'Oh my God. Girls, he called us girls,' Jesse says. 'We're fifteen, we're not girls anymore.'

'So then, Alex, is it? Well, where do you work, how long have you worked there, what are the latest games you have made?' Amy reels off her questions with the authority of an expert in the field.

'Ah, what?' is all Alex can stammer.

'Your qualifications? What are they? How many games have you made? Were any of them any good, would we know any of them?' Jesse adds.

Alex looks from Jesse to Amy to Kelly, not sure how to answer. 'It's very simple, Alex. What are your qualifications for helping Jesse?' Amy asks.

Before he can answer, two teenage boys saunter into the room, the ones he saw from earlier, both still carrying their rolled-up newspaper swords.

'What's all this about qualifications?' one of them asks.

'Luke, Ryan,' Kelly says, 'this is Alex, he's here to help Jesse with her wish.'

'Is he now. So, are you going to answer Amy's question? What makes you qualified to help?' Ryan asks.

Alex feels put on the spot, and Kelly isn't helping. She's looking at him with a 'come on then, show us what you've got' expression on her face and clearly enjoying his discomfort.

He clears his throat.

'Well, I was the sole creator on earlier games for the company I work for, but we've now moved into 3D CGI. That's combining traditional filmmaking techniques with advanced CG and AI. I've done some virtual reality stuff but it's out of date now.'

'What's the name of the company you work for?' Luke asks.

'TriOptic Studios,' Alex answers.

'Funny name, where'd it come from?' Ryan joins in.

'Well, the marketing guys tells us "Tri" incorporates 3D, suggesting seeing things in a new dimension, "Optics", light, and together they convey creativity alongside technology.'

The four teenagers all burst out laughing and Kelly looks highly amused.

'Did you have to learn that in case someone asked about the name?' Amy asks, still giggling.

Alex allows himself a small smile. 'Yeah, we did, actually. How did I do?'

'Gold star!' Luke says.

The teenagers relax a little bit and their expressions soften. 'OK, we get the picture. So, what's your experience with teenagers, girls in particular?' Amy goes on.

'Amy,' Kelly says sternly, 'that's not appropriate.'

But Jesse has buried her face in a pillow, stifling laughter.

'It's all right,' Alex says. He can feel his face turning red. 'Ah, none, I have none, no experience with girls.'

'What, you've never had a girlfriend?' Amy throws at him.

'That's enough, Amy,' Kelly says. 'You three are coming with me. Let's leave Jesse to tell Alex what she needs in peace.'

Kelly, Amy and the boys depart, leaving the door ajar behind them. With their departure, the atmosphere becomes less frantic and a lot more serious. To help compose himself, he wanders over to a pinboard on the wall next to Jesse's bed.

He feels Jesse's eyes on him as he studies the photos carefully: Jesse, pretty as a picture, long, light brown hair, building sandcastles on the beach with who he presumes are her parents and a younger brother. *A perfect nuclear family*, Alex thinks ruefully. Something he's never known. Jesse racing on an athletic track, out in front, hair streaming behind her. Jesse standing on a small podium with two other girls, a gold medal around her neck. Jesse in a ballet leotard, her hair piled tightly on top of her head. Jesse with her father, cheeks touching, eyes closed, sharing headphones. Jesse and her brother lying on their stomachs painting on one piece of paper. Jesse with her mother dressed up at a formal event.

'Your family?' he asks, turning back to face Jesse.

'Yep.'

'You're an athlete?'

'I was.'

'And a dancer?'

'Was.'

'Is there anything you can't do?'

'Get better. That's why you're here.'

'I'm so sorry.' Alex's voice breaks. Are those tears welling up in his eyes? He needs to pull himself together, but he can't. He takes a step backwards as if to leave.

'You can come closer, you know; you won't catch it from me.'

Alex nudges the chair beside her bed a little further away before sitting down.

'Can you tell me what you want from me, please? No one has filled me in on the wish, on what it actually is.'

'I don't think anyone really gets what I want. I've talked to Kelly about it, and I think she's trying to understand, but I can tell she doesn't really *get* it. I need someone who can not only build my wish but who sees my vision. Does that make sense?'

Alex nods. He's in safer waters. This is something he comes across in his daily work.

'You want a proof of concept.'

'A what of what?'

Alex grins. 'A proof of concept. It's like a plan of how to build something. So, in my line of work, someone might come to me saying, "I want a game where all the possums in the world turn into zombies."'

Jesse rolls her eyes. 'Oh wow, another zombie game. How original.'

'Hang on,' Alex says. He's enjoying chatting to this kid. 'That's just an example. But let's say someone does want a game where all the possums turn into zombies. They'll tell me what they want, including what they want it to look like, how zombies work in this world, what the aim of the game is, and then I'll go away and think about how I could make it work. I'll do some drawings, write up a plan – that's the proof of concept – and if it matches with the idea they've got in their mind, I'll go ahead and make it.'

Jesse nods thoughtfully. 'So that's what I want from you, at least at first. A proof of concept. I want to make sure you get what I want.'

'OK then, hit me with it.'

Jesse takes a deep breath. 'Well, here's what I'm thinking. I want a video, like a story of my life, with all the happy things my family and I have done, something that they can be part of, then watch if . . . when . . . I'm not here. Kinda like when you take a lot of photos and make a slide show but more complex than that, I want to relive some of the photos we have and make them into a story of my family when I was in it. Something they can experience. Something so they don't forget me.'

'Don't forget you,' Alex repeats. It's hard to think that this vibrant, intelligent girl doesn't have much time left. It feels wrong. 'Is there any chance that you might get better?'

'Do you know what the word terminal means?' Jesse says sharply.

Alex rubs his forehead. Life is so crap. And he understands now why Kelly was so prickly with him before – it would be so much worse if he promised he could help Jesse but didn't deliver. What Jesse is asking for is amazing – beautiful even – he can see it in his mind's eye, but it's also incredibly ambitious and, if he's honest, he just isn't confident that he can do it.

'I'm so sorry, Jesse, but I don't know what I can do. It sounds like you want to make a movie, and while we partner with production companies, helping them make films and miniseries, this isn't our area.'

'But you make games, I've seen some with your company's name on them.'

'Used to. We've moved on from them for the most part, now we only make high-end CGI games for arcade use.'

'But you do it, you make the same game over and over. Oh yeah, you change the characters and scenarios they play, but they are basically the same game.'

'You know your stuff!' Alex says with growing admiration.

This is something he's thought for a long time – he's even raised it with Ian, but his boss has zero interest in investing in innovation. Alex feels he's slowly watching TriOptics lose whatever edge on the market they once had, when Frank was in charge, before he retired and handed the company over to his dead-beat son-in-law. He thinks of the project he has been working on at home.

'I've been doing my research. What else am I going to do, sitting in this bed? My dream was to be a game designer. That's not going to happen now, but with your help I'd like to design just one thing.'

'Look, I'm sorry you're sick, I really am, but I can't promise that I can make what you want. It's really ambitious. I'm afraid you're going to be disappointed.'

'Disappointed? So, you're not even going to try?' Jesse's voice is full of disbelief and anger. 'Because I might be disappointed? Don't you think I know about disappointment?'

Alex is at a loss for words.

'Why would you come here if you don't even want to try?' She shakes her head, on the verge of tears. 'You don't want to be here, do you? You don't want to help me. You never did.'

'It's not like that.'

'So, what are you doing here?'

'My boss told me—'

'Your boss, I see. You're not interested in helping me, you're just here because you were told to come. Well, I don't want to waste any more of your precious time.'

Before he can respond, Kelly rushes into the room, grabbing Alex by the arm. Forcing him to his feet, she marches him out of the room as Amy comes in and runs to Jesse. Out in the hall, staff, visitors and patients, including Ryan and Luke, stop and watch as Kelly drags Alex to one side.

Away from the observers, Kelly releases his arm. 'What just happened in there?'

'I don't know. We were talking, and she told me to go.'

'What did you say to her?'

'I told her I thought that what she was asking for was too ambitious.'

'So, you told her she can't have her wish?' Kelly folds her arms, blue eyes blazing.

'Well, not in so many words . . .'

Kelly turns from him, shaking her head in disbelief.

'Look, I never wanted to be here in the first place.'

'Whether you want to be here or not is beside the point—'

'I don't need this,' Alex cuts in, storming off. The last thing he hears as he punches through the double doors towards the lifts is Kelly calling after him.

'And clearly Jesse doesn't need you!'

Kelly turns around to see she has an audience. Ryan is staring at her with his mouth open as if he can't quite comprehend what he has just witnessed, and Luke is looking down at the ground.

Sandy comes over to Kelly. She has helped make wishes happen for too many children. She knows the toll it takes on everyone involved. The patient, their family, the staff who work on the ward, the people who volunteer to help. 'You were pretty hard on him. Hell, it was probably the first time the poor guy has been on a kids' ward, let alone met a child with a terminal illness,' she says softly.

Kelly looks away, competing emotions playing out on her face. She wants to hide from them all. 'He can't help her, you heard him.'

'That may be, but did you give him a fair chance? Come on, I'm due a break, let's go to my office.'

Kelly follows Sandy who shuts the door behind them. Kelly drops into a chair facing the desk as Sandy pops a capsule in her coffee machine, placing a cup under the spout. Hearing Kelly sniffle, Sandy takes a box of tissues from her desk and tosses them to her. Kelly takes a tissue and blows her nose loudly, feeling slightly sheepish.

'Want to talk about it?' Sandy asks as the steaming coffee pours into the cup, the aroma filling the room.

'No. No, I don't,' replies Kelly, aware that she sounds a bit like one of her teenage patients.

Sandy hands Kelly the coffee and pulls the chair from the other side of the desk to sit beside her.

'I should never have let him near her,' Kelly finally blurts out.

'What happened?'

'He upset her.'

'Looks to me like Jesse wasn't the only one he upset.'

'I should never have let him near her if he couldn't help. Right?'

Sandy half-heartedly nods.

'I mean, what was the point, you either want to help or you don't. Right?'

Another small nod from Sandy gives Kelly nothing.

'OK, maybe I could've prepared him better, could've found out what exactly she wanted, but that was his job. Right?'

A not-so convincing nod from Sandy.

'It was his whole attitude, from the minute he arrived, he never wanted to be here.'

Sandy sighs, takes a sip of coffee, then says, 'Kelly, you're a brilliant social worker. Your patients, their families, the staff here, all love and admire you, but you are very attached to Jesse, we all are. This was never going to be easy for you.'

'So, it's my fault, is that what you're saying?' Kelly looks at Sandy, not sure she wants to hear her reply.

'I'm not saying that exactly . . .'

'You wouldn't. Still, we're better off without him, he's not the right person to help Jesse.'

'And Jesse's wish?' Sandy asks. 'How are we going to make that happen?'

'I'll find a way.'

'Kelly, listen to me. I've been on this ward for over eight years and you, what, three?'

'Nearly four,' Kelly mumbles.

'Right. Not long in my book. For the record, you are the

best social worker I've worked with. You have compassion and empathy for everyone, including the staff who I know go to you for a sympathetic ear.'

'Only sometimes, and only when you're not around.'

Sandy smiles in acknowledgement. 'What I'm saying is that, unfortunately, there will be many more like Jesse who will come into your life. You will make a difference. But it's not easy for *anyone*. You need to help guide them through this crazy world we work in. Do you get what I'm saying?'

Kelly can't make eye contact and looks around Sandy's office seeing Alex's helmet on the floor. 'No,' she groans, 'he's left his bike gear behind.'

'I'll take care of it,' Sandy says, collecting the helmet and leaving her office.

Alone in Sandy's office, Kelly cringes at the memory of her confrontation with Alex. She knows she wasn't fair on him. She probably owes him an apology. She thinks about Dean, and his reaction to hearing of Jesse's wish, and how unreasonable she thought it had been at the time. She's no better, she proved that today. But the thought of Jesse and how little time she has left . . .

Kelly balls the tissue in her hand. Whatever she has to do, even if it means swallowing her pride and apologising to that jerk, she'll do it. She'll do everything she can so Jesse can get her wish fulfilled.

CHAPTER 7

Alex strides out of the hospital, his head buzzing with all the things he should have said to Kelly. He's annoyed with her, and himself for letting things go too far. But mostly, he feels sorry for Jesse. Why didn't anyone explain her vision to him before he met her? Possibly because Inspire a Wish, the nurses, Kelly, don't have his knowledge of what's needed to pull off such a huge undertaking. They don't understand the enormity of the work; they probably thought it would only take a couple of days, tops.

The work. Alex has reached his bike now and looks at it unseeingly while his mind is lost in the intricacies of what Jesse had proposed. It's not impossible, but it *is* ambitious. Too ambitious? Although he has a niggling feeling that he's not up to the task, ideas start popping up into his mind. The possibilities are endless, exciting, even – but does he have the capacity? The skill set?

It's only when he's about to get back on his bike that he realises that he's left his helmet in the hospital. In Sandy's office. He can picture it there, on the floor where he'd dumped it. Bugger. *Bugger, bugger, bugger,* he thinks to himself. He visualises Kelly's face, her blue eyes triumphant, as she silently thrusts his belongings at him, then the humiliation of slinking back outside, his tail between his legs. But there's nothing else to be done. He turns around and reluctantly walks towards the hospital entrance once more. He's approaching the front desk when the charge nurse, Sandy, comes bustling up to him, carrying his helmet.

'Oh, thank goodness,' she says, 'we wouldn't want you out on the road without this!'

'Thank you,' he says, his face reddening. 'Erm, I'm sorry about . . .'

She bats his apology away with her hand. 'Don't be. I think we all could have handled that a bit differently, a bit better, don't you?'

'Yeah,' he agrees quietly. 'Well, thanks again,' and turns to leave.

'Just . . .' she calls after him, and he turns to face the older woman. She sighs and gives him a warm smile. 'Just take some time and think about it, before saying no. Jesse's a wonderful kid, and we all care so much about her. Maybe there is a way to help her? Maybe if you just think about it a little more?'

Alex nods his head. 'OK,' is all he can manage.

'Well then,' Sandy says, 'I hope to see you soon. And take care on that bike of yours, OK?'

Alex takes the long way back to work. Finding himself riding alongside the beach, he pulls over and sits on his bike, staring at the blue water, the breeze creating white tops on the waves. Above him, a hot air balloon glides down the coast.

He envies the people inside, travelling above the world without a care.

As the balloon disappears from sight, Alex knows it is time to face the music. That said, he's in no hurry and takes his time, ignoring the horns blasting at him for going too slow. Back at work, Alex sneaks into the office and to his cubicle. Dropping his helmet beneath his desk, he quickly fires up his screens.

'So, they didn't talk you into donating your body to science then?' Steve asks, resting his arms on the cubicle wall between them.

'I know whose body I'd like to donate to science,' Alex mutters.

'That would be Ian's, I'm thinking.'

'Followed closely by a certain social worker.'

Alex hasn't heard Ian approach and jumps at the slap on the back Ian likes to greet everyone with.

'Everything all right then?'

'No, not really. Look, Ian, I met the girl and she kinda kicked me out. I wanted to manage her expectations – her wish, well, it's amazing, but far too ambitious.'

'So, what you're saying is that you're not up to the challenge. I should have known. All sizzle and no sausage.'

Steve raises his eyebrows and makes a low whistle.

'It's not that I can't do it, it's more that—'

'If you can do it, then what's the problem?'

'It's going to take time, resources, money . . .'

'Those are just excuses. You know that Frank is backing this, right?'

Ian waits for Alex to nod, which he does with a heavy sigh. 'So, anything to do with resources and suchlike will all be signed off by him,' Ian says. 'So, I ask you again: what's the problem?'

'Yeah, look, if it's all right—'

'No, it's not bloody all right. I sent you there to do a job and you didn't do the damn job. Get yourself back there. What part of this did I not make clear enough to you? We want the publicity from this kid, it'll give us the edge.' He speaks to Alex like he's five years old. 'God knows we need it right now.'

Alex says nothing. He looks pleadingly at Steve, who gives a tiny shrug. He can't help. Alex is on his own with this one.

'Now go back and see the kid. Apologise, do whatever you have to, then let me and Frank know when it's finished so I can contact the media. And Steve, get back to work. This little show is over.'

That night, Alex and Max don't go to his office after their run. Instead, they sit on the couch, Alex with a microwave meal in front of him, Max gnawing a chew toy. An old black-and-white movie ready to stream on the TV. Before he hits play, Alex spends several minutes rubbing Max's tummy, scratching him behind his ears, knowing all his special spots for attention.

'So, I've got this problem, buddy. I met this girl today, Jesse. She's only fifteen and she's really, really sick. She wants me to help her make something for her family. I don't know if I can do it, I've never done anything like this before. I've never met anyone like her before. What do you think I should do?'

Max listens intently, then he thumps his tail on the rug.

'But that's not all, Max, I also met this social worker. Her name is Kelly. I thought she'd just be like the social workers I met when I was a kid. But she's not. They were just doing a job, but she's involved, she *cares*, probably more than she should for this girl. I don't know what to make of her. I think I may have been out of line the way I spoke to her. Do you think I should apologise?'

Max thumps his tail yes.

Alex watches Max to see if he wants to continue the conversation. He doesn't, he is now focused on the television, waiting for the movie to start. Alex presses play on the remote, picks up his plate, now cold, and takes a bite before putting it back on the coffee table in front of him. The credits to *Great Expectations* roll.

CHAPTER 8

A lex stares at his bike, parked in the same place as yesterday, working up the courage to go inside the hospital. He needs to have it out with Kelly before he speaks to Jesse. *One fight at a time*, he thinks. Although he hopes not to fight with her today, remembering Max's advice to apologise. At the main reception, Alex asks for the social work department and is directed down the corridor with instructions to follow the signs. All signs eventually lead to social work, the exhausted receptionist tells him.

Staff, visitors, patients in wheelchairs or being pushed on beds, others trudging slowly hanging onto loose pyjama bottoms or in gowns gaping at the back, waltz around each other with varying speed and intent. Alex walks through them, dodging and weaving. Seeing Kelly, he slows his pace before stepping in front of her.

'How can I help you, Mr Daniels?' Kelly asks, walking on, Alex now beside her.

'I'd like to talk to Jesse.'

'Not going to happen.'

'Why not?'

'She doesn't need to be upset by you.'

'I promise I won't upset her, OK? I just need to ask her some more questions about what she wants to see if I can help. I want to help.'

Kelly stops abruptly and turns towards him. Once again, those bright blue eyes seem to pierce right through him.

'OK,' she says, 'I'm listening.'

Alex gestures towards the side of the corridor, stepping out of the flow of people. Beyond the glass a beautiful garden invites anyone needing the comfort mother nature provides in abundance. Dappled sunlight dances on the faces of worried and distressed patients and their loved ones, sitting beneath the trees, on the grass or on benches.

Finally, Alex speaks quietly. 'I'll be honest with you. This job – it's a lot. Yesterday, it just felt too much, too . . .' Alex searches for the word but it eludes him. 'I took on board what you said about letting Jesse down. I don't want to do that, of course, but it's . . . it's ambitious. I know I'm here to do a job and I will do it to the best of my ability. But . . . I'm going to need your support to do it. To make that wish a reality.'

'You really want to help?'

'Yeah, I do.'

'Then come with me,' Kelly says, turning and walking towards the lifts.

Alex hesitates then scurries after her.

Walking side by side, Alex and Kelly enter 6 East, heading purposefully to Jesse's room. On the way they pass Amy,

Luke and Ryan who are helping staff rearrange some of the children's paintings strung around the nurses' station.

'Two minutes, I give him two minutes,' Ryan announces.

'Five, I reckon,' Luke confidently replies.

'You're both wrong,' Amy says.

'What do you mean?' Ryan asks.

'Kelly will leave first,' Amy tells the boys.

'It's a bet,' Ryan says with bravado, his hand outstretched for Amy to shake.

She takes his hand in her, and they shake.

As Kelly and Alex approach Jesse and Amy's room, an immaculately dressed, middle-aged woman intercepts them, smiling warmly at Kelly.

'Kelly, have you got a minute?' she asks.

'I shouldn't be long; can it wait a moment?' Kelly asks.

The woman notices Alex.

'Oh, I'm sorry for interrupting.'

'This is Alex Daniels,' Kelly says. 'He's here to see if he can help Jesse fulfil her wish.' Turning to Alex, she says, 'This is Dr Christine Taylor, Jesse's doctor.'

The doctor extends her hand to Alex, who takes it, blushing despite himself. He feels five years old again in her calm yet commanding presence.

'It's nice to meet you, Alex. Call me Christine – everyone does. Thank you for helping Jesse. You have no idea how important supporting our patients in this way can be at a time like this.'

'It's nice to meet you, Doctor, but we're not quite there yet.'

'Oh, you'll be fine, and you've got Kelly here to help you. She's the best.'

She turns to Kelly. 'I'll leave you to it then. Kelly, I'll catch you when you're free.'

'She doesn't look like a doctor,' Alex says, watching Christine walk down the ward.

'What should she look like?'

'Wear a white coat and have a stethoscope hanging around her neck, I guess.'

'This isn't an ordinary hospital ward. We're much less formal than most hospitals and that's something we're super proud of. Now, come on. Jesse's finished her treatment for the day. We never want to give up but, just to prepare you, there is only so much her young body can take.'

As Kelly and Alex enter Jesse and Amy's room, Jesse looks up from the book she is reading. She's pale, Alex notices, there are deep rings under her eyes, and she's rigged up to an IV. For the first time he properly registers just how unwell she is. It hits him like a blow to his gut. How could he have been so blunt with her yesterday? She's still a child and she's . . . dying.

Alex attempts a smile and Jesse scowls back. Kelly grabs the spare chair next to Amy's bed and pulls it alongside Jesse's bed, indicating for Alex to sit. Jesse slowly places a bookmark in the book. Closing it carefully, she puts it down on her bedside table and gazes at the two of them, waiting.

'Jesse, Alex has asked if he can talk to you about your wish, he'd—'

'Let him speak for himself,' Jesse interrupts, staring intently at Alex.

'I'm sorry I upset you yesterday,' he says. 'I'd like to talk to you some more about your wish. Maybe I can make it come true for you after all.'

'Who made you come here? Was it Kelly?'

Before Kelly can reply, Alex jumps in.

'No. Sorry, no, it was my boss.'

'What'd they say?'

'In less than polite language, he said that I have to make your wish come true.'

'Or else he'd fire you. Is that it?'

'Something like that, yeah.' Alex grins ruefully.

'Do you think that's a good reason to be here?'

'As good a reason as any. Kind of motivates me, don't you think?'

For the first time since Alex and Kelly had entered the room, Jesse smiles. Alex relaxes a little and smiles back.

Jesse turns to Kelly. 'Thanks, we'll be OK now.'

'I'll just stick around for a bit,' Kelly says.

Alex turns to Kelly, trying to keep his annoyance in check.

'Like Jesse says, I think we'll be OK, but thanks for the vote of confidence.'

'I think he's going to behave, Kelly. He's going to take my suggestions seriously, and we're going to do this together. Aren't we, Alex?'

Alex is surprised to see a hurt look on Kelly's face. She returns her chair back to its place beside Amy's bed and silently leaves the room, keeping the door wide open behind her.

'So,' Alex says, 'where shall we start? We have a virtual reality suit and games at the office, I could drag one out—'

'No, Alex, that's not the kind of thing I want. I don't want my family to be locked into their own suits with goggles, wandering aimlessly around and unable to engage with one another. I know you can create moving backgrounds of places and scenes for people to walk into together, and experience a moment already lived or dreamed of. I want to be part of the scenes, and I want them to be able to enter them without me. Does that make sense?'

'Yes, absolutely. But you're going to have to give me more background.'

'Go and look at my pinboard. Really look at it.'

Alex walks over to the pinboard, but this time lingers over the contents. Several drawings are pinned up alongside the photos. Childish but with a clear message. A family of four building sandcastles on the beach, a woman, a young girl and a boy close together, a male figure sitting apart with a phone in his hand, a dog further away. Three stick figures playing a board game.

He points at them. 'Who did these?'

'My little brother Sam. He's eight. They make me sad when I look at them, they tell me how our last holiday together as a family was for him.'

'Wasn't it a happy holiday?' Alex asks.

'It should have been, we were away from all of this,' Jesse says, waving her arms to indicate the hospital room. 'It was a beach holiday, and it was during term so there weren't many people around, and we had the whole beach to ourselves. Dad took time off work, but he didn't leave his work behind. He'd sit on the beach with us or go to a restaurant with us but most of the time he wasn't with us, if you get what I mean.'

'I think I do.'

Alex takes a piece of paper from the pinboard, a poem. He starts to read. The effects of the words play out on his face, which he has turned away from Jesse.

My sweet Jesse, my love, my precious one,
The days we've shared, the joy, the fun.
I see you fight, so brave, so strong,
Through every night, you still hold on.

Should time fade and seasons change,
My heart will stay, my love remain.
In every breath, in every sigh,
You'll live with me, with no goodbye.

You are my daughter, so pure, so bright,
And in your eyes, I see the light.
No matter where this journey goes,
I'll hold you close, through all our woes

'Who wrote this?'

'My mum.'

All Alex can do is nod. He doesn't trust his voice. Slowly, he starts examining the photos he had seen yesterday from a distance. He lifts a photo from the board taken at the beach, Jesse wearing her favourite floppy hat.

'Nice hat.'

He doesn't need to be told that the young boy photographed so often with his arms around his big sister's neck is Sam. There is no doubt that the beautiful woman with the same features as Jesse is the author of the dazzling poem: her mum. He spies a photo which includes a man, Sam on his shoulders, Jesse beside him, all three of them laughing together.

'Your dad? He's not in many of the photos.'

'That's because he's behind the camera.'

'Ah, of course.'

Alex returns to the bedside but doesn't sit down.

'It's a bit . . .' He looks around the room. 'Is there any chance we can go somewhere else to talk?'

'Don't like being in a sick room, is that right?'

'Something like that.'

'Imagine how I feel.'

'Oh, I didn't mean—'

'It's OK, I'm messing with you. Follow me, I know the perfect place.'

Jesse slides off the bed, slips her feet into a pair of sandals. From a drawer in her bedside table, she takes out a large sketch book and a pencil case. With practised ease, she wraps her right arm around the pole with a hook at the top, where the bag of liquid that's connected to the IV in her arm is hanging. The trolley and pole become part of her as she walks to the pinboard where she removes several of the photos, a drawing and the poem. Tucking them into the sketch book she walks towards the door. Alex quickly follows her.

As Jesse steps into the doorway, Amy, Ryan and Luke scurry away. Looking back, Ryan and Luke throw a thumbs-up to Jesse, while Amy blows her a kiss.

Alex and Jesse take the lift to the ground floor. Jesse pushes open the glass doors that lead out to the garden he and Kelly stood looking out on earlier. An elderly man sits on a nearby bench, a woman who Alex presumes to be his partner, in a wheelchair beside him. They hold hands, their faces turned to the warmth of the sun; only they can know the thoughts, the memories they each embrace in silence.

Alex follows Jesse to a far corner of the garden, hidden from view and set away from passersby. A picnic table with benches either side is tucked away between the bushes. Sitting on one side, Jesse indicates for Alex to sit opposite her.

'My office,' Jesse says with a grin. 'This is where the dream team hang out when we want some peace and quiet.'

Alex is struck by the realisation that Jesse has spent so much of her short life here, in hospital, and of how hard she and her friends have worked to make it fun and normal. He feels small in the face of their courage and determination. He thinks of how he tried to wriggle out of helping her and feels ashamed.

Opening the sketch book, Jesse carefully places the photos, drawing and poem on the table. The drawing is one of Sam's beach scenes. Turning the sketch book to face Alex, she shows him illustrations of places, their names painstakingly written beneath each one. Playgrounds with meticulously sketched play equipment, a boy on the beach making sandcastles. The drawings are beautiful. Most of them are Jesse's family out of doors, many, like Sam's, scenes of sand and surf.

'Your family really love the beach, huh?'

'Yeah, we're really lucky we live right on it, we just walk from our backyard onto the sand. It's been my playground since I was a baby.'

'Is that where you want your wish to be set?'

'Of course, but not the only place. I don't have room on my board for photos of everywhere I'd like the wish to explore. These are the special places my family and I have visited, where we share awesome memories. I want you to make those memories come back to life so they can be relived forever,' she tells Alex, stumbling over her words in a rush of emotion.

Alex flicks quickly through the book. 'Are all these nearby?'

'Yes, we've not gone far since I was diagnosed. My grandparents and cousins all live hours away so they come to us. One of my grandparents has a farm and I used to love going there, it's so different from the city. You will be able to go to all of these places and film them, won't you?'

'Ah, sure. I presume you have other photos taken at these places?'

'Yes, and I can get them to you.'

Alex points to a sketch of a park with a rotunda in the middle. 'Tell me about this.'

Jesse's face lights up. 'We went there one day, played in the park, then had a picnic lunch in the rotunda. It was

60

winter and the flowers that should have covered the rotunda were dead, but the bare branches were entwined all over it. I remember Mum saying how beautiful this would look in summer covered in flowers, but I quite liked it all stark with no colour. I heard her whisper to Dad that she could imagine me getting married in such a place.'

'Married? But you're just a kid.'

'Yeah, I know. She was looking to the future. A future she's now not going to get unless you and I can give it to her. Do you see what I'm talking about?'

Despite the warmth of the sun, Alex's body chills, he feels numb. His mind races. What has he agreed to? What are the implications if he can't give this mother and daughter the imagined future that she's so desperate to create?

Placing his hands on the sketch as if to draw strength from the scene, he stares deeply into Jesse's eyes.

'I understand what you want, Jesse. I just don't know if it can be done. You need to know that usually when we do this, it's not just me, there's a whole team of colleagues I work with, and we each have our own expertise. There are digital artists, environmental artists, terrain artists, effects artists just to name a few. I would need to involve others and I'm not sure I can, it might be right at the limits of our abilities. I've been working on a simplified version of the software, something that can be made available to anyone wanting to make a 3D CGI story, but I haven't perfected it yet.'

'You can do it; I believe in you.'

Alex is stunned. No one has ever told him they believed in him. He knows he's useful to Ian, but only in a purely transactional way. Max needs him and loves him, of course, but he's a dog. Alex struggles to think of a human who has placed their trust in him. He takes a deep breath. He's going to give this his best shot. It's all he can do. Jesse, it seems, is going to help him through sheer force of will. If he can pull this off, maybe he'll finally have something to show for himself.

'OK, let's give it a go. Can I use one of these blank pages to make notes? You'll have to help me; tell me which scenes are the most important to video in case I can't do them all; I don't want to be the one to make that decision. Deal?'

Their eyes meet. Jesse pauses then holds out her hand. 'Deal.'

They shake on it. The tension breaks. They're a team now, and there's a lot of work to be done. Alex still has no idea if he can give Jesse what she wants, but he's prepared to do everything he can to make it happen. He's not thinking about TriOptics or Ian or even his job now; he wants to do this for Jesse.

There's just one thing he doesn't know and is afraid to ask: how long does he have?

CHAPTER 9

The sun reflects off the glass surrounding them, casting shadows over the sketches and photos on the desk. Jesse feels a burst of happiness, and of hope. Together, it seems, she and Alex are going to make something special, she believes it. She begins pulling pages from the book, sorting the sketches into two piles.

'The definites and the hopefuls,' she says with a cheeky grin.

Alex writes down the names of the parks, gardens, beaches, restaurants and cafés Jesse puts into the definite pile. Once completed, they spread the sketches out on the table, adding photos where they were taken. Jesse places Sam's drawing on top of a photo. Lost in their studies of the places that will make up Jesse's experience, they don't hear Sandy until she stands beside them.

'Someone said I might find you two here. How's it going?' she asks.

'It's going,' Alex replies smiling at Jesse.

'It's just the beginning, Sandy, but Alex can do it, can't you, Alex?' Jesse challenges.

'*We* are doing this. The two of us.'

Jesse grins. 'Yep, *we're* doing it.'

'That's wonderful, Jesse, however, I hate to break this meeting up, but . . .'

'Can I come back tomorrow?' Alex asks.

'Tomorrow?' Jesse says.

'I'd like to, if you let me.'

'Oh, I don't know,' Jesse says teasingly. Inside she's bursting with gratitude and excitement. 'I think we can let you, just this time. What do you think, Sandy?'

'Oh, I'm sure something can be arranged,' Sandy replies with a wink. 'But not too long – we don't want to wear you out.'

Jesse and Alex stand up, Alex gathering up the papers from the table. Before she knows what she's doing, before she can stop herself, Jesse gives him a quick, fierce hug. She's surprised him, she knows, because when she lets go of him, he looks as if he doesn't know quite what to do or where to look. For someone almost twice her age, it's like he's never been hugged before. Adults never fail to surprise her – it's like they're never as certain or as straightforward as they pretend to be, even to themselves.

Jesse follows Sandy, pushing her IV as she goes. She turns round to give Alex one last wave and sees him sitting back down on the bench, face turned up to the sunshine. She doesn't know what he's thinking, but in her mind she's certain: he's the one for the job. Alex is going to make her wish come true.

CHAPTER 10

That evening Alex sits in his home office surrounded by banks of computer monitors and equipment, totally focused on playing several games simultaneously through his PlayStation. Someone else toiled to make the games he has enjoyed and played for a long time. This is his time out, his relaxation. When he is forced to focus on the games, everything else disappears. A pizza box beside him is untouched. Max sleeps at his feet, a toy stuffed under his chin. Blindly Alex reaches for a piece of pizza, takes a bite and shivers, it is cold. Max opens one eye and licks his lips. As Alex goes to put it back in the box, he sees Jesse's sketches and photos. Closing the pizza box and moving it aside, he replaces it with the sketches, wipes his hands and begins studying the images once again. Reaching down he scratches Max on the head.

'What have I agreed to, Max?'

Back in her room, Jesse lies in bed, a dinner tray in front of her, her favourite pasta with a tub of ice cream. She can only stomach the ice cream. Amy's family has taken her downstairs to the canteen, so Jesse's on her own for now. She pushes the pasta around on her plate, lost in thoughts of project plans and proofs of concept and how they all tie in with her memories. Her mind is whirring with possibilities, but she's also aware that she's more tired than usual. She is brought back to the room when her mum and Sam appear at her door.

Sam jumps on Jesse's bed hugging his sister tightly. Her mum joins in on the hug.

'Well, sweetheart, you're looking a bit brighter this evening.'

'Mum, you missed him. He came back. Sam, he came back!' she squeals with delight.

'Who did we miss, honey?' her mother asks.

'Alex. He came—'

'The person you sent away yesterday. The one who upset you?'

'Yes, he came back and guess what, he's going to help me with my wish.' Jesse notes the concern in her mother's eyes. 'You don't need to worry, Mum. His name's Alex and he really gets what I want to do. He understands my vision in a way that no one else has before.'

Sam wriggles out of his hug looking at his sister with big eyes. 'Your dream's coming true?' His voice is full of wonder.

'It looks like it,' she says, ruffling her brother's hair.

Jesse hears the heavy footsteps that can only belong to her father. 'How's my baby girl?' Dean asks as he kisses Jesse on the top of the head.

'Dad, Alex came back, we're going to make my wish.'

'*What?*' Dean says too firmly, looking from Jesse to his wife.

'My game, well, my experience, my wish—'

'Don't you think you should be concentrating on getting better? Not some silly game!'

Jesse blinks, stunned. *It's not some silly game*, she thinks. Her dad doesn't realise how cutting his words can be. She looks to her mum for support, to find her already studying her face, taking in her hurt and disappointment.

'Dean, that's enough,' Mandy says, taking one of Jesse's hands in hers. 'Jesse was just telling us about Alex's visit.'

'Who is this guy, *Alex?*' Dean spits out. 'What do we know about him?'

'Dad!' Jesse cries out.

'He's the person who wants to help Jesse get her wish. Don't worry, he's been vetted by the hospital and the foundation,' her mum says, clearly trying to pacify her husband.

But Jesse's father is not to be mollified. 'Wasn't he the one who walked out on you yesterday? Why are we trusting someone like that?'

'Dean,' her mother says firmly, 'you're being unreasonable. Let's just hear Jesse out.'

'Oh, *unreasonable*, am I?' He laughs hollowly. 'Yes, it's so *unreasonable* of me to expect a level of caution when it comes to young men hanging around my daughter—'

'Stop it. Stop it!' Sam yells, pulling away from Jesse.

'Look what you've done!' Jesse's mum snaps.

Going on the defensive, Dean backs away, hands raised. 'OK, I'll shut up. Forgive me for giving a damn.'

'Yes, that's right, you shut up, you're good at that, really good at not saying what you're thinking or feeling except to criticise—'

'Stop it. Jesse, make them stop,' Sam pleads, his hands over his ears.

Dean attempts to reach out to his son, but Mandy steps in his way. 'I think it's best if you go now.'

'Fine, I'll see you all later,' he says, walking out of the room.

Jesse has been watching all this in horror. Just a few minutes ago, she was buzzing with energy and excitement; now she's watching the people she loves most in the world – the people this wish is for – tear each other apart. She touches Sam on the shoulder, and he crawls up into her arms. When their mother attempts to hold him, he flinches.

'Leave Jesse and me alone,' Sam stammers.

'Darling, I'm so sorry. I didn't mean to fight with your father.'

'I said leave us alone.'

Jesse nods at her mother, indicating that she's got this.

Mandy stands, helplessly looking at her children. Sam's words are like knives to her heart, and tears spring to her eyes.

'It's all right, Mum, I'll look after Sam for a while. It'll be all right.' Jesse's voice is calm but firm. Mandy registers how their roles are reversed. Her child is taking charge of the situation, as her parents squabble like teenagers.

Fighting back tears, Mandy stumbles to the door. She turns to see Sam sliding under the covers with Jesse, her arms enfolding him. Outside the room, Mandy leans against the wall trying to compose herself. Visitors walk past, seeing her visibly upset, they look down and hurry on – they can only guess what she's dealing with. Everyone in this ward is facing the unimaginable. Looking up Mandy sees Dean enter the nearby Parents' Room. She follows him, wary of another outburst but unsure what else to do.

At the door, Mandy watches as Dean scans the room. Two distinct groups are gathered at each end. He looks at the group of mothers, nods at the ones he recognises. The women are drinking coffee, sharing concerns about their children, comforting each other where needed. At the far end of the room, the fathers congregate. A game of football plays quietly on a big screen and all eyes are on it. Dean gets himself a glass of water and joins the men. Mandy continues to stand at the doorway, not yet ready for Dean to see she's there. They are only a few metres apart, but the distance between them could be continents wide.

'How you doing?' several of the men ask Dean as he approaches.

'You know how it is,' he answers.

All the men murmur in agreement. Yes, they all know exactly how it is.

'Great mob, that Inspire a Wish foundation,' one of the men says quietly, not making eye contact with anyone.

Dean stares grimly at the screen, not answering.

An awkward silence surrounds the men for several moments before one of the fathers changes the subject.

'So, who's your money on here, Dean, think our boys can pull it off?'

Mandy registers Dean relaxing a little and so goes to join the women. She sees his head turn towards her but chooses not to meet his eye.

'How are you bearing up, Mandy?' It's Lauren. Her little boy is only seven but has been in and out of hospital almost as often as Jesse has.

'I'm getting there. Good days and bad days, you know?' She takes a deep breath. 'Jesse, though, she's amazing. I wish I had an ounce of her strength.'

It's all she can do to stop herself from crying. She feels Lauren's hand on her shoulder, another hand patting her back. She lets the tears come. These women *know*, they understand, in a deeper way than any of her well-meaning friends and colleagues who sympathise but can't comprehend what she's going through. These other mothers do, and she's grateful to all of them.

Someone sits her down, another woman offers her a glass of water. Mandy feels held here, her feelings acknowledged and allowed to flow – no judgement, no blame. She senses Dean looking at her again, and this time she raises her eyes to his. He doesn't seem angry any longer, just deeply sad. He holds her gaze but then, in a gesture of defeat, he turns back to the football game.

This is Dean all over, she thinks to herself. His fear of losing control, of uncertainty, of the prospect of loss. His blunt refusal of anything that might remind him of Jesse's prognosis. His lack of acceptance, stuck forever in the anger part of the grieving process. She cannot fix him; she has given up trying.

*

'I'm home!' Mandy burst into their house. 'And I have a surprise!'

It was an evening in July. Mandy was late. She had driven from the dealership, buzzing with the excitement of a new purchase. Her first car bought from new, not second-hand, the kind that she had been dreaming about for years: leather interior, heated seats, a state-of-the-art sound system. It handled like a dream. And it was, not a reward, exactly – she checked herself. Actually, yes, why not? It was a reward – for the promotion in April, to publishing director, her family had been too sad to celebrate. For her birthday in May that went unmarked – which was understandable, given everything that was going on at the time, with Jesse's health and with Sam playing up at school – but it was her fortieth. Even though she told them the family dinner Dean, Jesse and Sam cooked for her was enough, the handmade cards from them all, including the one Dean had been bullied into making with his daughter and son, had touched her deeply. But then again, there was the last eighteen months of hell.

'Good of you to drop by,' said Dean, under his breath.

It was his turn to cook tonight, and he made his usual fare of pasta bolognese, heaped with veggies and so much cheese it could never be called healthy. But it was delicious – Mandy loved it when he cooked. Carbs galore. But just like everything he did these days, his dinners were loaded with resentment and anger. He acted sometimes like he was the only one affected by Jesse's illness. They had been a great team, once upon a time, parenting together effortlessly (it seemed from this vantage point) through sleepless nights, the terrible twos and countless *everyday challenges, but now his emotions, his fury, were taking up all the space, burning up all the oxygen in the room. It was tiring and unnecessary and she didn't know how much longer she could cope with being his sparring partner.*

Jesse and Sam were already sitting at the dining table, waiting to be served. Mandy jangled her keys. 'Want to see my new ride?'

The kids gasped at each other with delighted, surprised looks on their faces. Sam jumped away from the table, tearing through the door and taking the steps down to the driveway two at a time. Jesse stood up more cautiously but no less enthusiastically, squeezing Mandy's arm as she went by. She was growing stronger, Mandy felt, but it was slow. So much slower than Amy's progress. She checked herself: she shouldn't be comparing Jesse's recovery with Amy's. They were two different girls with different battles to face.

Dean barred her way to the outside, arms folded across his chest. 'So when were you going to talk to me about this "new ride",' he demanded, the last words laced heavily with sarcasm.

Mandy sighed. 'We did talk about it, Dean.'

'And I thought we agreed that now wasn't the right time.'

'We didn't agree anything,' Mandy was careful to keep her voice to a low hiss. 'Yours is not the only opinion that matters in this house. I needed a new car, and we can afford it. I don't see what your problem is.'

'A black car? You said you wanted a black car.'

'Oh, for goodness' sake. You're being ridiculous.'

She pushed past him and walked down to the car. He was not going to spoil this for her, she wouldn't let him. She felt his presence behind her, heavy and dark, but focused instead on her

children: Sam, lolling across the bonnet of the car as if hugging it;
Jesse, standing a little way off, laughing at her brother.

Mandy pasted a smile on her face. 'Who wants a quick spin?'

Sam jumped up with his hand in the air. 'Shotgun!' he called.

Jesse dashed to the front passenger seat. 'You'll have to fight
me for it!'

'Dad?' Sam called out. 'Are you coming?'

Dean was scowling, the muscles in his jaw working furiously,
staring daggers at her beautiful, expensive-looking, chic black car,
the kind of car she always wanted. She was over feeling angry
about his anger, which seemed so random to her, so aggressive
and unreasonable. If anything, all she felt now was exhaustion.
'Dinner will be cold,' he said, turning back up the path, away
from the car and his family.

Mandy hoped that the kids didn't notice the tension at dinner.
If anything, they were too hyper, laughing and giggling about
the short drive along the bay road, Sam extolling the virtues of
the sound system, the way the car took the curves, the comfort of
the front seat his sister allowed him to have. Jesse talked about
all the places she could drive her to – the cinema, the mall and
athletics, once she was well enough to start back – which made
Mandy laugh and say that she hadn't realised her job title had
changed to personal chauffeur. Dean sat silently at the table but
separate from the family conversation, forking pasta into his
mouth, while Mandy tried to keep the atmosphere light. But
her children were quicker than usual to take their plates into
the kitchen and clear the table. Sam seemed eager to go to bed
straight away, while Jesse kissed her mum on the cheek before

heading off to her room to do homework, leaving Mandy and Dean alone, together.

Dean scraped his chair back, getting up and heading to the kitchen. He started loading the dishwasher noisily, pointedly. Mandy followed him, standing in the doorway watching him clean up, dreading the conversation they were about to have. That they needed to have.

'We need to talk, Dean,' she said finally.

'Oh, I thought my opinion didn't matter,' he shot back.

'That's not what I said, and you know it.' Mandy took a deep breath. 'You're acting unreasonably about this. We weren't talking about it, not properly, just going round in circles, there just didn't seem to be any point in continuing. The dealership was running an offer, so I decided why the hell not. With my promotion, we can afford the repayments, and you never outright rejected a new car. I didn't tell you before now because I was afraid of your reaction.'

'Afraid of my reaction.' His voice sounded calm. Flat.

'Yes, to be completely honest.'

'Well, perhaps we could have used all this new money you've got to fly out to Cyprus, see if we could have got a cure there.'

'That's unfair, Dean. That's something we definitely did talk about — there is no treatment in the world better than what she's receiving here, and you know it.'

He turned to face her, his eyes swimming. 'I asked you not to buy a black car,' he said, using the same controlled tone as before.

'What? Oh, for God's sake,' Mandy said. 'What is your problem? I've always wanted a black car, you know this. I think they look stylish. What's wrong with that?'

'It's not just a black car though, is it?' The anger that Dean had been barely suppressing came to the fore, and he punctuated each word by stabbing his forefinger on the kitchen counter. 'It's the colour of a hearse. You are going to be ferrying around our daughter – our sick daughter – in a fucking hearse.'

Mandy stood still, as shocked as if her husband had slapped her across the face. Dean stalked past her, his expression fixed and grim. She finished loading the dishwasher, then wiped down the benches and swept the floor, all the while their argument going around and around in her head. They were both exhausted, both angry. They were misunderstanding each other and not giving each other grace. But to make things right would take more energy than Mandy could spare at this point in time, especially as she wasn't sure Dean would be able to meet her halfway. If Jesse's illness had taught her anything, it was that some problems are insurmountable and some problems are not yours to fix. She put the broom and dustpan into the cupboard, ran a cloth around the sink and the taps, then leaned both hands against the counter and stared at her reflection in the dark glass of the window, readying herself for the next confrontation.

She found him in the living room, his head in his hands. When he looked up at her, his eyes were red-rimmed, but she didn't think that he had been crying. She knew he wouldn't let himself. Her heart ached for him in that moment, especially as she knew she was about to hurt him more.

'I'm sorry,' she said softly. 'Not for the car, not for its colour, but I should have told you that I had bought it. I'm sorry for springing it on you like that.'

Dean nodded, running his hand over his head. He seemed very subdued. All the fight had gone out of him. For now.

'I think you should see someone, Dean,' Mandy said gently.

He snorted. 'Like that's the solution.'

'We can't go on like this. It's got to stop,' Mandy told him, feeling strangely emotionless. She knew the tears would come, the guilt at breaking up her family. But this conversation was long overdue.

Dean looked down at the floor, rubbing his hands together, the muscles in his jaw working. 'I know we can't,' he said finally.

Mandy sat next to him. 'By "we", I meant the kids, and me. We can't keep being held hostage by your moods. It's not fair, on Sam and Jesse most of all.'

Dean let out a deep sigh, as if he had been expecting this. 'I know.'

He pressed his thumb and forefinger against his eyes, shuddering. Mandy placed her hand on his back. There was still love there. But right now, it was buried under anger, resentment, sadness and fear. In the face of Jesse's uncertain prognosis, Mandy was putting everything she had into making life better for her kids. She needed to look after herself too, in order to show up for them in the way they needed her to. And Dean? He wasn't letting the ones who loved him, love him. He was so intent on being strong that he wasn't letting himself be cared for. And Mandy saw, with sudden clarity, that if he wasn't going to let her care for him, then it was a job she could no longer take on.

He looked round at her, eyes red. 'Seeing someone. Counselling. It's not going to fix it, is it?'

She rubbed his back. 'You never know. It might. If you give it a chance.'

He sniffed again. 'That's not what I meant. It's not going to fix her, is it? What's the good of counselling, what the point of making myself feel better, when . . .'

He left his sentence hanging, unable to say the words as he put his head back in his hands. They sat there, the two of them, on the couch, touching, but as far apart as they had ever been.

Lauren brings Mandy a cup of tea from the machine. 'One sugar,' she says with a smile.

Mandy takes it gratefully, and sips. She's so thankful for the support of all these mothers, all who have similar worries, similar fears. She knows what Jesse's prognosis does for the other families on this ward because she felt it too – huge grief and concern for the children and parents involved mixed in with the fear that death might touch them too, that it was catching. And it's obvious that this is what Dean's unreasonableness about it all – her car, Alex, Jesse's wish – is all about: fear of death.

Finally, Dean breaks away from watching the football game with the other fathers, catching Mandy's eye. She nods at him – it's time to go back and be parents to their children. She gives Lauren a hug goodbye, whispers 'thank you' in her ear, and waves at the others.

Together, they walk silently back to Jesse's room. Amy is stretched out on her bed reading; she looks up from her book and throws them a warm smile. Jesse and Sam are sleeping in each other's arms. Mandy is overcome with love for her children. They fight and bicker, just like normal siblings, but it's moments like this, the quiet moments where their love for each other shines so beautifully, that Mandy wants to bottle it up, to keep it safe for a moment in the future when she needs to access that memory.

'I don't want some stranger spending time with her when we don't know how much longer we've got,' Dean whispers, breaking the moment.

Mandy fights back anger, determined to remain calm. She wishes Dean could move past his fear to see how badly Jesse needs to have her wish come true.

'Jesse knows what she wants and what's she's doing. We have to trust her,' Mandy says, not making eye contact.

They regard their children in silence for a few more moments. 'School tomorrow,' Mandy says finally.

'I'll take Sam back home and wait for you there,' Dean says.

Kissing Jesse on the forehead, Dean carefully picks up Sam. Cradling him in his arms he carries him out. Jesse wakes and struggles to sit up. Mandy gently pushes her back onto the pillows, stroking her daughter's forehead, like she used to do when she was a toddler. 'It's all right, darling, you sleep.'

'Mum, my wish—'

'You'll have your wish, darling, I promise. I'll not let anything stop you and Alex.'

'But Dad—'

With a conspiratorial smile, Mandy whispers, 'You leave him to me.'

Jesse giggles. 'How many times have you said those words to me?'

'Probably too many for your father's liking.'

'So, you'll meet Alex?'

'We'll all meet him and do everything we can to help the two of you make your wish come true.'

'It will be worth it, Mum, in the end it will be worth it, I promise you.'

'I know. Now shush, go back to sleep, I'll sit here a little longer.'

The smile doesn't leave Jesse's face, even as she falls asleep. Mandy looks over at the pinboard, noticing gaps she's sure weren't there before. She looks questioningly at Amy, who smiles a secret smile and goes back to her book.

CHAPTER 11

'Alex, long time no see!' Steve calls out.

Dammit, Alex thinks. He didn't want to draw attention to himself – it's been days since he's shown his face in the office as he's been doing some deep diving into Jesse's project. It's turning out to be even more work than he thought it would be at first. Truth be told, he's a bit daunted by it.

He strides across the office floor, acknowledging his colleagues with a nod or flick of his hand. At his desk, he gets down to business as quickly as possible, logging on before he even has his jacket off. He wants it to look as if he has been at work for a while.

Steve leans over the cubicle. 'So, how are you getting on?'

'Good, yourself?' Alex answers, facing his monitors.

'I'm good, considering we've all had to cop Ian's bullshit every day you're not here. What are you up to?'

Alex sighs and swivels his chair round to face Steve. 'I think I can do it, but I'm going to need help.'

'Anything, mate, you just have to ask. Have you talked to Ian about it?'

'I was hoping to circumvent him, you know what he's like. He'll want to string me along before he says yes.'

'That's true,' Steve scratches his head. 'I've got a deadline coming up, but I could work on it after hours. Maybe back here after dinner?'

'Or at my place, if you're up for it? I've got a pretty good set-up.'

'I'm sure you have.' Steve leaves his cubicle and pulls up a chair. 'How about you tell me about this game you're designing, this wish.'

Alex winces. 'Ian got that wrong. It's not a game; it's an interactive 3D video experience.'

'Whoa.' Steve whistles. 'Tell me more.'

'Jesse has shown me photos of her family at their favourite places. I'd like your help to go to these places and film them. Then, with the other material she has given me – drawings by her brother, poems from her mum, family photographs – we create a film for them. Next up, we bring them into the studio to recreate their special moments. What do you think?'

'So, are you saying we're going to be using the studio? We'd need permission from Frank for that.'

'Permission shouldn't be a problem – I'm doing what Frank asked me to do. I'll ask Frank about the studio when we get to that stage of development.' Alex thinks, but doesn't say, *if we get to that stage* . . . He needs to stay positive about this. 'Would it help if I show you what I've done so far?'

Steve nods, so Alex goes onto the server and navigates to a private folder. Here he's scanned in Sam's drawings, the handwritten poetry. He's created mood boards and references, trying to establish the visual tone and atmosphere of the piece, something realistic, but also charming, like stepping into your very favourite day. He's put together some concept art and sketches, based on their conversations and used some 3D models to roughly block out shots and camera movements.

Steve whistles. 'You've got this done in a few days when it takes weeks to put together a three-minute commercial? Are you sure you need me, mate?'

Alex laughs. 'I absolutely need help. I'm having trouble with the coding between the life shots and the animated. I need a specialist effects artist to work with me.' He grins at his friend. 'You don't happen to know someone, do you?'

'I can do it. The issue is *when* I can do it. Ian's constantly peering over our shoulders to see what we're up to, he'll never go for it.'

'Well, in that case, you're probably not going to like what I'm going to say next . . .'

Steve leans back in his chair and folds his arms. 'OK. Hit me with it.'

Here goes nothing . . . Alex thinks to himself. He's been building up to ask Steve this question. 'So, like I said, at home I've got a lot of the equipment we need. I'm just missing the team that brings it together.'

'The team. So more than just me?'

'Yeah.' Alex is feeling a bit sheepish now. 'I was hoping you would have a word with Phil and Sarah, and maybe Charlie too, to see if they're interested in helping us.'

'We're officially an us, huh?'

'Steve.' Alex sighs. 'Look, eventually, I can get this all done on my own. But even with your help, I'm going to be pushed for time. And Jesse . . .' Alex peters out. He's not sure he can find the right words.

Steve's expression turns serious. 'it's OK, man, I get it. I'm in. I'll have a word with the others. If coding's your problem, Sarah's your answer.'

'Thanks, mate. Appreciate it.' The two men sit in silence for a moment. 'There's just one other small thing I'm worried about.'

'Alex?' Ian shouts out from the far end of the room.

'Speak of the devil,' Alex says wryly.

'How's it all coming along?' Ian asks, slapping him on the shoulder with his usual half-aggressive fake friendliness. 'With all that time you're taking off, must be almost done by now.'

Alex shrugs off the hand. 'It's a big job, Ian. I'm actually on my way out.'

'Out. Out where?'

'I'm going back to the hospital. I need a bit more information for the, ah, game.'

'That's the attitude boy, good work. So, it's looking good?'

'Yeah, it's good, Ian. I might need to borrow some camera equipment; I need to shoot some live scenes to help make it work. Wouldn't mind if I could borrow Steve at some point too?'

'Yeah, sure, take what you need, hope you're not making a miniseries though,' Ian says, laughing at his own joke.

'Not a series Ian, just a feature,' Alex laughs back at him before turning to Steve, who shakes his head, knowing now what Alex is planning.

As Alex walks away, Ian calls out to him.

'Just let me know when you're done, I've given your current assignment to Bronwyn to finish, she'll probably do a better job than you would have anyway.'

'See you, Ian,' Alex calls out as he leaves, hearing the usual encouragement Ian gives to his colleagues yelled out:

'Now get back to work the lot of you.'

CHAPTER 12

Back on the ward, Alex enters Jesse and Amy's room to find it empty. He wonders if Jesse is with Kelly and is surprised at how the thought of finding the two of them together pleases him. He's hovering outside, not sure what to do, when Sandy walks past, does a double take, and stops. 'You came back then?' she states with a grin.

He shrugs. 'I said I would.' He clears his throat. 'Do you know where Jesse is?'

Sandy checks her watch. 'She should be just about finished with treatment. Are you in a rush?'

Alex doesn't quite know how to answer this – the fact is, he wants to get on with the project, but he needs to chat a little more with Jesse before he can. 'Sort of,' is all he can manage. 'I just need a bit more background before the next stage.'

Sandy nods. 'Well, then, why don't you wait in her room while I see if I can track her down? I'll be back shortly.'

Alex steps into the room, feeling uncomfortable. He's not sure he should be here really, and is about to head back out, to wait outside, when he's drawn to the family photo on Jesse's bedside table. Picking it up, he stares at the faces of a family. A family bound to each other physically and emotionally. This photo was taken when Jesse had a head of beautiful hair. He stares at the photo for a long time, so caught up that he doesn't hear Jesse enter the room, wheeled in by an orderly.

'Have you got any photos of your family I can see?' Jesse asks, startling him as she steps out of the wheelchair, grasping her IV pole, and standing beside Alex. He quickly replaces the photo before turning to face Jesse, putting on a fake smile, shaking his head no.

'You should carry a photo of your family with you.'

Jesse steps closer to the bedside table and studies the photo he has just replaced.

'When I'm not feeling so good I look at them and know they love me and that I must be strong for them.'

Alex tries to read her face as he watches her, looking so lovingly at her family. 'Aren't they meant to be strong for you?'

'That's not the way I see it.'

Jesse climbs onto her bed, drawing her knees up under her chin.

'What's wrong?' Alex asks as he pulls up the chair and sits beside the bed.

'There's something I should probably tell you about my family.'

Alex fiddles with the bag in his lap, giving Jesse the time to decide what she will say.

'My parents are separated; they don't live together

anymore. Sam and I, well, when I'm not in here, we live with Mum, but we still see Dad a lot.'

Alex nods. 'I'm sorry.'

'My dad has trouble with me being sick. He just can't deal with it, and he and Mum were fighting all the time, so he moved out.'

'That's rough.'

'Do you want to know what they were fighting about?'

'I presume it was about you.'

'Yeah. It was all sorts of things, really. Like, my dad was spending all his time researching cures in other countries, contacting hospitals here, there and everywhere. Once, he even flew to Cyprus because they had a hospital that claimed it could cure me.'

'And your mum?'

'She got several opinions, of course, but they were all saying the same thing.'

'What about you, what did you want?'

'You know, you're the first person to ask me that. It was like they were the parents, they knew what was best for me even if they couldn't agree.'

'So would you—'

'Have liked to go to another country? I never really thought about it as I wasn't asked, I just overheard all the fighting. And I couldn't do that to Sam, drag him away from his school and friends. I spoke to Sandy and Christine and asked them what they thought was best.'

'What did they say?'

'They showed me the other countries' data relevant to my

situation, and no one had treatment better than what they were giving me here.'

'So, you stayed here and your dad doesn't like it?'

'It was more that he couldn't accept that Mum wouldn't even try, but she was trying, trying to make these past two years as easy on me as she could. My mum's not a quitter.'

'I bet you take after her.'

'I hope so. I didn't really want to be around strangers. At least here there's Amy, Ryan and Luke.'

'I'm sorry, Jesse.'

'You already said that.'

'Would you like me to come back when you're feeling better?'

Before Jesse can answer they are interrupted by the sound of her name being called out as a young boy runs into the room, a woman right behind him. Alex recognises them from the photos. Sam and Jesse's mum, Mandy. Sam stops stock still when he sees Alex, a look of apprehension on his face.

'Hey, Sammy, come and give me a hug,' Jesse says to her brother. 'There's someone here I want you to meet.'

Walking slowly to the bed, his eyes never leaving Alex, Sam hops up and is enveloped in a hug by his big sister.

'Is this him?' he asks Jesse cautiously.

Alex stands as Mandy walks towards him, her hand outstretched.

'Hello, you must be Alex. I'm Mandy, Jesse's mum, and this is Sam.'

Alex takes Mandy's hand and gently shakes it, not knowing what to say.

'This is Alex,' Jesse proudly says.

'It's a pleasure to meet you, Alex,' Mandy says with genuine warmth.

'Nice meeting you too, Mrs—'

'Mandy is fine.'

'Thank you, Mandy.' Alex turns to Sam who hasn't stopped looking at him. He holds out his hand. 'Hi, Sam.'

Sam shakes Alex's hand while Mandy is making herself comfortable on Jesse's bed. She hugs Jesse tightly, kissing her on both cheeks, then hugging her some more.

'How are you, my darling?' she finally asks. 'I've just spoken with Sandy and Dr Christine; they said you tolerated the chemo really well today. How are you feeling?'

'I'm fine, Mum, but you have to let me go so we can talk to Alex.'

With her arm still around Jesse, Mandy turns to Alex.

'I want you to know how grateful I . . . I mean, we, are for your making Jesse's wish come true. It's so important—'

'Mum, he's not doing it on his own, he's working with me, we are doing it together.'

Mandy gives Alex a conspiratorial look, as if to say, 'That's teenagers for you!' but Alex knows she's not criticising her daughter. She just seems to want to be beside her, hug her, comfort her. Sam is acting the same way. Alex is not used to such overt displays of affection, though he recognises that these are special circumstances.

'Well, we won't interrupt you any longer, we just stopped by on our way to Sam's tennis lesson. We'll be back later. Will you still be here, Alex?'

'Yes, he will, he needs to meet all of you. *All* my family,' Jesse answers firmly for Alex.

The look of concern on Mandy's face doesn't go unnoticed by Alex. But with one final hug, Mandy takes Sam's hand and helps him down from the bed. Then, calling out goodbye, they leave. Sam hasn't said a word.

'Did my mum make you feel uncomfortable? I mean, you looked uncomfortable.'

'I don't know what you mean,' Alex says, his tone defensive again.

'Didn't you like your mum hugging you?'

'Which one?' Alex says bluntly.

'Huh?'

Looking down at his lap, Alex says, 'I had about ten "mothers".' He looks up into Jesse's face. 'My mum died when I was seven. I hardly remember her.' He immediately regrets having been so honest.

Jesse looks down, begins fiddling with a blanket. 'And what about your dad?' she asks softly.

'Never knew him,' Alex says. 'But hey, that's all ancient history. I just know you're very lucky.'

Amy enters the room and sees Jesse and Alex, both with their heads down. 'Somebody died?' Amy asks with a gleam in her eye.

Jesse begins to laugh. Alex is shocked when Amy walks up to him and pokes him in the side.

'Nope, not dead, but not exactly full of life. How's the wish coming along?'

'We keep getting interrupted,' Jesse says still laughing.

'Well, I'll put a stop to that,' Amy says, climbing up on the bed to sit cross-legged opposite Jesse. The two girls immediately carry on as the fun-loving teenagers they are. Alex cannot fathom the dramatic emotional changes around him and walks back to the pinboard, focusing on the photo with Jesse and her father listening to music through shared headphones. He turns back to the girls.

'Jesse, I need to start filming some of the places in the photos, how about I come back later?'

'When you come back later this afternoon, Alex, make it quite late. My dad should be here then and you two need to meet,' Jesse says.

'Meeting the father, that's huge, Alex,' Amy says playfully.

'Stop it, Amy, you'll frighten him off,' Jesse answers with a giggle.

Alex has had all the teen teasing and emotional roller-coasters he can take for the moment. Gathering up his bag he mutters, 'OK, I'll try. No promises,' and hurries from the room.

CHAPTER 13

'So, Jesse,' Amy says, once Alex has left. 'I . . . um. I've got some, um, news.' She's not meeting Jesse's eye. Instead, she's playing with the hospital blanket, weaving it around her fingers. Jesse has an immediate pang of fear for her friend. She looks well – she seems to have been responding to treatment, she has more energy than usual, is louder, more active. With the sun coming in from the window and lighting up her freckles, the only giveaway that she's ill is her head, covered in downy hair. But Jesse knows how quickly things can change.

'What is it, Amy? You're scaring me.'

Amy shakes her head, presses her lips together. 'No, it's nothing to be scared about, it's not scary, I mean, it's a bit scary, but . . .' She looks up at Jesse. There are tears in her eyes, but she's not looking sad, not exactly. If Amy's expression reveals anything, it's hope. She's hopeful. And in that moment, Jesse knows. She experiences it as a great lurch in her stomach, almost painful. A swell of anger, of jealousy, of fear. But also, relief, and happiness. Happiness for her friend.

'You're in remission,' she says softly, not trusting her voice.

Amy nods, and grasps both of Jesse's hands. 'My parents . . . they're telling your mum and dad tonight. But I wanted to be the one to tell you, I wanted to be the one to let you know.' She gulps and wipes her eyes with the heel of her hand. 'I'm so sorry, Jesse, I'm so, so sorry . . .'

Jesse feels the tears spring up. 'Don't be sorry, I'm happy for you, honestly I am. Come here.'

They hug, Amy sobbing hard, Jesse stroking her friend's back and telling her not to worry. It's all going to work out. It's all going to be fine. She's saying this as much for herself as she is for her friend. They have been through so much together, they have whispered in the darkness all their hopes, their dreams, their fears. They have confided in each other, shared secrets, played video games. They've even been snarky at each other, or silent, when the treatment got too hard. And they've never needed to explain, because they know, better than anyone else, what the other is going through. It's always been the two of them together. And they are about to travel on very different paths. But right now, it's just Jesse and Amy, Amy and Jesse, BFFs. Best friends forever.

'You don't hate me, do you?' Amy asks, pulling away from Jesse.

'Course not, you big idiot,' Jesse says, playfully punching her friend in the shoulder.

'You know, it's because your blood is just too posh. Whereas mine . . .' Amy points her thumbs at herself. 'Plebian, through and through.'

'Common as muck,' Jesse agrees, grinning.

The two laugh for a moment, then fall silent, Amy tracing the pattern on the blanket with her finger.

'I really am sorry,' she says, after a while.

'I know,' Jesse replies.

'It still could happen, for you I mean. They still could find someone.'

'Yeah,' says Jesse. 'Yeah, they could . . .' Jesse settles back into her pillows and looks out of the window.

CHAPTER 14

'Over there, that looks like the place,' Alex tells Steve as the two of them, each carrying a high-end camcorder secured around their necks, wander through the park. Alex looks down the viewing pane in front of him, adjusting the angle from wide to tight and back.

'So how do you want to do this?' Steve asks.

'The photos show them under those trees having some sort of picnic. They're on a rug and there's food. It's the right park, just need to make sure it's the right spot,' Alex tells him. 'I want to walk with them to the spot, then we'll do some panning scenes from where they were sitting. You know the drill. You do the wide shots; I'll go in for the close-ups.'

Steve nods. 'Sounds good.'

'Turn the sound off. We don't need it as we'll be superimposing them into the scenes in the studio. We'll get all the audio we need then.'

'Which angle do you think we should come in from?' Steve asks.

Alex looks around, sees the car park in the distance.

'I reckon they would have parked there,' he points out. 'Come in on that angle.'

As Steve walks towards the car park Alex calls after him, 'I don't want anyone in the shot – you might have to wait so you avoid those families coming in.'

'Yeah, yeah, I know what I'm doing. By the way, you did get a permit for us to be filming today, didn't you?'

'Sure,' Alex calls out.

'No, you didn't. Guerrilla filming again. One day we'll get caught,' Steve mutters to himself as he looks down into the lens of his camera, framing the shot he's about to capture.

Alex and Steve separate, each filming different parts of the park and playground. After a while they come together again, cameras still rolling, sound off. Without looking up Steve coughs to get Alex's attention.

'So, I was thinking, maybe you'd like to come to a small gathering I'm having for Lydia. It's her fortieth next month and I thought I'd surprise her with a party. I was thinking we would have it at home but now I'm thinking this could be a great place, plenty of room for kids to run around and the playground, and well, do you think you'd be up for that?'

Caught off guard, Alex takes his time to answer, concentrating on the viewing pane showing him what he is filming. 'Forty, eh?' He whistles. 'You there yet?'

'Yeah, a few years ago. It was lockdown and our youngest was just a baby, so it was just the family.'

'The family? You know, I don't know if you've got any siblings,' Alex asks. 'Do you?'

'A brother and a sister, one lives out in the country, the other overseas. What about you?'

'None that I'm aware of. But who knows what my old man got up to in his day? For all I know you and I are half-brothers.'

'You clearly haven't met my dad. So, what do you say? It'll be quite quiet – just Lyd's folks and two sisters – sorry, man, they're both married – and a couple of friends. I was thinking about inviting Sarah too. She and Lydia have met a couple of times and kind of bonded over soy-milk lattes or some such concoction.'

'Yeah . . . I dunno . . .'

'Go on, mate. What else have you got to do? And it'll get Lyds off my back. She's always banging on: "When are you going to bring home your work bestie? When can I meet your work bestie? Why are you hiding your work bestie from me?"'

Alex stops short. *Work bestie?* he thinks to himself.

'So, yeah, she's obsessed,' Steve continues, 'so you'll be doing me a favour by showing your face. She's starting to think I made you up.'

'Work bestie?' Alex wonders, this time out loud. '*Me?*'

Steve stops, takes a spare bottle of water out of his bag and hands it to Alex. 'Course you are, you dickhead.'

Alex shakes his head, grinning as he realises that, yeah, it's true. If there is such a thing as a work bestie, then Steve fills the brief. He discovers that he likes it. 'Let me know the date. I guess if you're having it here, I know where to come.'

'Sure, no problem.' Steve doesn't seem to realise how

momentous this revelation has been to Alex. 'I'll let you know when I've organised it a bit better. I'll probably have to get one of her sisters to help me.'

'I think we're just about done here,' Alex says. 'I'm going to take some still photos to show Jesse where I've been, then I'm going to head back over to see her. I'll come into the office in a bit and get the hard drive from you. Thanks for your help, Steve, I mean it.'

'You're welcome, I'll see you back in the office.'

As Steve walks back to the car park Alex flicks a switch on his camera from video to photo and snaps away.

Buoyed up by his first day filming, with some still shots to show Jesse, Alex walks through 6 East smiling. The ward is full of family and friends surrounded by those young patients mobile enough to be out of their rooms.

'Hey, Alex, what are you up to?' Ryan calls out. He's with two adults, and a younger girl and boy.

'Hi, Ryan, I'm just going to see Jesse.'

'Will you come and say hello to my family?'

Alex walks over to the family.

'This is my mum Gaylene, my dad Norm.'

Ryan wraps his arm playfully around his younger brother, 'And this is Ash, or Ashton as Mum and Dad call him, and my kid sister Sienna.'

'Hello,' Alex greets them all gruffly.

'We've heard about you from Ryan,' Gaylene says, extending her hand for Alex to shake.

'And Dean,' Norm says, shaking Alex's hand. 'Sorry,

probably shouldn't have mentioned that,' he adds, looking sheepish.

'That's OK, it's nice to meet you. Good to see you, Ryan, I'd better go.'

'Sure, say hi to Jesse for me, and don't forget, no upsetting her,' Ryan says, gently punching Alex on the arm.

'We're going down to the cafeteria to get milkshakes to have in the garden. Nice to meet you,' Gaylene says. 'Oh look, there's Luke and his family. Norm, go and ask them if they'd like to join us.'

Alex slowly walks away, watching as Ryan's father greets Luke and his family. Luke looks over at him and waves.

Alex spies Amy with a couple he guesses are her parents and she waves for him to go on into her room. He watches as Amy tells her parents who he is, and they turn and smile back at him.

There's no sound coming from Jesse's room, so Alex enters slowly. He freezes, unsure of whether to go in or turn and go home. Jessie is lying on her bed, propped up with pillows. The man Alex recognises as her father lies beside her, their faces almost touching. Jesse holds her phone, and each of them is wearing one ear pod. Both are clearly lost in music.

Alex watches for several moments before deciding to leave. Turning, the bag he carries knocks against the wall. Jesse opens her eyes and sees him. Jerking to sit up, she pulls out her ear pod. Dean sits up and follows Jesse's gaze to Alex.

'I didn't mean to disturb you,' Alex blurts.

Dean scrambles from the bed. 'Well, you did. You are?'

Jesse struggles to sit up on her pillows. 'Dad, this is Alex. I told you about him.'

'What? Oh yeah. Alex. Look, now's not a good time—'

'He's come here to meet you, please, Dad—'

'OK, honey, calm down. Alex, let's step outside for a few minutes,' Dean says, walking through the door, clearly expecting Alex to follow him.

'Dad . . .' a worried Jesse calls out.

'It's OK, Jesse, I'll be back in a minute.'

Alex looks at Jesse who shrugs her shoulders, so he follows her father.

Dean walks towards the doors leaving the ward and stops to the side to prevent them opening. Turning to Alex he talks quietly, but firmly. 'Sorry to waste your time, we're all good here, Jesse's good.'

'I don't understand, I'm here for Jesse, I'm making her wish come true.'

Hearing the word wish Dean struggles to control himself, clenching his fists, fighting internally.

'I just said, we don't need your help.'

'I don't mean to upset you, you are Jesse's father, but I've been asked by Inspire a Wish—'

'Don't mention that name, you hear me?' Dean has his finger in Alex's face. They are almost the same height, but Alex gets the sense of the older man looming over him. 'If my daughter wants something, anything, I'll be the one to get it for her, not some stranger.'

'Please, Mr Morgan, I'm not trying to take anything away from you and your daughter, quite the opposite, I'm wanting to help her give something to you and your family. A wish, a gift that I admit I didn't want any part of initially, but now, now that I've got to know Jesse and believe in what she wants for you, I want to do this.'

'Well, you don't get to do "this" for her, I told you: her family will get whatever Jesse wants, whatever she needs. Get outta here, pal, and don't come back.'

Alex holds his anger in check; all he can do now is protect himself as he says the words he doesn't truly feel. 'OK, settle down. I'll go and tell Jesse you don't want me helping her, and, what the hell, I was just sent to do a job; if you say I'm not wanted . . .'

As Alex moves towards Jesse's room, Dean cuts him off. 'I'll be the one to tell her,' Dean says putting a hand up to stop Alex advancing.

'Look, the project's going really well, but we need to keep going. I've been told there's not much time to do this for Jesse,' Alex is almost pleading.

Dean gets in his face, furious now, shouting. 'Who the hell do you think you are, saying that to me?'

'OK. I'm out of here.' Alex realises there's no reasoning with him, and turns to leave.

It's only now that he sees Mandy and Sam, frozen, standing outside Jesse's room and looking at them both in horror. With a giant wave of shame, Alex realises that everyone on the ward – and, worst of all, Jesse and her family – have overheard this altercation. The two men glance at each other, and Alex wonders if Dean is just as mortified as he is.

Sam struggles out of his mum's grasp and runs towards

the two men. 'Stop it. Stop it, leave him alone, Dad!'

'Sammy, it's OK, I know what I'm doing—'

'We can't help her, Dad. *He* can.'

Dean kneels and attempts to pull Sam into an embrace. 'Jesse doesn't need him, she's got us.'

Sam pulls free from his father and runs towards Jesse's room. Staff, patients and visitors look on with concern. Dean goes after Sam, Mandy hurries after them both. Alex hesitates before slowly following them. As he passes the nurses' station Sandy mouths a 'sorry' as she picks up the phone, dialling.

Alex pauses at the entrance to Jesse's room. Her parents watch on as Amy comes over to him and gently takes one of his arms. Together they look into the room. Sam is cuddled up with Jesse, her mother sitting on her bed, stroking Sam's hair. Dean stands apart looking out the window.

'Show me, come on,' Jesse says tenderly to Sam.

From inside his jacket, Sam produces several drawings which Alex and Amy struggle to see from their position. As Jesse looks at each one, she places them on the bed.

'You did all these today?'

'Yep,' Sam says.

'They're great, Sammy, really great. What else did you do today?'

Sam looks over at his father.

'It's all right, Sam, we both know Dad loves us.' She looks over at her father and sees him flinch. 'He just has trouble sometimes knowing what's right for us.' She looks down at Sam. 'Don't you agree?'

Sam shrugs a maybe. Jesse looks up and sees Alex and Amy standing in the doorway.

'I'll sort things out with Dad later and don't worry, Alex will still help me with my wish.' She looks directly at Alex.

'But I heard Dad tell him to go away,' Sam says.

'I probably shouldn't have asked him to come back tonight. This is our time, family time, right?'

'But you need him,' Sam tells her.

'I need you, and Mum and Dad more,' she tells him. Alex glances at Mandy, who is wiping away a tear. When he looks at Dean, the pain that is written all over his face is so clear to see. This is a man who loves his family, Alex realises, even if he doesn't know how to help them.

Alex startles as Kelly taps him on the shoulder. She indicates for him to follow her.

Alex follows Kelly to a far corner of the hospital cafeteria. 'Coffee? Tea?' she asks.

'I'll take a coffee. Long black.'

Kelly nods and heads over to order. The barista makes a joke and Kelly laughs – Alex can't help but notice what a pretty smile she has. As he waits, he looks around the café. Families and friends sit with patients, many in pyjamas and gowns, several have IV poles beside them, watching their visitors drink and eat, envy on many of their faces.

Kelly places the coffee on the table and throws two sachets of sugar at him, for which he's grateful.

'How old is she again?' Alex asks, dumping both sachets of sugar into his coffee.

'Fifteen.'

'She puts most adults to shame. Did you see the way she was with Sam?'

Kelly nods.

'She'd just heard that her father's not going to let me make the one thing she wants happen, and she's comforting Sam.'

'Maturity and wisdom don't necessarily come with age, Alex. That's one of the first things you learn here, it's life experiences that make us who we are, not years lived.'

In silence they drink their coffee, Kelly watching him go through a range of emotions, contemplating what to do next, what to say to her, to Jesse, to Ian.

'Is this too much for you, Alex?' Kelly asks finally.

He glances up at her words, but he sees no judgement there, just concern.

'This is hard stuff, and it's going to get harder,' Kelly continues. 'There is no shame in walking away at this point. You have to take care of yourself too.'

'Yeah, it's a lot, but no, I'm not going anywhere. I'll stop when Jesse says stop.'

Kelly nods, as if this is what she expected Alex to say. 'I'm happy to hear that. But we need to factor in Dean. Saying that, I know how difficult he can be.'

'At what age can a patient make their own decisions?'

'That would be eighteen, unless there are exceptional circumstances. But don't forget, Jesse has two parents, and Mandy is on board.'

'I've met Mandy, she's really nice.'

'Mandy is a very special person. She's doing the best she can, in the circumstances,' Kelly says.

'So, what do we do from here?' Alex asks.

'We just have to hope that Jesse and Mandy will be able to talk Dean round, I guess. But I'd just get on with it, if I were you. Don't stop until Jesse says you can stop.'

Alex looks at Kelly, seeing her for the first time as someone other than a social worker. Maybe she's not so bad after all.

Finishing his coffee he stands. 'Thank you for the coffee and the chat. I better get back to it.'

Offering a smile, Kelly says, 'Goodnight, Alex.'

At the doors to the cafeteria, Alex looks back to see that Kelly is watching him. He raises his hand goodbye.

And thinks of her smile all the way home.

In the dimly lit room he calls his office, Alex runs the two sets of filming he and Steve shot earlier in the day. On a third screen he cuts and pastes a portion of the long-range scene, splicing it with the up-close video he filmed under the trees. Repeating this process, he settles on one scene combining the two. Adjacent to the scenes he makes system notes: insert a Sam drawing, merge it into video; talk to Sarah to help with special effects, possibly change the seasons to show multiple visits.

'Aw, Max, what have I got myself into?' he murmurs.

Max rises and places his two front paws on Alex's lap. He's rewarded with an intense rub behind the ears.

'Fancy a late-night run?'

Before Alex can get out of his chair Max has bolted for the front door. By the time Alex gets there he is holding his lead in his mouth, ready to go.

'Slow down, boy. How would you like a ride in the car?'

Alex and Max drive to a park Alex has spotted near the hospital which is sign-posted as dog friendly. He's decided his buddy should try a new place to roam free.

Leaving the car in a suburban street across the road from the floodlit park, Alex and Max spend the next hour walking, running and playing. Alex can't help thinking of Jesse, her family and the playground he and Steve filmed earlier that day. It's well into the evening when Alex hooks up Max's lead and together, they cross the street and walk towards the car. Night revellers walk around them, several of whom pat Max, and he obliges with a wag of his tail and a friendly lick.

'Alex! Is that you?' a voice calls out.

Five women are walking towards him in the dim light. It takes him a moment to recognise the woman who called out to him. Sandy.

'Hi, what are you doing here?' he asks.

'I could ask you the same question. We've been out to dinner and are now heading to a club. I'd invite you to join us but I'm afraid dogs aren't allowed.' Bending down, Sandy pats Max. 'He's lovely. He is a boy, isn't he?'

'Yes, this is Max. Wow, you look different.'

The other women stand a little way off watching Sandy talking with Alex and Max.

'Kelly, aren't you going to say hello?'

Alex turns to see Kelly walk from the group of women,

towards them. She looks very different away from the hospital. 'Hi, Alex, how are you?'

'Kelly, hello, this is a surprise. I brought Max here for a run in the park.'

Kelly bends down to pat the dog. 'Well, hello, Max. My name is Kelly.'

Max wags his tail furiously, licking and nuzzling Kelly.

'You like dogs?' Alex asks.

'You could say that. I paid for my university education dog-sitting and dog-walking. I didn't know you had a dog, though.'

'There's a lot of things you don't know about me,' Alex says, cringing as the words come out of his mouth.

'I imagine there is. It's good to see you.'

'So, you're going clubbing?'

Kelly rolls her eyes. 'Sandy thinks I needed to get out more. Normally, I'm a stay at home and watch a black-and-white movie kinda gal.'

'Me too, I love old movies.'

'One more thing I now know about you.'

'Kelly, are you coming?' one of the women calls out.

'I'd better go. Have a great evening, I'll see you at the hospital,' she says.

Alex watches Kelly join the other women. Only when they are out of sight does he open the car door for Max to get in the back so they can go home.

CHAPTER 15

A bleary-eyed Alex enters 6 East, heading towards Jesse and Amy's room. From behind the nurses' station, Sandy steps out to meet him.

'Have you spoken to Kelly today?'

'No, should I have?'

Sandy gives him a warm smile. 'She's asked to see you before you see Jesse.'

'Why?'

Her smile is comforting, but Sandy doesn't give anything away. 'She's in her office. Ground floor. I think you know the way?'

Alex catches the lift down to the ground floor and follows the signs to the social work department. Greeted by the receptionist, he is immediately shown into Kelly's office. He is feeling uneasy about all this. Has Kelly brought him down here to tell him his services are no longer needed? He pales, thinking of what that might mean.

A late night shows on Kelly, her eyes tired, her hair a little messier than usual as she comes around from her desk and, thanking the receptionist for bringing Alex to her, closes the door. Alex stays standing as she sits back behind her desk.

'Is Jesse OK?' Alex asks.

'Oh,' Kelly says, 'I'm so sorry if you were worried. Yes, she's OK. Well, much the same. I've been talking to Mandy, and we think the time is right to give you some context and background.'

Alex sighs in relief and sits down in one of the chairs opposite Kelly. He slept very little last night, and he feels he can finally see a way to create what Jesse wants. Now he is frustrated by the sudden formality. He just wants to see Jesse and show her the work he did last night, all there on the laptop tucked away in his bag.

'How long have you known her?' he asks.

'About two years, since she was first diagnosed.'

'What's actually wrong with her?'

Kelly sighs softly. 'I'm sorry we've not told you anything before, but Mandy thought now was the right time for you to know about Jesse's diagnosis and prognosis, and she's asked me to tell you. It's quite hard for the family to explain over and over again what's happening to their child.'

Alex nods, dread pooling in his stomach.

It looks like Kelly also finds this news difficult to impart. She laces her fingers together, her gaze on the table, as if she's reading from an invisible script. 'Jesse has ALL, which stands for acute lymphocytic leukaemia.'

'Sounds bad.'

'It can be. In Jesse's case, it is. In children and young adults, it has a high success rate of remission and cure but unfortunately for Jesse she has not responded to the many rounds of treatment. A little over a year ago she had a bone marrow transplant from Sam. He was the closest match in the family but sadly it failed. She has a rare blood combination of both her parents, making neither one of them a match. She's never stayed in remission for very long and her only chance is another bone marrow transplant but that doesn't seem to be available.'

'What's so difficult about it?'

'It's not like a blood transfusion if that's what you're thinking. It involves taking bone marrow from a donor and transferring it into the patient. But here's the thing: there are a lot of markers that need to be met before it can be attempted. The compatibility indicators between the donor and patient must be high.'

'And Sam's wasn't high enough?'

'It was as high as we could get from any of Jesse's family. Just about every adult member of her extended family all over the country was tested and only Sam was close enough to try.'

'So, you need to be a family member then?'

'Mostly, though occasionally a stranger with the right markers can work. It's so hard to find suitable donors that register for bone marrow. We are constantly searching the database for new donors registered.'

'What about Amy and those two boys I've seen with the girls?'

'Ryan has ALL, and he is responding to treatment, Amy and Luke have CLL which has a better success rate of cure, and . . .' Kelly takes a deep breath. She looks as serious as Alex has ever seen her. 'There's something else you should know, something that Mandy wanted me to tell you before you next saw Jesse. Amy has officially gone into remission; she will be discharged shortly.'

'Oh,' Alex says, leaning back in his chair. 'Oh no, poor Jesse.'

'We are pleased for Amy, of course we are. And Jesse is taking the news well – you've seen how mature she is. But still, it's a difficult time as you can imagine.'

Alex is not sure he can. He likes Amy, likes her buzzy energy, but he's here for Jesse, and can't quite comprehend how difficult this news must be for her. Poor kid. He wants to get back to Jesse and get on with the work.

'Is this why you wanted to see me?'

Kelly sits back in her chair. 'I'm afraid we have a problem.'

Alex looks directly at her. The ball is in her court.

'Dean has left instructions with the staff that you are not allowed near Jesse,' she blurts out.

'How is that my problem?'

Kelly stares back at him, clearly at a loss. 'Well, how can you make Jesse's wish if—'

'Look. This is how I see it. I was asked to do a job, I'm here to do it and if you have a problem getting me access to Jesse, then that's your problem, not mine.'

'You're being unreasonable, don't you understand . . .'

'Oh, I understand. Either you make it possible for me to see Jesse or there is no wish. You have to deal with the father, not me.'

Kelly stands, clearly outraged. 'You're refusing to help here, is that what you're saying?'

Alex also stands, placing both his hands on the desk, leaning towards Kelly, who doesn't budge.

'I'm going back to my office now to tell my boss I was here twice yesterday, when I was verbally attacked by Jesse's father, and again today but unfortunately the social worker has been unable to get me access to the patient, to Jesse.' His voice changes to sorry and pathetic. 'I tried my best, boss, I truly did but her father won't let me see her, according to the social worker, that is.'

'What if Dean doesn't find out? What if you work with Jesse and Dean needn't know?'

'Sneak around behind his back, looking over my shoulder in case he sees me and comes after me, is that what you're asking me to do?'

'No. Yes, kind of, just be careful but do what you can for Jesse.'

Alex shakes his head in frustration. He turns and leaves.

As Alex leaves the office Kelly comes around from her desk and calls out to his retreating back, walking down the department corridor, 'I was right all along, you are an arrogant—'

'Arrogant what?' Alex says, turning back to look at her.

'Person, male, thing, whatever.'

Kelly slumps into the chair Alex has just vacated and her colleague George from the office across the corridor comes in, sitting in the second chair.

'Well, that didn't go well then,' he says, 'anything I can do to help?'

'Why are men such jerks?' she asks.

When he doesn't answer Kelly looks at him apologetically. 'I'm sorry, George, not all men, just some.'

'That one, huh?'

'Yeah.'

'What are you going to do?'

'I have to talk to Jesse; I've got to tell her about her father refusing Alex access to her and see if there is something else we can offer her for her wish.'

'What's the issue?'

'I'm just . . .' Kelly looks down at her lap, sighs. 'I can't seem to do the right thing. Dean wants to refuse Alex access to Jesse. Although everyone else wants Jesse to have her wish, he's just putting up too many roadblocks.'

'I've got to say, I wouldn't want to be in your position. That's tough. Has Mandy tried talking to him?'

Kelly sighs. 'I think everyone has tried talking to him. He's just not budging.' She pulls the sleeves of her cardigan over her hands, a habit that she's had since she was a child. 'Last night, they almost came to blows. And that's why Dean has told the staff not to give Alex access.'

George's expression is serious. 'You all want to help Jesse, but you're coming at it from different directions.'

'It should be what Jesse wants, right? She should have the final say.' Kelly puts her head in her hands. 'I just don't know how I feel about going against her father's wishes, however much I disagree with him.'

George nods. 'What are you going to do?'

Kelly sits up, takes a long deep breath. 'I have to talk to Jesse; I've got to tell her about her father refusing Alex access to her and see if there is something else, anything else, we can offer her.'

George reaches over and pats Kelly's arm. 'You've got this. And if you need some support, you know where I am.'

Kelly smiles wanly and stands up to do what she has to do.

In the hospital parking garage, Alex sits on his bike, helmet in hand, not knowing what to do, where to go. He's been drawn into the world of Jesse, her family and friends, and then there's Kelly. Why does she mess with his head?

'You all right, mate?' a passing stranger asks. In this location this is a perfectly understandable question to ask. Everyone coming and going from this car park is a patient, friend or family member of a patient. Compassion and empathy come with admission.

'Yeah, fine, thanks,' Alex responds, putting his helmet on and pulling the visor down, covering the eyes that threaten to make a liar out of him.

Exiting the hospital grounds, Alex turns away from the direction of his office and heads to the beach.

Kelly pauses in the entrance to Jesse's room, unobserved.

Jesse is sitting on Amy's bed, showing her Sam's latest pictures. A piece of paper with neat feminine writing falls from the pile she is holding.

Amy picks it up and begins reading. 'What's this? Did Sam do this?'

Jesse looks up. 'No, that's from Mum, another poem.'

'They're so personal.'

'Yeah, they are.'

'Then why do you have them on your board where anyone can see?'

'Dunno. I guess I can lie here, look over there and see them and in my head read them. I know them all off by heart.'

'Oh, Jesse, that's so beautiful.'

'I've seen Dad look at them, but I don't think he's ever read them. I showed one to Alex and he seemed to get upset.'

Kelly shifts uncomfortably – maybe it's time that she announces her presence.

'I thought the last one you showed me was the most beautiful thing I've ever read. This is, well, it's your mum and your relationship in the most beautiful words,' Amy says, wiping a tear away.

'I showed Alex the other one.'

'You what? You let him read a poem your mum wrote about her love for you?'

'Well, yeah, what with him losing his mum so young, I thought maybe he might like to read what mine writes.'

'Or get totally freaked out and upset. I don't think that was such a good idea, Jesse.'

'What's not a good idea?' Kelly says, full of smiles as she joins the girls at Amy's bed.

Jesse quickly grabs the poem from Amy's hands.

'Hi, Kelly, nothing, we were just talking,' Jesse hurriedly says.

'It's OK, girls your age *should* have secrets. I get it. But, Jesse, can I talk to you a minute?'

'Sure.'

'Can we go into another room?'

'No, you can say anything in front of Amy, she's my best friend, you know.' Jesse gives Amy a wink. 'What's up?'

Feeling cornered, Kelly shuffles her feet before beginning. 'It's about Alex . . .'

'What about him?' Jesse interrupts.

'Well, he won't be back, I'm afraid, we're going to have to rethink your wish . . .'

'What did you say to him?' Jesse demands.

'I just told him he couldn't see you anymore, but Jesse—'

Clambering from the bed, Jesse stands, hands on hips, glaring at Kelly, fire in her eyes.

'I knew you didn't like him. This is all your fault, Kelly. He could do it; I really believe he could do it and you've sent him away!'

Taken aback, all Kelly can do is stammer. 'I . . . it's not like that, Jesse, it's your father who's objecting—'

'I know that but all you had to do was convince Dad that Alex could make my wish, how hard did you try? Or maybe convince Alex to do it without my dad knowing, at least in the beginning.'

'I know this isn't what you want to hear, Jesse, but I have to respect your parents' wishes.'

'But you don't seem to respect my wish!' she snaps. 'I want you to leave now!'

Kelly has never seen Jesse like this – perhaps, she thinks, she's underestimated the teen's determination. 'I'll come back in a bit and maybe we can discuss this more, once you've had a think about it. See if there is a wish we can do that everyone is in agreement with.'

'It's just my dad who doesn't want this,' Jesse mutters. 'And you, apparently.'

Kelly takes a deep breath. 'I'll come back soon,' she says, 'we'll sort something out. I promise.'

But Jesse has turned away from her, her back shaking. Amy comes over, flashes an accusatory look at Kelly, and gives Jesse a hug.

Kelly heads for Sandy's office, knocking and entering without waiting for an answer. Dropping into a chair opposite Sandy's desk she waits while Sandy finishes writing in a patient's record. A pile of similar records in front of her, waiting for her attention, are pushed aside.

'How did it go?' Sandy asks sympathetically.

'Not well, to say the least. First Alex tells me it's my fault, and Jesse now thinks the same. They both say I should have done more to make it happen and keep Dean out of the way. But I can't do that, can I? It feels wrong to go against Dean like this. And Alex . . .' She turns her head away, her brain buzzing.

'What about Alex?' Sandy prompts.

'Oh, I don't know.' Kelly shifts in her seat, she can't get comfortable. Her clothes feel too restrictive. 'He's so prickly. He's hard to pin down.'

'Well . . .' Sandy looks like she was about to say something but thought better of it.

Kelly looks up sharply. 'What?'

Sandy leans back in her seat. 'Just that you could have been nicer to him. Made him feel welcome on the ward, offered to run interference with Dean, been supportive of Jesse's wish, helped—'

'Hey, slow down. I came in here looking for comfort.'

'Kelly, listen to me. It's not just me saying this. Others have noticed too. We're worried about you. Is everything all right?'

'I'm fine, it's just this guy rattles me, I don't know what it is about him, he just . . .'

'Represents what you and Dean can't face: Jesse running out of options.' Sandy looks into her friend's eyes with deep concern. 'Kelly, do you think you've become too attached to Jesse?'

'No!' Kelly rubs her forehead. 'Yes . . . Maybe. I don't know.'

'Don't take this the wrong way, Kelly. Would it be better if one of your colleagues could step in with Jesse and navigate her wish? I have to say – I am worried that Jesse's wish is becoming too much of a focus.'

Kelly's stomach lurches. She knows what's at stake. Passing this on to someone else feels like a cop-out, an abdication of her responsibilities. But perhaps Sandy is right: she hasn't been putting Jesse's needs first and foremost. 'No, that's not necessary, Sandy. I want, no, I need to sort this out and see it through. I owe it to Jesse. I'll make sure not to let my personal feelings get in the way anymore.'

Sandy nods. 'OK. I'm here if you need me. You can always run anything past me first. Remember, you can't do everything on your own. Sometimes you're going to have to give up control.'

Kelly understands this, but it's hard. She's always been independent, always made her own way in the world, without the help of her family. She says goodbye to Sandy and heads out the door. Determined that whatever she does, she must find a way to make Jesse's wish come true.

She picks up the phone and dials a number. 'Hi, Mandy, it's Kelly. As you know, Dean is making the staff stop Alex from seeing Jesse. I need your help to make sure she gets her wish.'

CHAPTER 16

After Kelly leaves the room, Jesse climbs back on Amy's bed. She feels bad for shouting at her, no one is listening to her, no one – none of the adults, at least – can understand what she is creating with Alex. Why don't they get it?

'Don't worry, Jesse. I'll fix this for you. You will get your wish,' Amy says full of confidence.

Jesse bursts out laughing.

'What's so funny?' Amy asks.

'You. I'm picturing you fixing this for me while lying in bed receiving chemo. You know the drill, just because you're in remission doesn't mean you immediately stop the drugs and chucking.'

Amy joins her laughing. 'All right, so I can't fix it straight away, but you get me the name of Alex's company and I'll fix it.'

'All I want is a simple wish to help bring my family back together. Something for my family to remember me by. I want them to be a family again. Is that too much to ask?'

As the two girls hug, Ryan and Luke wander in.

'What's going on?' Ryan asks.

'Amy's going to tell my dad and Kelly that Alex is coming back, and they can't say no. Can you imagine my dad's face when she says that?' Jesse says giggling.

'Jesse needs her wish,' Amy tells the boys.

'And Jesse is going to get it,' Ryan says looking at Amy and Luke.

'Dream team assemble!'

'We saw your dad and Alex fighting last night,' Luke tells the girls. 'It wasn't pretty.'

'Oh, groan,' wails Jesse.

'Luke, have you got your phone with you?' Ryan asks.

Luke pulls his phone from his pocket. 'Yeah, do you want it?'

'Yes, I do. Now what's the name of the company Alex works for, Tri something?'

'TriOptic Studios,' Jesse says. 'Why, what are you going to do?'

Ryan searches on Google. Finding what he is looking for he hits 'call'.

'Hello, hi, can I talk to whoever is in charge, please?' the others hear Ryan say. 'Well, if he's not around, can I speak to the next person in charge, please?'

'Good manners,' Amy whispers.

After a short while, someone comes to the phone.

'Hi, Steve, is it? Well, my name is Ryan. I'm calling on behalf of my friend Jesse, she's in hospital and one of your employees, Alex something . . .'

'Oh, you know him, good. Well, here's the deal. He's meant to be helping my friend Jesse . . .'

'Oh, you know about that. Well, good. So can you please tell him to stop being a moron, get his butt back to the hospital and get on with making Jesse's wish.'

Ryan listens for a while.

'Yeah, but he's not going to let a little problem like her dad stop him from doing what he's paid to do, is he?'

Ryan listens some more.

'All right, thanks, Steve, I knew I could count on you. OK, you're right, I don't know you, but I was sure once I made this call, we could sort it out. Yeah, you have a word with him, and we'll see him back here as soon as possible. Thanks, Steve, you're the man.'

He presses the end button on the phone with a flourish, grinning to the rest of the group.

'"You're the man"?! What are you thinking?' Amy groans.

The others are in varying states of hysteria; Jesse is laughing so hard she has tears rolling down her cheeks.

'He sounded like a dude, so I was trying to sound like him.'

'Not a sixteen-year-old kid, huh?'

'Hey, he's going to tell Alex to come back.'

'Thank you, Ryan, that was the funniest thing I've ever heard. But I'm pleased you've spoken to someone who might be able to get through to Alex,' Jesse says, giving him a quick hug.

'My turn,' says Amy, taking the phone from Ryan.

'Who are you calling?' Jesse asks.

'Your dad. Someone needs to set him straight.'

'Please, Amy, don't call my dad. You'll only make it worse.' Her stomach is in knots.

'Are you sure?'

'Yes, please don't.'

'Well, can I say something to your mum when she comes? Let her know that we are doing our best to get Alex to stay on the project and make your wish, and that it shouldn't be us having to be the grown-ups, making your dad see sense?'

'Yes, you can talk to my mum anytime about anything.'

'You got it, sister.'

Ryan is on the bed next to Amy and they're starting to play a video game. Luke has got his phone back. 'Group selfie?' he says. 'Get in, Jesse!'

He holds the phone out and they take photo after photo, laughing together, making funny faces, pulling dramatic poses. When they're done, they crowd round Luke's phone, hooting at how hilarious some of the photos have turned out, applying filters and stamps, making the colours pop. Jesse sits back, observing them for just a moment, her friends, brought together by a terrible illness, but finding joy in being together. She's so lucky to have them, so grateful.

'Jesse!' Luke's voice brings her back into the room. 'I reckon you should have this one made into a T-shirt.'

In the photo, Jesse is pulling a face, tongue sticking out, eyes bulging. She laughs and playfully bats Luke on the arm, turning away from her thoughts and back into the company of her friends.

CHAPTER 17

Her legs curled up underneath her, *The African Queen* playing on a muted television, Kelly looks at her phone before slamming it back on the sofa. Glancing at the television screen, she plays with the remote, volume on, volume off. She picks up the phone and looks at the blank screen. Grabbing a small piece of paper from the side table she jumps up, untangling herself from a blanket and goes to the window, staring out at the night sky.

'Damn it!' she mutters before punching in the numbers on the piece of paper.

Max raises his head at the sound of the ringing telephone. Alex is playing a shoot-em-up game and ignores it. Max gives a gentle woof. Annoyed, one hand manipulating the console, Alex snatches up the phone. 'Hello.'

Silence. He stares at the phone to see if he missed the call.

'Talk or I hang up,' he says.

'It's Kelly.'

'Who?' he says, out of surprise. Kelly was the last person he expected to hear from.

'Kelly. From the hospital.'

'How'd you get my number?'

'You gave your number when you signed in to be a permitted visitor for Jesse; before Dean . . .'

'What do you want?'

'You to come back and help Jesse make her wish.'

Alex says nothing. The silence drags on.

'Look, I'm sorry for the way I've behaved towards you. I've spoken to Mandy, and she's given her permission for you to help make Jesse's wish.'

'What about her father?'

'Well, although you have permission from one parent, it might be best if you try to avoid him. Will you please come back?'

'I'll see you tomorrow,' Alex tells her, disconnecting the call.

Turning to Max, Alex shakes his head. 'Women,' he mutters.

It is enough for Max, who goes back to sleep. Alex closes the game he was playing and finds the file he wants, marked JESSE.

Closing her phone, Kelly returns to the sofa, wraps herself in the blanket, turns up the sound on her movie. 'Men,' she mumbles to no one.

CHAPTER 18

Turning off his computer, Alex swings a bag onto his shoulder and leans over the cubicle. He's excited this morning and filled with determination. Time is running out and he's not going to let Jesse down – too many adults did that to him when he was her age. He's going to show them what he can do, all of them, Kelly and that father in particular. He's also started to feel really excited about the wish. He doesn't want to curse it but this could be groundbreaking stuff. If he can pull it off, then he may have created something that can be used the world over by people, young and old, wanting to leave behind an immersive, interactive experience for their loved ones. His inward smile disappears as the memory of the only photo he has of his mother, with a seven-year-old Alex sitting on her knee while she reads him a story, threatens to overwhelm him. What would he give to have the very thing he is creating for Jesse? He pulls himself together as he realises Steve is looking at him over the top of the cubicle.

'Now that I've got your attention,' Steve says to him, 'I took a phone call yesterday that was meant for Ian. It was from a kid called Ryan. I take it you know him because he knows you.'

'Ryan, yeah, he's one of the kids on the ward with Jesse. What did he want?'

'He's a smart kid. He rang here looking for your boss. Thank God Ian was out so I told him that was me. He wanted me to tell you to pull your head out of your ass and get on with making Jesse's wish.'

Alex laughs in appreciation. 'Shit, Steve, these kids, barely teenagers, are smarter than you and I put together. They see us adults being hopeless and they're not afraid to call us out. I'm so impressed. I'll tell him I got your message: you slapped me around and I'm back in the game.'

'Does that mean I get to slap you around?'

'No. It means, I'm on it. This afternoon still OK for you?'

'Yes, I'll meet you in the car park and you can take us to the part of the beach where Jesse and her family hang out, below where they live.'

'Would you bring a drone with you, and we'll get some aerial shots as well?'

'Sure, no problem.'

Walking past his colleagues, they all call out various forms of: 'See you. Good luck, Alex, you've got this.'

For once, Alex waves and smiles back.

They're just nearing the exit when Ian appears. 'Alex, wait up,' he calls out.

With obvious disinterest in any conversation with Ian, Alex stops walking, forcing Ian to come to him.

'Heading out?' Ian asks.

'Just doing what you told me to do.'

'So, how's it going?'

'Do you want to hear anything other than spectacular?'

'Come on, Alex, we're on the same team here.'

'Yeah, right, sure we are. OK, Ian, anyway, got to go. Oh, by the way Steve's coming out with me again this afternoon.'

This said as a statement, not a request.

'Back up a minute. This was something given to you, it's bad enough you're not here doing your job, but I can't let you have Steve or anyone else, we're behind in the work we have to do for real, paying clients.'

'Well, you said that Frank wants me to do what I need to do to make Jesse's wish, and that includes using Steve's expertise or I'll never finish it in time . . . if you get what I'm saying.'

Ian's expression changes and Alex can feel him trying to work out how to back down without losing face.

'You think you can run this show, don't you? Just hurry the hell up and finish the job. I'm meeting with a TV network later this week. Publicity, Alex, which means sales and a nice big bonus for us all.'

Disgusted, Alex walks away, shaking his head. Behind him, he hears Ian calling out, 'Back to work, the lot of you.'

The sooner he can get out of here, the better.

Walking through 6 East, Alex slips a camera from the bag over his shoulder. Jesse and Amy are sitting together on Amy's bed. Raising the camera he takes a photo. The girls look up at him, smiling.

'Hey, you didn't get my good side!' Amy squeals, while immediately striking a pose.

Alex snaps another photo.

'What about video?' Jesse asks Alex.

'That too, one at time, Jesse, you have to be patient,' Alex says, smiling.

'I am patient, I am a patient,' Jesse says, laughing. 'You know what I mean.'

Amy strikes another pose, and Alex obliges with another click of his camera, just as Sandy enters the room.

'What's going on?' Sandy asks, looking from Jesse to Amy to Alex.

'Alex needs to take some photos, is that all right?' Jesse asks.

'Sure, just make sure you get permission from everybody you photograph, Alex, and that means permission from parents too.'

'Yeah, I know. I have releases in my bag for everyone to sign. If they don't, then I won't use their images.'

'I take it this is for your wish, Jesse?'

'Yes, it is, and Sandy, you're in it. Can we have your photo, pleeease?'

'Oh, all right then.' Sandy sheepishly shrugs her shoulders, turning to Alex who takes a photo. She's much more self-conscious in front of the camera than the two teenagers.

'Again,' he says.

Sandy relaxes into laughter as Alex gets his shot.

'I'll get your details and put them in a release for you to sign,' he tells her.

'Well,' Sandy says with a twinkle in her eye, 'if you two ladies are going to be in a photoshoot, what do you say to a little bit of makeup? I know you have some, Amy, would you like me to send in someone to help you with it?'

'And our hair, we'll have to get our hair done,' Jesse says, teasing.

Even Alex laughs as she pulls at the tufts of spiky hair on her head.

Sandy turns to Alex. 'Will you excuse us for a few minutes? Kelly's just outside, maybe you'd like to shoot her.'

The girls laugh, miming firing pistols at each other. Realising the double meaning of what she's said, Sandy rolls her eyes.

'Film, photograph . . . you know what I mean.'

With Jesse and Amy giggling hysterically at Sandy's remark, Alex backs out of the room, unable to conceal his amusement. Glancing up, he sees Amy reaching into her bedside drawer and bringing out a mirror and a lipstick and other things unrecognisable to him.

Alex finds Kelly sitting behind the nurses' station, writing in a file. Leaning over, he takes a close-up photo of her.

'Sandy says I have to get your permission to photograph you.'

'And if I say no?'

'Then Jesse doesn't get her wish.'

She gives him a look. 'We can't have that, now, can we?'

Alex focuses the lens, taking a few more photos. 'Just need a head shot or two.'

Kelly smiles, grimaces, turns away laughing. When she

sees Alex has stopped shooting, and placed the camera on the desk, she turns serious.

'Do you really think you can do this?'

'I don't know, but I'm going to try.'

Alex sees Kelly look beyond him and follows her gaze. Sandy is heading towards them with Jesse and Amy, IVs removed, now changed into trendy clothes, glossy lips, subtle eye shadow, Jesse batting her eyelids, Amy putting a floppy hat on and off, both girls laughing. Alex gasps. All he can think is they should be on a beach, or at a shopping centre, wherever girls their age hang out.

Their eyes meet. Both look away again quickly, feeling their cheeks burn.

He turns to Kelly. 'They shouldn't be here.'

Kelly whispers back, 'I know. My only advice is just do your job, don't think about it, it's the only way to get through.'

'That's easier said than done.'

Picking up the camera, Alex forces a smile at the girls. 'With or without hat, Amy?'

'Both, of course!'

'I hate to interrupt, but this isn't the most appropriate place for a photoshoot,' Sandy says.

'Oh, of course, I'm sorry, perhaps we could go . . .'

'. . . to the garden, dream team HQ,' Jesse finishes his sentence.

'That would be much better, perhaps Kelly should go with you?' Sandy suggests. 'And don't forget the releases, Alex, you can leave Jesse and Amy's with me, I'll have their . . .' She pauses looking at Jesse. 'Their mothers sign them.'

'Let's go,' Amy says impatiently, pulling Jesse along and forcing Alex and Kelly to scurry after them.

As they walk to the garden, Alex asks Kelly if there is a room in the hospital he could borrow as he needs some video footage of Jesse and her friends and family alongside the stills. He would need to hang a green screen, which he can bring in. She tells him the ward has a conference room which only gets used occasionally – she's sure Sandy will let him use it. It is private and reasonably soundproof.

'What about Dean? Can this work without him?' Kelly asks.

'I want to do what I can and then, with help from Mandy, you, whoever, maybe we can bring Dean in later. One step at a time, Kelly.'

Kelly smiles and nods. He's right. And she's pulled along by the girls' excitement, and Alex's determination.

Today, the garden is filled more with birds than people. Alex tells the girls to pick where they want their photos taken while he sets up a tripod. He wants to control some of the shots with a steady hand – close-ups, candid moments.

As he adjusts the tripod, Jesse picks up the camera, puzzled. It's not like her dad's, where you look through a viewfinder from behind. The viewing screen is on top. She peers down into it, trying to work out how to frame a shot.

Alex kneels beside her, showing her how to use it. Just as he's demonstrating, Ryan and Luke appear with a nurse.

'Excuse me, Jesse,' the nurse says. 'Ryan and Luke asked where you were. Sandy said you were down here having your photo taken. They want to know if they can join. It's up to you. I can take them back.'

Ryan and Luke have already made themselves part of the action. Ryan dives into the bushes with Amy, both of them yelling, 'Boo!'

'I've got a camera. I love taking photos. Can I help?' Luke asks Alex.

Jesse smiles, watching the chaos. 'They're fine. I want their photos. We'll bring them back with us, won't we, boys?'

'I'll make sure they behave,' Kelly tells the nurse.

'Hey, Jesse, take a photo of me!' Ryan calls, now wearing Amy's hat.

Alex shows Jesse how to press the shutter. She snaps the shot.

The next hour becomes a free-for-all. Jesse plays with Kelly's hair; the teens trade off posing and taking pictures. Kelly ends up in some, both staged and candid. Jesse insists on taking photos of Alex and Kelly, catching them mid-glance, laughing.

Amy gets creative when it's her turn. She lies on the ground, shoots from picnic tables, angles everything.

Then Jesse hears her name, and Sam and Mandy appear.

'We were told you'd be here. What's going on?' Mandy asks, grinning.

They join in the fun, and Alex snaps a flurry of joyful moments: Jesse laughing with Mandy, Jesse lifting Sam, the two girls kissing Sam's cheeks, a sweet family portrait.

'Mandy, Sam, do you mind if I get a few shots of Jesse with Amy, Luke and Ryan?' Alex asks.

'Of course not. Come on, Sammy, let's watch,' Mandy replies.

Mandy and Sam stand with Kelly. The other three don't need an invitation to join Jesse and for the next while the four teenagers do what teenagers do, joke, push, poke, hug.

'It looks like the girls are practising flirting with the boys. Safe environment to do it in with us here.'

'I think you're right. I also think the boys are doing the same. This is quite a privilege, being here, observing them. I feel overwhelmed at what they are letting us in on, letting us witness.'

Mandy hugs Kelly, wiping away the tear that spills down Kelly's cheek.

Jesse pulls Alex aside. 'Can you take a picture of me with Mum and Sam?'

'Sure,' he says, and snaps away. At first, Mandy is hesitant, but then she warms up, and her resemblance to her daughter really shines through, the same dark brown eyes and warm smile. Sam starts goofing around and Mandy and Jesse join in. He takes shot after shot after shot. *There will be some brilliant footage for the wish here*, he thinks.

Jesse breaks away. 'My turn,' she says, holding out her hand. 'I want to take some pics of my friends and you now.'

He hesitates, then gives in, handing her the camera.

Amy, Luke and Ryan rush to help Jesse line up the shot, all pretending to be old hands at this game before jostling to stand next to Alex, and posing.

'Kelly, get in too!' Jesse calls.

'No, you don't want me in these,' Kelly says.

'We do,' Amy insists, grabbing her hand, pushing Ryan out of the way and placing her next to Alex.

Camera angles and poses create a wonderful experience for Jesse as her mum and Sam join the others in their antics. Amy breaks away and takes the camera from Jesse, telling her she wants a go snapping her mother and Sam, Alex and Kelly.

Jesse hands the camera to Amy. The two boys crowd behind her, giving advice. But Amy slyly frames the shot to exclude Mandy and Sam, focusing instead on Alex and Kelly.

Jesse stumbles slightly, and Mandy steps forwards. 'I think it's time to go back upstairs.'

Sam protests, but Kelly steps in. 'We can do this again, but she needs rest.'

Alex starts packing up, but something makes him pause. Amy, Luke and Ryan are group-hugging Jesse. He quickly pulls out his phone and captures it.

Jesse sits on a bench, suddenly pale. Kelly vanishes, returning moments later with a wheelchair. Jesse doesn't object.

They leave in a lovely little procession: Mandy pushing the chair, Sam in Jesse's lap, the other kids walking behind.

Alex and Kelly watch from a distance.

'I didn't say goodbye. I'll head back up for a minute,' Alex says.

'I'll come with you. We need to finalise some forms to make this party legal.'

Inside, Mandy and Sam are at the nurses' station. Kelly stops with them, nodding for Alex to go ahead.

'Sam and I are heading off now. Thank you, Alex, this has been, well, the most fun any of us have had here in a long time,' Mandy says.

In the room, Amy calls out, 'Thanks for today!' before returning to her book.

Jesse is quiet.

'What's wrong? Didn't you have fun?' Alex asks.

'It was amazing. I never thought I could have so much fun in hospital. It's just . . .'

'Just what?'

'We have photos of everyone but my dad.'

Alex thinks. 'He won't let me photograph him. But maybe he'd let you.'

Jesse shrugs. 'Maybe.'

He hands her the camera. 'Give it a try. I'll pick it up tonight.'

'You're the best,' she says.

'If he asks, you may need a cover story.'

'Maybe Kelly lent it to me to take photos of my "home away from home"?'

'Not my call. You'll have to ask her. But I get the feeling she can't say no to you. See you tonight.'

At the nurses' station, Sandy and Kelly are sorting releases.

'I need a favour,' Alex says.

They exchange a look.

'Can I come back later? Jesse wants to photograph her dad.'

'Think that's a good idea?' Kelly asks.

'Probably not. But maybe he can't say no to her.'

'That's fine,' Sandy says.

'There's more,' Alex adds. 'She might tell him the camera is yours, Kelly. I said she should ask you first.'

Kelly sighs. Sandy nudges her.

'OK. No problem. This wish is getting us into some irregular territory.'

'But it's worth it, right?'

The three share a look. Then Kelly blurts, 'Can I buy you a coffee or something?'

She instantly regrets it.

'I'm busy,' Alex says, awkwardly.

'Of course. Forget I asked.'

'No, sorry, I mean . . . I'm filming this afternoon at the beach where Jesse lives. But later?'

'Sure.'

'We can walk to a café down the street. Better coffee than here.'

'Thank goodness. Six o'clock?'

'Six.'

The café is noisy. The street is crowded. Alex and Kelly find a table outside.

'Menu?' the waiter asks.

Kelly fumbles. 'Uh . . . I hadn't—'

'Just a drink will be fine, thanks,' Alex quickly rescues her. 'I'd like a beer, a lager if you have one. Do you want a glass of wine, or did you really want coffee?'

'If you're having a beer, I'd love a glass of wine, your house sauvignon blanc, please,' Kelly says.

When the waiter leaves, they sit in silence, fiddling with napkins.

'We've seen a lot of you lately,' Kelly says.

'Is that a problem?' Alex asks.

'No. Though isn't work getting tricky for you?'

'I didn't volunteer for this, remember. This is my work. Though it's become something more.'

'Oh, I see. So, there's no problem then?'

'We're good.'

'Good. Good.'

'Why'd you invite me here, isn't there some rule about you seeing people you work with outside the hospital?'

'I'm pretty sure the rule is more about patients and their families, seeing them outside of the hospital. I'm sure you see people you work with away from the office.'

'So, this is all right then?'

'I think we're OK.'

Alex nods, not sure of what to say.

The awkward moment is saved by the arrival of their drinks. Thanking the waiter they both play with their glasses, moving them around the table, each unsure if they should offer to 'cheers'. Neither do and they both take a sip.

'Did you grow up here, in the city?' Kelly asks.

'Yeah. You?'

'I grew up on a dairy farm, watched my parents work from sun-up to sun-down and beyond twelve months of the year and couldn't wait to get away. Not the life for me.'

'Sounds idyllic to me. You don't like getting your hands dirty?'

'It's not that, I don't mind hard work, I don't mind long hours, but there's no let-up because the cows have to be milked twice a day, every day of the year. I knew at an early age that life wasn't for me, so I studied hard to get good grades, move to the city and find a career.'

'So, you're a country girl. I thought there was something different about you,' Alex says, studying her, forcing Kelly to look away.

'What do you mean by that?'

He looks at her appraisingly. 'I'm not sure but I think it's something about the way you dress.'

'What's wrong with the way I dress?'

'Nothing, it's lovely. It's just different and I'm the sort of bloke who doesn't know what's different, just that it is.'

'OK. You're right actually, I prefer clothing from previous decades, the sixties and seventies, and I mainly thrift my clothes. I'm all about recycling.'

'Good on you. I saw how you were with Max, comfortable, not scared. I take it you had dogs on the farm, too?'

'Well, yeah, we had dogs, but they were working dogs not pets. But yes, I love dogs, cats anything with four legs that doesn't argue back.'

'Ah ha, now I get you.'

They are startled when someone calls out Alex's name. His colleague Sarah and her wife Claire walk towards them.

'Sarah, hey. First time here. This your local?'

'One of them,' Sarah says warmly.

'Kelly, this is Sarah. We work together. Sarah, this is Kelly.'

'Nice to meet you,' Sarah says. 'So, how long have you two been seeing each other?'

Alex and Kelly exchange uncomfortable glances. 'What? No. She's the hospital social worker. We're working together.'

'Ah . . . Well, it was nice meeting you, Kelly, see you at the office, Alex,' Sarah says, taking Claire's hand and walking off, an amused expression on her face.

Alex looks around, aware he had been too blunt in introducing Kelly. 'I'd better get going. Dean's probably left by now.'

'OK, I'll take care of this. See you there.'

Alex lingers watching her searching for her wallet in an overcrowded handbag. She looks up triumphantly when she finds it and he smiles a thank you before heading off.

As Alex walks towards the hospital entrance, he looks up at the wards above. Figures walk past windows; some patients and their visitors can be seen on a small balcony outside their rooms. Alex tries to recall if Jesse and Amy's room has a balcony. Most rooms are brightly lit, he sees a series of windows where only dim lights filter out into the night, and wonders what that ward might be. His gaze continues up to where the brightness of the full moon and stars competes with the lights of the houses and buildings below. He sighs. He used to drive past hospitals and barely register them. Now he feels that powerful sense of all those lives within the building, living through tragedy, pain, loss – and sometimes recovery. It's overwhelming to him.

Walking past the nurses' station, Alex gets the thumbs-up from Sandy. He finds a beaming Jesse sitting on her bed, waving his camera at him. Taking the camera, he nods towards the glass door. Sliding from her bed she lets him lead her out onto the balcony from her room.

He positions her at the railing. She tilts her head up. He lies on the ground, framing her with the night sky. Her face is calm, dreamy. She waves to the moon. Twirls. Hugs herself.

Suddenly overcome with exhaustion and emotion, Alex stops shooting and slumps against the wall, transfixed by Jesse, lost in the moment, in herself, it's as if she could fly away from all the pain and heartache that makes up her short life. Sadness threatens to overwhelm him. Jesse senses he has stopped shooting and stops twirling, turning to Alex with a beaming smile that drowns out the moon and stars. He can't help but smile back at her.

From inside the room, Kelly watches the beautiful scene playing out on the balcony. She sees Alex slump against the wall and Jesse finally stop and look at him. This is her cue to step outside so Jesse and Alex can end the moment. She helps Jesse back inside where Amy waits for her.

After a few moments Alex comes back into the room. 'Thank you, Jesse. Now, you get some rest.'

'You too, Alex. This was one of the best days ever.'

'Hey Alex, you're actually pretty OK,' Amy calls.

'Thank you, Amy, you're pretty OK yourself. I'll see you, girls.'

'WE'RE NOT GIRLS!' they yell in unison.

Alex mimes shooting himself in the head.

'Would you like me to walk you out?' Kelly quickly says.

'No thanks, I know the way,' Alex says, throwing Amy a wink. He turns back, suddenly feeling shy. 'So, um, thanks for tonight,' he says.

'Yeah,' she says softly. 'Yeah, it was nice.'

'I'd better, um . . .' He points towards the door. 'Lots of work to get through tonight.' He colours, feeling the eyes of Jesse, Amy and Kelly on him, looking at him, it seems, with amusement. 'But we should . . .' he says helplessly.

'Yes,' Kelly says, rescuing him. 'We should. Let's chat soon.'

'Totally,' Alex replies. He glances at Jesse and Amy who are grinning at him like Cheshire cats. They're not making this easy. 'I'll see you all tomorrow, then.'

'Bye, Alex!' the girls chorus, and their laughter follows him out of the ward.

Back in his home office Alex works furiously, downloading photos, sorting them out into the 'to be used' and 'just for fun' files. He then goes through the beach videos he and Steve made earlier, once again mixing long shots with close-up scenes. Videos and still photos merge and change from one screen to another. He places still photos of Jesse, Mandy and Sam on the beach as he anticipates filming them in the studio, looking at the skyline, the receding tide, manipulating the photos so it seems the family are interacting. He likes what he sees. When a photo of him and Kelly side by side, each casting a sideways look at the other appears, he is shocked. He smiles to himself, knowing this was the work of Amy. A ping on his phone tells him it is midnight and breaks his concentration. It also wakes Max who stands, stretches and wanders over to Alex, knowing it is time for a last trip outside for the night. Placing his head on Alex's lap he looks up to see Alex concentrating on one photo. A photo of Kelly. Max wags his tail approvingly.

CHAPTER 19

Working in her office, Kelly is disturbed by the department receptionist leaning in the doorway, smiling.

'What?' Kelly asks her.

'Anything you want to tell me?'

Kelly puts her head down pretending to work. 'About what?'

'You know what. Last night.'

'Last night. It was a quick drink, it was nice.'

'Nice. Just nice. A tuna sandwich is nice.'

'It's complicated, OK!'

'And you don't want to talk about it.'

'It's not office gossip, Rose.'

Rose is distracted by someone walking towards her. 'I think that's about to change. Oh, by the way, he's here.'

Kelly jumps to her feet. 'What? Why didn't you say so?'

'I just did,' Rose says, walking away from Kelly's office towards Alex. Kelly frantically pushes wayward hair from her face and smooths her skirt before sitting back down.

Kelly tries to act casual, looking up as Alex appears in her doorway. He stands staring at her, and she stares back.

'You can come in, take a seat,' Kelly says.

'No thanks, good where I am.'

'What, standing in the doorway as if you're just passing by?'

'Well, I am, just passing by.'

'On your way to where?'

'To see Jesse.'

'This is not on your way.'

'My mistake, I must have got lost. Have a nice day.'

He turns and walks back the way he came, grinning widely at a colleague who returns the smile. Looking ahead she sees Kelly appear in her doorway to watch the retreating Alex.

'Was there something you wanted?' Kelly calls out after him.

Without turning around Alex calls out, 'Nope.'

The colleague stops beside Kelly and together they watch Alex leave the department.

'Was that who I think it was?' she asks.

'I've no idea who that was,' Kelly snaps back, returning to her chair.

Upstairs in ward 6 East, Mandy sits beside Jesse's bed, gently playing with her daughter's fingers, trying to mask the agony that tightens her chest every time she looks at Jesse's pale, tired face. Today, her hands are colder. Her breathing is more strained. The decline is undeniable, and Mandy feels the weight of it pressing in.

Across the bed, Sam enthusiastically lays out his latest

drawings for Jesse. They spread them out on the bed between them along with two poems Mandy has written.

Jesse reads one slowly, her eyes lingering on each word. She sinks back into her pillow, moved, though she says nothing. Mandy watches, pretending not to notice.

My darling girl, my heart, my soul,
Through every tear, you make me whole.
Your strength, your smile, your gentle face,
You've shown me love and light and grace.

Should time be short, and skies grow dim,
You'll be my life, my constant hymn.
Nothing can change what's always true –
My love, my heart, will stay with you.

Should you soar beyond this world,
I'll feel you near, my precious girl.
In every place, however far,
You'll be with me, bright shining star.

Watching Jesse read her words while Sam rambles on about his art, unaware that Jesse isn't really listening, fills Mandy with a bittersweet kind of joy. This moment – this exact moment – feels impossibly precious. How can she hold onto it forever?

A soft click breaks her reverie. She turns to see Alex approaching, camera in hand, having just captured the scene she was trying to sear into memory. For a moment, she isn't sure whether to thank him or be annoyed at the intrusion – but she chooses gratitude and gives him a warm smile.

'I'm sorry, am I interrupting?' Alex asks gently. 'I can come back.'

'No, I'm glad you're here,' Jesse says, her voice softer than yesterday. 'I want to show you something. Mum and Sam said it was OK.'

As Alex steps closer, he notices the bandage on Jesse's arm – one that wasn't there before. It stretches from her upper arm down to her wrist, and something about it instantly worries him.

'What happened to your arm?' he asks, his concern sharp as he moves nearer.

'Oh, nothing. I'm fine,' Jesse says quickly, but Alex hears the crack in her voice – weakness that wasn't there the day before.

'The vein collapsed this morning,' Mandy explains gently. 'They were giving her a small dose of chemo. The pressure bandage is just to protect it.'

He hears the weariness in her tone – more than exhaustion, it's a kind of quiet resolve, like someone bracing for a storm they can't stop.

Alex glances at Jesse again. The change is obvious. He looks to Mandy, searching for some cue, some direction. Her sad smile is all he needs. She knows. He must say nothing.

Trying to redirect the energy, Jesse lifts the poems and drawings. 'Look, Alex. These are the poems Mum wrote for me. And Sam's drawings from last night. I want to include them in my wish.'

'If it's OK with you, Alex,' Mandy adds quickly.

Alex picks up one of the drawings, studying it before glancing at Sam, who's still hunched over, absorbed. 'These are great, Sam. Really – these are amazing.'

Jesse hands him the poem she just read. He scans the opening lines, then pauses.

'Are you sure you want me to read this? It's . . . it's personal.'

He hopes she'll take it back, take away the ache he already feels building in his chest.

'I know,' Jesse says simply. 'That's why I want it. It's personal. It's us.'

Alex turns away from them to read it properly. Mandy watches his shoulders rise and fall, his breath coming quicker.

When he finally turns back, his eyes are damp. 'It's beautiful. Truly,' he says, meeting Mandy's eyes. 'Are you a writer?'

Mandy lets out a small laugh. 'I wish. I did some creative writing after my English Lit degree, but then I got a job as an editor . . . and life got in the way.'

'You're a lucky girl, Jesse,' Alex says, though he's still looking at Mandy.

'No, Alex. I'm the lucky one,' Mandy says firmly.

There's a pause. Then Mandy asks gently, 'Jesse told me you didn't grow up with your parents?'

'I never knew my father. My mum died when I was seven.'

'Did anyone in your family take you in?'

'No,' Alex says quietly. 'It was just mum and me. And then . . . just me.'

'I'm sorry,' Mandy says, her voice sincere. 'Everyone deserves a family.'

From the doorway, Kelly steps in, having heard the end of the exchange.

'Fourteen,' Alex says, still focused on the poem in his hand. 'That's how many homes I was in – until I aged out. Some just for weeks, some longer.'

'And school?' Mandy asks softly.

'Lost count. They tried to keep me in the same district, but it never really stuck.'

Before Mandy can respond, Kelly reveals why she came.

'Dean's on his way up.' She turns to Alex. 'Let's get you out of here.'

Sam suddenly leaps onto the bed. 'No! Don't send Alex away – we need him!'

Jesse grabs him, giggling. 'Hey, Sammy – maybe we should hide Alex under the bed!'

Sam bursts into laughter as Kelly pulls Alex gently by the arm.

In the hallway, she steers him towards the exit – too late.

Dean is already inside, talking to another parent. Kelly curses under her breath. 'Come on. I'll take you to the playroom. It's safer.'

The door shuts softly behind them, sealing Alex into a space that feels both safe and suffocating. The hospital playroom is bathed in the soft colours of forgotten childhoods – dolls, puzzles, finger-painted drawings pinned to the walls. The air is still. Heavy. Alex stands awkwardly in the middle of the room, surrounded by symbols of a childhood he never got to experience.

Kelly glances through the small window in the door, making sure Dean hasn't spotted them. 'No one usually comes in here during visiting time. You're safe.'

'I don't want to be safe,' Alex murmurs, but before Kelly can respond, the door opens again.

Sandy appears, urgent and matter of fact. 'Sorry, Kelly. We need you. Christine wants to speak to Mandy and Dean together. Sam needs to be taken out of the room.'

Alex's expression shifts instantly. 'What's happening?'

Kelly's eyes soften, but there's no comfort she can offer. 'The consulting doctors always speak to both parents when it's serious. Christine wouldn't ask unless she needed to. I'll be right back,' she adds, and follows Sandy out the door.

Alone, Alex wanders further into the room, unsettled by the quiet hum of fluorescent lights. The toys sit as if they, too, are waiting. He walks past a half-finished puzzle, past an easel where a rainbow has been started and abandoned.

Minutes later, the door creaks open again. Kelly enters with Sam in tow.

As soon as they step in, Sam pulls his hand from hers and runs to the far corner, where he sits at a table facing the wall. Alex looks to Kelly, whose face betrays what he already fears: Jesse is out of time. Grabbing a piece of paper and a crayon, Sam begins to draw. Despite all of her training, Kelly's eyes fill with tears. Alex sees this and feels himself well up.

He turns to Sam, seeing a mirror image of himself,

someone who retreats into his own world instead of inter-acting with others. Going over to him, he pulls up a chair. Sam slides a blank piece of paper towards Alex and hands him a crayon. Alex begins drawing, not the human figures Sam is creating but a dog. Max. Kelly remains at the far end of the room watching, unsure of her ability to do her job in this instance. She's the one who should be looking after Sam.

Alex and Sam finish their drawings and wordlessly push them aside. Sam gives Alex another piece of paper and again they draw. Sam draws people, Alex another version of Max. Alex pushes his piece of paper alongside Sam's, extending his drawing on to Sam's, a small dog now appears with what is obviously a drawing of Sam's family. Sam attempts to do the same, put people into Alex's drawing, and their arms tangle as they draw across each other. Sam begins to giggle and nudges Alex who exaggerates the nudge ruining the drawing with a large line across both pieces of paper. Kelly takes this as her cue to join them.

They welcome Kelly, who pulls up a chair beside Alex as Sam shows her what they are doing. In demonstrating, he nudges Alex who leans into Kelly. Both are shocked as bare arm touches bare arm. Alex then nudges Kelly who loses balance on the small chair and reaches out and grabs Alex for support. Sam is laughing loudly at the game he started. Alex nudges him a little too hard and reaches out to grab him as Sam threatens to fall from the chair. He holds him in an embrace for a moment longer than he should and Sam relaxes in his arms.

Feeling the need to regain composure, Kelly stands and

takes a few steps away. Alex glances at her before putting a blank piece of paper in front of Sam.

'Why don't you draw a picture of us for Jesse?' he suggests.

As Sam begins drawing, Alex joins Kelly.

'You continue to surprise me,' Kelly says quietly.

Alex stares at her, not helping her discomfort. 'Boys I get along with; after all, I was one myself once.'

'I see. Not so long ago maybe,' Kelly answers.

'Yeah, boys I get, girls are a whole other matter.'

Kelly feigns indignance. 'Girls are easy, we say how we feel, we say whether we're happy or sad, unlike you guys who have to be forced to talk about anything deeper than cars or sports . . .'

'Whoa there.' Alex looks over at Sam. 'Hey, Sam, come on and help me out here, we're under attack. What d'you say, Sam, who's easier to get along with, boys or girls?'

Sam stands up straight and commands: 'Girls are yuck.'

'Well, I wouldn't go that far, but boys are definitely easier to get along with, right, Sam?'

Sam walks over to Alex and leans against him. 'Boys rule,' he says, smiling at Alex.

Alex smiles down at Sam and places a comforting arm around him.

'Well, if you two are going to gang up on me, I'm going to, I'm going to . . .'

'What are you going to do, Kelly? Cry?' Sam says, laughing.

'Yes. No. I don't know. I'm going to leave,' Kelly says playfully.

Before he thinks about what he's saying, the words leave Alex's mouth. 'Don't do that.'

Kelly looks at Alex, searching for the meaning behind the words.

'We're sorry, Kelly, aren't we, Alex? You can stay, you can even draw with us if you like,' Sam says.

Before Kelly can respond, the moment is broken by Mandy and Dean stepping into the room.

'What the hell is he doing here? Get away from my son!' Dean yells at Alex. His grief at what he's just heard from Christine turns immediately to rage.

Mandy steps in front of Dean, stopping him from advancing on Alex, who lets go of Sam and takes several steps away. Kelly moves towards Mandy and Dean.

'Dean . . .' the social worker says.

Turning on Kelly, Dean points his finger at her. 'I told you to keep him away from my family,' he says tersely.

'Stop it, Dean, we need him right now,' Mandy implores.

'I told him to stay away . . .'

'Alex is making Jesse's wish. I gave him permission and there's nothing you can do about it. Do you hear me?'

'But I gave instructions he wasn't . . .'

'And I overruled you.' Standing in front of Dean, Mandy places a hand on his chest. 'Please, Dean, please don't be like this, not now,' she whispers.

Shocked, Sam watches his parents argue. Slowly he backs away, back to the desk he and Alex were sitting at. Carefully, deliberately, he picks up their drawings, cuddling them in a protective manner.

Alex steps cautiously towards Kelly. 'I don't understand, what's happening here?' he asks no one in particular.

Mandy walks over to him, speaking quietly. 'Christine just told us the last round of chemo hasn't worked.'

'But what does that mean? Can't they do it again?'

Mandy begins to tremble, her eyes moisten. 'It means, it means . . .' is all she can stammer.

Sandy walks into the room and sizes up the situation. Seeing Sam alone in the corner of the room she goes to him and, taking his hand, leads him out. The others just watch them leave.

'No, Alex. There is no more treatment we can offer Jesse. She's had bone marrow transfusions, she's on the bone marrow register but there are no compatible donors, and she's had too many rounds of chemotherapy for her young body,' Kelly tells him.

Kelly's words wash over Alex like the tide on a beach, their meaning not sinking in.

'I still don't understand. What does that mean?' Alex asks slowly, knowing the answer but not wanting to believe it. He looks from Kelly to Mandy.

'Bloody know it all doctors, they don't really know a damn thing,' Dean says, the venom no longer in his voice. He turns and points to Alex. 'And you, stay away from my daughter, stay away from my family. You hear me!'

Dean storms out of the room. Alex looks at the others who all stare back at him. Then, he too runs from the room.

CHAPTER 20

'That had to be tough. I've got to tell you – having my own kids? I don't think I could've handled that.'

Alex barely hears Steve. He had come into the office that morning and spilled it all, the words coming out flatly, mechanically, like he was ticking off items on a checklist, as if describing someone else's night. Ward 6 East. Jesse. Dean. Mandy. The poem. The drawings. He tells it all like it's a story he once heard, not something he's just been through.

Steve watches him from over the cubicle partition, but Alex keeps his eyes on the screens. The flickering pixels blur together, meaningless shapes and colour. He stares until the movement starts playing tricks on him. None of it feels real.

For years, he's kept himself safe by staying detached. By choosing not to feel anything deeply – except loyalty to Max. He spends his life in simulated worlds, where outcomes are predictable and reset buttons exist. Reality is messier.

Steve's still talking. Alex hears the tone, not the words. He nods, hoping that's enough to make it seem like he's listening.

'So . . . what happens now? Have you told Ian?'

The moment Ian's name hits the air, something sharp snaps Alex into focus. He looks up, jaw tightening.

'This isn't about Ian,' he says, his voice clipped. 'Never was.'

Steve holds up a hand in surrender. 'Hey – I get it. This is hard. But good on you, mate, this is the most open I think you've ever been with me. I think I'll give my kids an extra hug tonight.' Steve pats him on the shoulder and adds, with a faint smile, 'Better get back to work. Someone's got to pay those dental bills. Ouch.'

Then he's gone, back behind the divider. Alex turns to the monitors again, though he still sees nothing. The day crawls by, and he can't focus on the project he was working on before Ian told him to visit the hospital. Images from last night flash through his mind in fragments – Jesse's bandaged arm, Mandy's voice breaking, Sam's quiet drawings. He stares at the partition wall as if he might find answers there.

His phone rings. He jumps.

The voice on the other end sounds distant, distorted. He pulls the phone away, looks at the screen like it might explain something. Then he ends the call and stands, grabbing his jacket.

He doesn't hear Ian approaching.

'Update, Alex,' his boss demands.

Alex tries to sidestep, but Ian lifts an arm, blocking his path.

'Going somewhere?'

Alex ducks beneath and walks off.

'All this bloody time out of the office – you better be nearly done with that pro bono,' Ian calls after him.

Alex doesn't stop.

'Listen, enough's enough. Bronwyn can't finish her project without your part. If we lose this contract, the whole company takes a hit. All because you can't handle one little assignment.'

Still walking, Alex looks over at Bronwyn. She gives him a small nod – she's got it covered.

'I've scheduled the media for next week, Alex! Next week!' Ian shouts.

Alex halts. Turns slightly. Takes a step back towards Ian – then stops, thinks better of it, and walks out.

Alex slows his pace as he nears the café he and Kelly had previously visited. He sees her sitting outside, playing with a glass of water. Stopping, he considers turning around and running, then realises she's seen him. Approaching the table, Alex stands holding on to the top of the chair opposite where she sits. A waiter approaches them.

'A flat white, please,' Kelly says to the waiter, smiling at him. He turns to Alex.

'Same. Thanks.'

'Please sit down,' Kelly says to him softly.

Pulling the chair out Alex sits, making no attempt to pull the chair closer to the table. He notices the second glass of water and takes a sip.

'Thanks for coming. How are you feeling?' Kelly asks.

Alex looks at her, shocked by her question. 'What?'

'After last night. How are you?'

Bluntly Alex answers, keeping his eyes fixed on the table. 'Fine. And you?'

If he was expecting an answer to how Kelly was, he doesn't get one.

'Are you sure? That had to be tough on you, hearing about Jesse's condition deteriorating.'

Before Alex can respond the waiter reappears and places two coffees on the table. 'Can I get you anything else?' he asks.

They both shake their heads no. Picking up their cups they drink, looking down at the table, each avoiding eye contact. It's a busy day out on the street, but the silence between them feels deafening.

'She doesn't deserve this!' Alex blurts out.

Kelly keeps her eyes lowered, uncertain how to answer.

'She deserves to be a typical teenager, be a pain in the neck to her parents; fight with her little brother, experience her first kiss if she hasn't already.'

He pauses, still not meeting Kelly's eye. 'She deserves to live,' he says finally, his voice barely above a whisper.

Kelly turns to look at him. She reaches out and touches his arm, causing him to look at her.

'We all deserve that, Alex,' she says. Despite himself, Alex feels the warmth and power of her compassion and empathy for him. He allows himself to raise his eyes and gaze into her lovely face.

'So why not Jesse? Why doesn't she get to live?'

'I don't have an answer to that,' Kelly tells him, and Alex hears the pain in her voice, senses her feeling of profound helplessness. He slumps his shoulders. This is just as hard for her – worse even. But he struggles to comprehend how she maintains her outward calm.

Alex empties his coffee cup. 'Doesn't she get to you?' he asks.

'Of course she does. They all do. But right now, I'm also worried about you . . .'

'This is not about me,' Alex snaps. 'Do you get that? This is about Jesse – or is this just an everyday thing for you? You'll shortly be moving on to the next unfortunate child who comes onto the ward?'

Alex's words hit Kelly hard, she struggles to respond, to stay professional. She's angry now and hurt. How could he think that about her?

'No, it's not. I can't begin to tell you how devastated I am that there is nothing more we can do for Jesse . . .'

'You wouldn't know it, sitting here having coffee, your world going on . . .'

'How dare you! You don't know me or how I feel about Jesse, and what I do is not just a job to me,' Kelly angrily replies. She flushes and her blue eyes fill with tears.

Realising he's gone too far Alex looks at her, his shoulders dropping, his voice quivering, not wanting to say the words he feels he must. His anger is gone and now all he feels is shame at having hurt the woman sitting opposite him, and despair.

'She's dying.'

Kelly sits back in her chair, controlling her breathing, calming herself. Softly she looks Alex in the eyes.

'It only takes a moment to die, Alex. The rest of the time we're living. Do you hear me? Do you understand me? We are living. Jesse is still living. Right now. You have to get that.'

The words sink in slowly. Something shifts in his face. She sees it.

'I should've told you sooner,' she adds. 'Most of my kids – they get better. They go through hell, but they survive. The few who don't? I have to be strong for them.'

'You called them your kids,' Alex says.

'You know what I mean,' Kelly replies softly.

He leans forwards, their faces close now. 'How can you do this job?'

Kelly closes the distance between them. He sees the freckles on her nose.

'Because I believe in it. Because these kids – they give more than I ever could. Jesse, her parents, Sam . . . they're the bravest people you'll ever meet. And now you've met them. So, you must agree with me too.'

Alex sits back, avoiding her gaze. 'How long does she have?'

'Not long.'

'There's really nothing else? No surgery, no drugs?'

'She's had every treatment. The transplant failed. The chemo failed.'

'What happened with the transplant?'

'It didn't work.'

'I get that. But you're saying there isn't a match for her – anywhere?'

'There isn't. She's been on the international bone marrow

register for two years. No match. As you know, Jesse's blood group is rare – a combination of her parents' antibodies.'

'What is it?'

'AB positive.'

He nods. 'So, the donor needs to be the same, or one of the universal groups?'

'Exactly.'

'What's involved in getting tested?'

'A cheek swab. And a blood test.'

'What are they looking for?'

'It's called HLA or tissue typing.'

He looks at Kelly for a long moment, her words scramble in his brain – chemo, HLA, marrow, AB – reorganise and register. Reaching into his pocket, he pulls out some cash, and sets it on the table.

'I've got an idea. I have to call in a few favours, but I think there's something I can do.'

Kelly looks like she's about to say something, but he quickly puts in, 'Just trust me, OK? I don't want to make any promises, and I'll need to check with Mandy first, but leave it with me. I'll see you later.'

'OK, see you then,' Kelly says. She looks shocked by his swift exit.

Alex hurries away. He will explain everything to Kelly later – but there's no time right now. Right now, he has a lot to do and not much time to do it in.

CHAPTER 21

O nly the dim light from a lamp casts shadows around
Alex's home office. Tonight, the bank of monitors and
screens which normally light the room in a kaleidoscope of
colour are blank. From his bed, Max watches Alex sitting
with his back to the screens, talking on his phone, making
notes on a small pad. Ending his call, he turns to Max.

'Come on, boy, time for your last trip outside tonight. I've
got an early start tomorrow and so do you – we need to get
some sleep.'

The first hint of light is visible on the horizon as Alex pulls
up in his car outside the hospital's main entrance. The dull
flashing of a nearby ambulance in the emergency bay is a
reminder that this building never sleeps. A security guard
approaches and after a brief conversation he nods for Alex to
head upstairs; he can leave his car where it is.

The swishing noise of the doors opening into the ward
seems too loud and Alex is struck by the quiet: it's usually
so alive with buzz and activity. He passes two cleaners who
barely glance at the intruder and makes his way to the nurses'

station. The charge nurse looks up at him, surprised.

Having explained his plans to her, the charge nurse gently wakes Jesse and waves Alex from the room. Helping Jesse from the bed she and Jesse look for clothes from the nearby cupboard. A few moments later they appear beside Alex, Jesse dressed in jeans, a jumper and jacket. A beanie on her head, shoes and socks on her feet. Together they leave the ward.

The security guard is waiting by the car and opens the door for Jesse once Alex unlocks it. He throws her a wink and a smile as if he is in on the adventure with them, and Jesse climbs in. As they leave the hospital grounds Jesse turns to Alex.

'So, where are we going?'

'You'll see. It's a surprise.'

They drive silently through the nearby suburbs, Jesse gazing out the window at the sleeping town. Alex drives through the gates of a park, making his way down tree-lined roads before pulling up in front of a small building. There is no sign of life. Parking the car, he runs around to open the passenger door, and gestures for Jesse to get out. Grabbing a camera bag from the back seat, shutting and locking the doors, he slowly walks off and Jesse follows.

'Why are we here?' Jesse asks, a note of anxiety in her voice.

'I wanted to do something special for you,' he tells her, carrying on walking – he's in a hurry to get to their destination.

Jesse stops walking, uncertain if she wants to go on. Alex doubles back to her.

'It's a surprise.'

His voice is calm, and reassures her that everything will be OK.

Taking her hand, he leads her to the back of the building where a large hot air balloon, fully inflated, is waiting.

'Alex, what have you done, why are we here?' Jesse puts her hands over her mouth in delight.

'Do I really need to tell you?'

'Yes. No. Oh my gosh, is this for us? Are we going in that?' Jesse asks pointing at the beautiful balloon in front of her.

Alex answers her by leading her to the balloon, scooping her up and placing her in with the pilot, then climbing in after her. The pilot forces a shot of helium into the balloon startling Jesse, who clings to Alex as the balloon slowly rises.

'Where are we going?' she squeals.

'I know you love the ocean, and your mum said you were fascinated by balloons, sooo . . .'

The pilot hands Alex a blanket which he wraps around Jesse's shoulders. Slowly the balloon rises. As it clears the tree line, the ocean gradually comes into view. Jesse leans out over the edge of the basket looking at the approaching water below them, lost in the moment.

The balloon sails to the coastline and follows it, out past the suburbs, until they reach a point where there is ocean on one side of them, forest on the other. Alex gestures to the spectacular panorama, his camera recording the scenery around them and focusing on Jesse looking out, laughing, oohing and aahing. Several times he tries to get Jesse to sit on the small chair in the corner of the balloon basket, but she refuses, preferring to stand, watching over the world below them.

Jesse goes quiet leaning out of the balloon.

'Hey, how about not leaning out so much? I don't want you falling out,' Alex says jokingly.

'I won't. Look, we're coming up to my home, it's just a little further on. There, there, can you see it? The one with the blue roof, and look, there's the swing Sam and I play on.'

Alex follows Jesse's gaze and sees the home with the blue roof and the swing in the backyard leading to the beach at the end. Feeling her hand grasp his arm and the slight shuffle closer to him, he gently puts his arm around her shoulder. Silently, they watch the Morgans' home as they slowly fly past it and it disappears from view.

'It looks like an amazing place to grow up in,' Alex finally speaks.

'It was. It is.'

Their moment is broken by the pilot pointing out a lone dolphin frolicking in the sea. They take the balloon down for a closer look. The dolphin leaps in the air, delighting Jesse.

They pass over a large container ship. Jesse waves enthusiastically to the crew, too excited to care that they don't respond. Alex watches with a satisfied smile on his face as Jesse takes off her beanie and throws it away, laughing. The two of them lean over the basket and watch it fall.

Looking ahead, Jesse laughs and points. 'Alex, that athletic track, I've been there so many times.'

'Tell me about it.'

'This is where the regional finals are held each year. I made the finals there every year I competed.'

'How many was that?'

'Well, I started when I was five and stopped two years ago when I got sick. What's that? Eight or nine years.'

'Did you have a favourite event?'

'Definitely middle distance running and cross country in the winter. For three years I won the 400 and 800 metres at State and went to Nationals.'

'Wow, your parents must have been very proud.'

'Yeah, they were. Especially Dad. He was an athlete, would probably still be if it wasn't for work and of course what's going on with me.'

'Did he compete?'

'Oh yeah, he's got boxes of medals and trophies.'

'So, he encouraged you?'

'Big time. He was involved at the club, training when he could and most Saturdays he came and helped out, either timing the races, or measuring at the jumps. He was never one to sit and watch; he had to be involved. I loved it. Made me feel special that my dad was actively involved with me and the club. Not that I ever told him.'

'Oh, I think he knows. It must be something else, having your parents involved and supporting you like that.'

'It is. It was. For the last two years I competed, he trained and qualified to be a starter at State level. I can still see the look on his face the first time I lined up on the track. He was wearing the official shirt indicating he was part of the event, he was given his own starting pistol, in a custom-made box with room for the caps. It had a red handle, and I stood in my lane watching him lining up the caps to ensure he gave us a clean start then he flicked the pistol closed, looked over at me and winked. He was ready, he hoped I was ready too. He called us up to our mark, I got down and placed my hands right on the line, not a millimetre behind. Usually, I kept my head down and focused on the track in front of me waiting, anticipating the word "set", knowing I needed to count to three and the gun would go off. This time I raised my head and looked over at my dad. I heard him call out "set" and raise the gun above his head. I counted to three, the gun went off and so did I. I ran a PB that day.'

'Sorry, what's a PB?'

'Personal best, the best time I'd ever run the 400 metres. I felt him running up behind me, then beside me then he was in front of me calling me on.'

'That's amazing. Thank you. Thank you for telling me that story, so many things about your dad and your relationship with him are becoming clearer to me.'

'He's my dad. I love him. I know he loves me so much and our love for athletics has made our relationship something special.'

'What about Sam?'

'No, he tried it, but he's more like Mum, you know, creative.'

They fall silent, watching the world below them gently pass by. Jesse feels a pang. 'Mum hates heights. The last thing she'd want to do is come up here with me. She'd panic.' She pauses. 'Dad, though . . .'

'This is more his kind of thing?'

She nods. Leaning against the edge of the basket, looking down at the coastline below her sparkling in the morning sun, she says, 'I'm not going to be able to tell him about this, am I?'

'Maybe later,' Alex answers.

'Later . . . I'm not sure how much of a later I have . . .' Jesse replies. She hopes there will be a later, that soon there will be a time where she doesn't feel like she has to go behind his back. She wants to talk to her mum about it, ask her advice. But the sun is shining on the waves below, the wind is a gentle breeze, ruffling her tufts of hair, the whole of the world is down there, in all its beauty and hope. From this distance, everything looks at peace; from this distance, everything looks like it will work out.

'Thank you, Alex.'

Her voice is filled with emotion: joy and excitement and gratitude. Alex meets her eye, then looks back down below them. Jesse nudges him playfully in the ribs and leans into him. Together they watch the scenery changing slowly below them as they float back down the coast, the sun now fully overhead in the sky.

CHAPTER 22

Parking his car once again in the main entrance to the hospital, Alex runs inside, returning with a wheelchair. The security guard from the early morning stop approaches apologetically, telling Alex he can't leave his car at this time. But he knows what Alex has just done for this girl, who he's got to know over the past few years, and he wants to help. Asking for Alex's car keys, he offers to park it for him, telling Alex to come to the security office next to the emergency department to get them when he is ready to leave.

'Valet service. Nice. That's never happened before,' Jesse says, impressed.

'Stick with me, kid, and you'll get the VIP treatment,' Alex tells her, giving the wheelchair a nice 360-degree spin as they head reluctantly back into the hospital and make their way to the lift.

As they arrive back at Jesse's room, they find Amy sitting on her bed playing with a bowl of ice cream, pushing it around, showing no interest in eating it. Jesse calls out to her.

'Amy, you'll never guess where Alex took me!'

When Amy doesn't reply, Jesse struggles to get out of the wheelchair, pushing away Alex's help.

'Hey, girl, are you OK?' Jesse says as she shrugs off her coat, dropping it on the floor, climbing onto the bed with Amy.

'How about I leave you two alone?' Alex says, seeing there is no place for him in the conversation that's about to happen.

'Alex, wait, can you come back tomorrow morning? Before I leave,' Jesse asks, stopping Alex in his tracks. He walks over to Amy's bed.

'Of course.' He looks from Jesse to Amy and back. 'Leave? Where are you going?'

'Home,' Jesse tells him.

Confused, Alex keeps looking from one girl to the other.

'There's no point in my being here, but I still need to see you about my wish.'

'But Jesse, I'm not sure I can . . .'

'Today, out there, I realised just what we have to do. Please, Alex, come back tomorrow morning.'

Alex stares at the teenage girl, with more bravery than he can imagine and barely manages a whisper. 'OK, OK, I'll be here. I'll see you tomorrow morning, right now I have to find Kelly.'

For the first time since they have entered the room, Amy looks at them with a smile and in a quiet voice manages a joke. 'Oooh, Kelly, I told you, Jesse.'

Making no attempt to hide his smile, Alex chuckles, 'See you, girls.'

'WE'RE NOT GIRLS!' comes the exasperated chorus.

Still smiling, Alex waves to the nursing staff as he passes their station. The assembled staffs' faces show surprise before exchanging looks as he strides past. They all know he is on the ward to make Jesse's wish, have accepted his lanky and slightly gloomy presence. But seeing him bounce past with a huge grin on his face is something very new.

Whistling now, Alex makes his way down to the social work department. The receptionist sees his smile and, without question, buzzes him into the department from her desk, with a knowing smile. He remembers which office is Kelly's, three down on the right.

Kelly is tapping away on her computer when she senses a presence. Looking up, she sees Alex leaning against the door frame, a silly smile on his face. She smiles back, waiting for him to say something or come into the room. Alex looks down at the well-worn carpet tiles that are so desperately in need of replacement. Kelly's smile fades as she puzzles over what is happening. Before she can say anything, Alex looks directly at her, smiling broadly before turning and walking back the way he came.

Kelly trips over computer cables as she rushes to the door, only to see his retreating back and the door to the department closing behind him.

'Damn it, I wish he wouldn't do that,' she says to the closing door.

'Getting to you, is he?' George asks from the office opposite. He has watched the interaction play out.

'He's so, so exasperating,' Kelly stammers at him.

'Looks like Kelly's met her match to me.'

Shaking her head, still trying to process a smiling Alex, Kelly returns to her desk. Turning her chair around she looks out the window. Why does the sky seem bluer today, the sun brighter, the flowers in the garden below more vibrant? She finds herself smiling as she gazes out the window.

CHAPTER 23

The last of the breakfast trays are being wheeled from the ward when Alex arrives back the next morning. He sees Sandy talking to a cluster of nurses, charts being handed between them, and recognises shift change over rituals. He's learning the ropes. Sandy sees him and calls out, 'They're waiting for you.'

Alex stops beside her. A flicker of concern dampens his sunny mood. 'They?'

Sandy only nods, motioning him to go on down to Jesse and Amy's room.

From the doorway, Alex freezes. Amy's bed is missing. His heart lurches. He stares at the empty space, dread tightening his chest – until he hears Ryan's voice: 'About time!'

Turning, Alex sees Amy's bed has simply been pushed next to Jesse's. Jesse and Ryan sit together on her bed. Amy lies in hers, an IV line snaking from her arm, and Luke is cross-legged at her feet.

'What's going on here?' Alex asks, unsure who to look at first.

'Alex, I want you to sit down and not say anything until

173

we've finished telling you what you need to do, OK?' Jesse says, nodding at a chair positioned on the other side of her bed so that he will be facing all four of them – a teenage interrogation panel.

'Umm . . . OK.' Alex follows orders and takes his seat.

'I said be quiet until we've finished!' Jesse says to the giggles of the others. 'You remember Sam's drawings and Mum's poems? And the photos and videos you've taken, right?'

Alex goes to says yes but sees the glare Amy is throwing at him and shuts his mouth.

Waving her hands over the drawings and poems on the two beds, Jesse continues. 'I want you to take copies of all of these. And I've written down the songs of the Spotify playlists that my dad and I like to listen to together.'

Luke pipes up, addressing Alex sternly, 'You got that?'

Alex once again goes to speak, stops himself and nods.

'Now I'm going to tell you what I want you to do.' Jesse pauses, taking several deep breaths. Her breathing's more laboured than yesterday.

'Because of my cancer my family's been torn apart. My parents split up, but I know they still love each other. My little brother Sam feels alone because all they do is worry about me and he deserves so much more. He deserves to have a normal childhood. He deserves to be happy. He deserves the puppy he wants but is not allowed because of my suppressed immune system.'

'That's where you come in,' Ryan adds.

'Thanks, Ryan,' Jesse deadpans. Then she looks straight at Alex. Her gaze is unwavering.

'You know I'm going to die. When that happens, things will get a lot worse for my family but hopefully only for a little while. My real wish is for us – together – to create something that helps them through it. Something they can keep. Something that makes it a little easier.'

Alex's throat tightens. Hearing Jesse speak so plainly about dying wrecks him. 'Jesse—'

'No, let me finish,' she says, softer now.

'Firstly, I've made peace with dying. The doctors and nurses can't do any more, and I can't fight it anymore. Believe me, I've tried.' She looks at her friends. 'We've all thought about it, haven't we?'

Amy, Luke and Ryan nod. They show no fear, no sadness – just quiet understanding.

'Everyone here on 6 East thinks about dying,' Jesse continues, 'or at least not being with their friends and family anymore. But you know what I think? I think death is just another transition to something unknown. My family will have to make a transition of their own that won't include me, but they will always have the memories we have made, and with your help, Alex, they'll get through it. They'll be happy again, I know they will.'

Amy picks up the thread as if it's been rehearsed. 'So, here's what we want you to do. Take copies of Sam's drawings and her mum's poems.'

Ryan chips in. 'I know the pin number to the ward photocopier.'

'Then, we want you to bring these and the videos and photos into the experience you're filming for Jesse and her family,' Luke adds. 'However your company does it, just do it how Jesse wants, OK?'

Alex nods, already forming ideas in his head. 'The poems – they need to be read aloud. Do you think your mum would read them? Or maybe you, Jesse?'

Jesse's face lights up. 'Mum. Definitely Mum. No one else.' She extends her hand. Alex takes it and they shake. The others nod in approval.

'You get it,' Jesse says. 'You see what we're trying to do.'

'I do,' Alex replies. 'Ryan, Luke – let's hit that copier. We've got work to do.'

'I trust you, Alex. But you've not done anything like this before, have you?' Jesse asks.

'No, not really. Not brought together in the way we're planning. We're usually given a script, producers' notes, camera angles, other kinds of details, and we work with them. This is . . . this is something else. But I know we can do it.'

'Thank you,' Jesse says, her voice barely above a whisper.

Amy struggles from her bed onto Jesse's, hugging her tightly, the IV pole threatening to topple over as the line pulls taut. Alex grabs it, holding it steady. Jesse pulls free from Amy and speaks quietly to her friend.

'Hey, Amy, can you go get Kelly? I think she might be able to help.'

'Great idea, let's get Kelly here,' Amy says, grinning at Alex and winking at Jesse.

Alex helps Amy untangle the IV line, hands her the pole and watches as she expertly wheels it out of the room. He turns to Jesse. 'How do you think Kelly can help?'

Jesse leans back into her pillows, exhaustion written all over her face and frail body.

'I didn't want the others to hear this, but Alex, I need you to hurry.'

Alex looks around the room. Nothing in his life has prepared him to hear these words under these circumstances. Nothing in his life has prepared him to spend time with teenagers facing life-threatening conditions, facing death. No one has told him the words he should say right now.

He feels Jesse's small hand take his.

'It's OK, Alex. I'll be OK, you'll be OK and thanks to you, my family will be OK.'

Amy and Kelly enter the room, breaking the moment.

'What's going on here?' Kelly says, seeing the two of them holding hands.

Jesse, without missing a beat, says, 'Nothing to worry about, Kelly, Alex is just reading my palm. He says I'm going to have a long and happy life. Aren't I, Alex?' The cheeky grin has returned.

A look of panic crosses Kelly's face as she and Alex stare at each other. He is completely overcome.

'Joking, I'm joking!' Jesse says. 'We were just saying goodbye to this place, weren't we, Alex? He's going to come to my home after the weekend when we know Dad is at work and won't be dropping in. He's just waiting for Ryan and Luke to bring him back some materials he needs for my experience.'

'Anything I need to know about?' Kelly asks, in a lighter voice.

'Best not,' Amy says, firmly.

'Oh, look – they're back. Did you do it?'

Ryan and Luke reappear at the door laughing and whispering. They spy Kelly and try to hide the large pile of papers behind their backs.

'Ah yeah, mission accomplished,' Ryan says. He clears his throat, glancing at Kelly.

'Alex, Luke's got something for you. Would you step outside, please?'

'What is going on here?' Kelly says in a voice that indicates she's asking as a formality: she doesn't really want to know what the friends are up to. Their energy and enthusiasm are infectious and she knows these moments are golden – they'll give Jesse strength for all that lies ahead.

'Nothing, nothing, just saying goodbye,' Alex tells her, managing to recover, and moving towards the boys, both of whom exaggeratedly walk outside the room.

As Alex walks past Kelly, he bends down and whispers in her ear.

'I'll see you next week, have a great weekend.'

Kelly feels herself blushing. 'Dammit,' she mutters.

Jesse looks at her and smiles broadly.

Walking from the hospital, Alex rings Mandy, wanting to talk to her about reading her poems for Jesse's wish. She invites him to pop over.

When he arrives, she takes him through the house to a large kitchen that opens onto the backyard. Alex hears the shouts and laughter of young boys playing.

'Alex, what are you doing here?' Sam runs up to hug him.

'Hi, Sam, I've come to talk to your mum. What are you lot playing?'

'Football! Mum's taking us to the beach soon.'

'Honey, do you mind if Alex and I have a chat?' Mandy says, ruffling her son's hair. 'As soon as we're finished, I'll take you to the beach.'

'OK, Mum, see you, Alex.'

As Sam goes back to his friends Mandy pours Alex a glass of water from a beautiful jug. He takes in the lemon and orange slices flavouring the water, the clinking ice.

Sitting opposite Alex, Mandy sips her own drink, watching the boys play. 'Thank you for coming. I wanted a chance to speak to you and when I got your call, it was like a sign.'

'Thanks, I want to tell you about—'

'Let me say something first: thank you. For what you're doing for Jesse.'

Mandy pauses, looking out at the boys in a tangled heap in the garden.

'What you have given her already is incredible. The balloon ride, for one. Her face lights up when she talks about you, and we haven't seen much of that from her recently.'

'She's remarkable. You and your husband must be so proud, you have clearly done a wonderful job as parents.'

'Yeah, well, Dean would say we failed. We can't fix her. And Sam's losing his sister, the person he loves most in the world.'

'That's being very tough on yourselves.'

'Alex, I don't want to go into too much detail, but I do want to tell you a little about Jesse's dad, Dean.'

'You don't have to tell me anything.'

'I know that, but I want to. When we first met, at university, I was the nerdy, English Lit student, he was top of his class in law, represented the uni in so many sports: football, athletics, swimming. I didn't know what he saw in me, but we dated and fell in love. The moment Jesse was born I saw something change in him. He held her and melted into the world of fatherhood; he didn't need to learn how to be a dad, he got it that first minute. The two of them formed such a bond that I have to admit, sometimes I was jealous of him, but not for long. Jesse makes everyone feel special.'

'I agree with that.'

'She was kicking a ball before she could walk, she never walked, she ran. He taught her to swim in the ocean as a toddler. She wanted to run all the time, not just run, but chase, Dean, me, the cat. We got her into athletics when she was five and she excelled, she was beating the boys her age for years. We didn't take much notice of the early symptoms. Occasionally she had a low-grade fever which never developed into anything serious, the bone and joint aches we put down to growing pains and pulled back on her training, we even ignored the occasional nose bleeds. They stopped. It wasn't until her times started going backwards in her best events at athletics, and I noticed her clothes were suddenly loose that we took her to a doctor.'

'Oh, Mandy, I'm so sorry, I can't imagine what that was like.'

'So, when you say we are good parents, we don't see it like that. We missed the early symptoms, and there's not a day goes by that I don't beat myself up for failing to be a good parent and getting help for Jesse sooner, and I know Dean feels the same way.'

'I don't know much about ALL, but you did nothing wrong. No one would know that those signs were symptoms, they sound mild.'

'They were, and she bounced back from every fever, or nose bleed. But still. When you become a parent, you have one job and one job only: protect them at all costs.'

Alex looks out at Sam and his friends kicking a ball between them. The noise of their play disappears as he travels back to his time as a boy. No loving mother, no friends to kick a ball with. He'd had so little, and yet somehow, he survived. Beautiful Jesse has it all, and yet now it seems it will all be taken away from her and her family, a family like he's never known. He looks at Mandy, who wipes silent tears from her eyes.

'Mandy, I don't know what to say.'

Mandy gives a little nervous giggle.

'That's OK, so many people don't shut up, but their words don't help. I appreciate the honesty, there is nothing to say.'

'I'm sure there is, I just don't know the words.'

'Actions speak louder than words. Alex, what you are doing for Jesse, for all of us, is beyond any words, beyond anything that could be done for us. It is Sammy, Dean and I who don't have the words to thank you.'

'I'm not sure Dean would agree.'

'He will. It's just hard for him. When she was first

diagnosed, he spent weeks researching cures. He wanted to take Jesse to Cyprus for treatment.'

'Jesse mentioned that.'

'Really? I guess I'm not surprised. She was only thirteen then, so young. We tried to keep our pain and worry from her, but I don't think we did a very good job.'

'She told me she was glad you didn't let Dean take her away for treatment. She trusts everyone on 6 East. She's made close friends there who really help her – she wouldn't have had that if she'd moved from hospital to hospital.'

'She said that? Oh, my goodness, I never knew that's how she felt. It's haunted me that I may have contributed to her condition by not taking her wherever there was the hope of a cure.'

'I think you knew it would be chasing false hope.'

'Oh, Alex, there's one thing I do know. There is no such thing as false hope, there is only hope.'

He shifts in his seat. He's never thought of it that way. 'Only hope,' he echoes.

'Mum, are you done?' Sam calls out.

'Almost, sweetheart. Sorry, Alex – I've been rambling. How can I help?'

'Thank you for telling me more about your family.' He leans forward. 'I wanted to know if you would be prepared to read the poems you have written to Jesse to include in her wish?'

'Is this what Jesse wants?'

'Yes. And me too.'

'Then of course I will. I'll record them on my phone and send them to you if that's OK?'

'Absolutely. I'll give you my number.' He stands up, holds out his hand, but Mandy ignores it, and hugs him.

After exchanging phone numbers, Alex calls out goodbye to Sam.

Driving away on his motorbike, Alex takes the next turn towards the beach. Stopping, he sits on his bike staring at the water. What Mandy has told him makes him understand Dean more. It's only been a few weeks, but he's become closer to Jesse than he ever dreamed he would – how must it be for her father? How dreadful must it be to see every dream, every hope for your daughter's future knocked down like dominos, one by one, until only false hope remains. And yet how natural to hold on to that hope. As Mandy said – can any hope be false?

He thinks of what he said to Kelly, just a few nights ago – that every day brings him another reason to fight for Jesse's wish, to make sure that it's everything she hopes for. And that is the hope he can give her. That he can give her family.

He wipes his eyes, kickstarts his motorcycle. It's time to get to work.

CHAPTER 24

Alex wakes early the next morning. Often on a Saturday he goes to the office to work in the quiet. Today he's decided not to, he needs to think without the influence of a thousand images crossing multiple screens in front of him. He needs to clear his head of all images other than those he will need to create Jesse's wish. In particular, he needs to work out how much of the end product will be special effects and how much will be live footage. He will need to find a way to talk to his colleague Charlie, TriOptics' environmental artist, to bring to the soundstage the props needed to complement the filming. Knowing he will be receiving many photos and videos from Mandy when he visits on Monday, he wants to concentrate on the visuals he has taken, the drawings and poems given to him by Luke and Ryan and listen to the songs on the list Amy gave him.

Pacing around his small kitchen with a cup of cold coffee – a prop in his hands, yet to be tasted – he looks at Max, who watches him from the doorway.

'OK, boy, fresh air! We both need fresh air.'

Seeing Alex put his running shoes on, Max excitedly pulls

his lead from a nearby hook, taking it to Alex.

Outside, Max watches as Alex goes through a routine of stretches. Recognising the last deep knee bends before he's ready to leave the property, Max positions himself at the pavement, poised for action.

Together, they gently jog past neighbouring homes, the normal Saturday activity of children in varying sporting uniforms being bundled into cars, hearing the ritual calls of parents: 'Have you got your water bottle? What about your cap?' What he would have given to have had an adult to remind him of such things, an adult who supported him to pursue and practise the many sports he'd loved and walked away from as a boy. As he was moved so often from home to home, he couldn't stay on the teams, or be consistent with training, and he'd eventually given up.

A boy sprays a garden hose across the pavement, laughing. It's hot so Max and Alex accept the mist gracefully. They pass a couple pushing a pram, their hands resting over each other's on the handle. Max slows, trying to sneak a peek inside. He loves babies. But Alex tugs gently on the lead, and they keep going.

In a nearby street, Alex hears cheers. He follows the sound to the local athletics track. Through the fence he sees children sprinting, launching themselves into sand pits, leaping at high-jump bars. Inside the inner field, javelins arc through the air under the wary eyes of supervising adults. Alex pauses, watching.

He shifts along the fence, eyes on a group of girls rounding the bend. He judges their age to be eleven, maybe twelve –

not much younger than Jesse. He smiles as they cross the finish line and wrap their arms around each other, no competition in sight, only joy. 'Wasn't like that in my day,' Alex says, ruffling his dog's head. Is that the difference between girls and boys? From his experience, there was only one winner. The rest? Losers. He remembers his only real rival in middle distance – a boy who sometimes muttered 'good race' or 'you deserved it' when Alex won. But mostly, he ran alone. No one in the stands. No team sport. Just him, the track, and the stopwatch. A private way to win or lose, with no one to blame but himself.

He doesn't see the young mother approach with her two children in club uniforms until she's right beside him.

'Are you looking for someone?' she asks.

Startled, Alex blinks. 'What?'

'Are you looking for someone?' she repeats. There might be a hint of suspicion in her eyes. Alex suddenly feels self-conscious. Does it look weird? A single man watching a group of teenage girls?

'I just . . . I know someone,' he stammers. 'She's not here. But she's a runner. I was thinking of her, that's all.'

The mother seems to relax at his explanation. 'She's an athlete?'

'Was,' he says. 'She's sick. Very sick. She asked me to help with something and – I don't know if I can.'

'That's hard. But trust your instincts. Be bold. Be brave. Do whatever you can, and you won't have regrets.'

'No regrets, huh?'

'It's something I tell my kids. When they come last in a

race, I say they still beat everyone who didn't show up to compete.'

Alex looks at the boy and girl beside her. He wonders if they know how lucky they are.

'Oh – sorry,' she says, and laughs. 'I talk too much. My husband says I could make friends with the devil.'

'No,' Alex replies, sincere. 'You've given me something to think about.'

'What's your dog's name?' the boy asks.

Max is sprawled on his back, paws in the air, basking in belly rubs from both children.

'Max. His name's Max. We should be going.'

'You and Max have a good day,' the mother says.

'You too,' he replies, smiling now. 'Good luck, you two. Have a great meet.'

Back home, Alex sits surrounded by glowing monitors. He layers music over the footage he and Steve captured. First, a track from Jesse's playlist. He watches. Listens. It's wrong. Another track. Still wrong. Again.

He drags visuals across screens, chasing timing, tone. It's still not working. Frustrated, he slams keys and Sam's drawings scatter to the floor. Max stays on his bed, looking worried, sensing the tension in the room.

Alex drops his head into his hands. Lifts it again and looks at Max.

The dog perks up, tail thumping once.

'I can't do this, Max, I'm not sure I have the knowledge or gear to pull this off. I'm not Marvel Studios.' He rakes his fingers through his hair. 'Help me out, buddy. Am I doing enough? If this falls apart – if we run out of time – will I be able to say I did everything I could?'

He accidentally knocks a keyboard to the floor. One screen goes black.

'Damn it!' he yells.

Max gets up, walks over, and rests his head on Alex's lap, reassuringly.

CHAPTER 25

Dean had driven over to the hospital alone, heart in mouth, trying to keep his breathing regular. Trying to keep it together. *She's coming home, she's coming home, she's coming home* runs like a mantra through his head, over and over. This is as positive a spin as he can put on it, pushing down another negative thought that threatens to overwhelm him: *they've given up, she's given up, I've let them.* But even that is better than the other, darker thought that comes to him at 3 a.m. when he's all alone in his dreary rented flat, a thought that torments him until dawn: *I've failed her.*

He's standing now, at the doorway, watching Amy and Jesse playing one last video game together, as roommates. Both girls are going home today, and Amy's side of the room has been packed up, suitcases neatly stacked along one wall. Even with their backs to him, the difference between the two girls is striking – Amy is sitting upright, the red-gold fuzz on her head shining like a halo, dressed in a red hoodie and jeans. She looks slender but strong, especially in comparison to Jesse who is slumped, leaning on her friend, her neck looking too delicate to hold up her head.

He walks away, giving the girls a moment, giving himself a moment too, because the contrast is too great and too unfair. He gets a coffee from the machine, welcoming its bitter, acrid taste. Amy's parents walk past him, holding hands. They have an air of bright hope about them, of relief. The danger is over, for now at least, and they're bringing home a daughter who may be weak now but who will get better, who will go back to school, find a job, fall in love. A daughter who has many years in front of her. Dean experiences an envy so vicious it feels like hate, which then makes him feel even worse. He knows he should be happy that at least one teenage girl gets to live.

They enter the girls' room. *It's time,* he imagines them saying, *it's time to say your goodbyes.* He waits, watching them, unseen. Amy's mum reappears, pulling along a suitcase and has her arm around her daughter's shoulders. Amy is wiping away tears, her mother kisses the top of her head. Amy's dad catches Dean's eye. His smile leaves his face, and he nods – there is nothing to say, no words to make it better, and he follows his family out of the ward.

Dean finishes his coffee and takes a few seconds to compose himself. He knocks on the door frame, and Jesse, who's now leaning back against the pillows on her bed, looks up at him and smiles, her eyes very large and dark. 'Hey, Dad.'

'Hey,' he says gently, and sits on the edge of the bed. 'Whaddya reckon? Shall we break you out of this joint?'

She laughs, then coughs, which forces her up off the

pillows and takes some time to subside. He rubs her back, feeling panic rise up in him. 'Do you want me to call a nurse?'

'I'm OK, I'm OK,' she says, giving him a shaky smile. 'Is Mum coming?'

'Of course, love.' Dean reaches for her hand, which, bird-like, squeezes his. 'She's on her way. I'm just early, that's all.'

'Amy's going to come and visit, is that all right?'

'Of course,' he says.

'Oh, before we go.' She takes her tablet from her bedside table and plugs in her earphones, giving one bud to him and placing the other in her ear. 'It's the new Mumford and Sons album.'

This is more his taste than hers, but he'd listen to Lady Gaga if Jesse wanted to. He leans back on the bed next to Jesse, her hand in his, listening together in their private ritual.

He's not asleep but nor is he fully conscious when he feels a soft hand on his wrist and hears a whispered, 'Dean?'

He opens his eyes. It's Mandy, staring down at him, her eyes so much like Jesse's. She smiles. 'Lost in music?'

'Something like that.' He smiles back and takes the ear bud out. 'Where's Sam?'

'Back home. Judith's looking after him. I thought that was best, given the circumstances . . .' She leans round to look at Jesse. 'Are you ready, darling? Thought I might take you round to everyone to say goodbye. Are you up for that?' Then, more gently, to Dean, 'Can you pack up her stuff?'

'Yeah, sure,' he says quietly. He's filled with an immense sense of gratitude – Mandy knows him so well, knows how difficult this is for him. She's giving him the space he needs.

They carefully help Jesse into a wheelchair and then Dean starts packing up. He takes all Jesse's belongings from the cupboard then moves to her pinboard. He stares at the photos, posters, his son's drawings, his wife's poems. He doesn't hear Sandy approach until she is standing beside him.

'I'm glad I caught you,' she says quietly. 'Have you got a minute?'

'Sure, not long though, I want to catch up with Mandy and Jesse.'

'And get out of this room no doubt.'

'It's nothing personal. I hate this place, I hate what it stands for, what it means every time we come here.'

'I know. Some days I hate it too.'

'Please don't get me wrong,' Dean says, turning to face Sandy. 'You and the staff here are the most extraordinary people I've ever met. You put the people I work with, both my colleagues and clients, to shame.'

'Thank you.' There's a slightly awkward silence. Dean wonders what Sandy is about to say next. Finally, she says, 'I'm glad we've got a chance to chat. I know this past week or two have been extremely tough on you.'

Dean nods, unable to speak.

'It's tough because there is no rulebook. I've seen so many families and so many different outcomes and each one is unique, because every family is unique, every child.' She speaks kindly, but firmly. 'And from each family, I've learnt something new. But one thing is very clear: it's important for Jesse to feel in control of this next stage of her illness, and it's also important for Mandy, Sam and you. All I ask is that you listen to your daughter, be guided by her and her wishes. You might regret it if you don't.'

'I think I know what's best for my daughter.'

'OK. I just ask you reflect on what I've said. Bye, Dean. It's been a privilege to look after your daughter,' Sandy tells him, turning and walking from the room.

Dean returns to removing the posters and photos one by one, placing them delicately on top of the clothes and toiletries. Removing one photo, he pauses, studying it. It shows Jesse running towards the tape being held by two adults on a cross-country run, hair streaming behind her, arms raised in victory. With a shaking hand he places it in the case with the others.

CHAPTER 26

It's time to leave.

Jesse feels strangely nervous, which is silly because she's been through this many times before. Maybe it's because it feels more final this time. It *is* final. It makes her feel slightly nostalgic for this place, where she's been through so much, but where she's also met such good friends. Amy, Ryan and Luke. Friends for life. Her life, at least.

As they approach the nurses' station, Ryan steps in front of them and clears his throat formally. Jesse struggles pulling herself out from the wheelchair to stand before him.

'I'm getting out of here next week; can I come and see you at home?' he asks.

'Of course you can, Ryan, anytime.' Mandy's voice is warm. 'You have your mother ring me and we'll make it happen, OK?'

Ryan simply nods. He looks at Jesse, reaches out and punches her oh so gently on the arm. Jesse kisses him on the cheek. Ryan turns very quickly and walks away.

Luke slowly walks towards Jesse and stops directly in front of her. His voice quivering, he asks if he can have a hug, the kind she gives Amy. Before he can move, Jesse wraps her arms around him, holding him as his body shakes with sobs. Eventually, a nurse gently pulls Luke from the embrace and hands him over to a colleague.

Dropping back into the wheelchair, Jesse quietly, says 'bye', as much to the ward as to anyone in particular. Her voice shakes, she tries to keep the tears in. Her mum places one hand on her shoulder as she wheels her away. 'Time to leave, my darling girl,' she says softly. 'Time to go home.'

In the car, Jesse turns off the radio, preferring to stare out the window in quiet contemplation, seeing the scenery go past as if for the first time. All those colours, all that life. On the coastal road, she sits up straighter. There, in the distance, a balloon floats high over the world.

'Thinking about your balloon trip?' Mandy says.

'It was amazing,' Jesse says, breaking into a big grin. 'Flying above everything like that. I could see the track, I saw dolphins . . . I think I even saw our house!'

Mandy laughs. 'That's great, darling. I'm so glad you had a good time.'

'It was the best.' Jesse smiles but then looks over to Mandy. 'Thanks for letting me go, Mum.'

'Well, Alex rang me asking if there was anything you liked to do; a place you liked to go, somewhere that he could take you as a surprise. I told him you were a beach bunny, but he knows we live on the beach and you can go there any time, so he asked what else you liked.'

'What made you say I liked hot air balloons? It's not something we've ever talked about.'

'The day I brought you back to the hospital, you were watching one fly over the bay. At the time I guessed you were wishing you could fly away from here, from your life, from the hospital, and it broke my heart.'

Mandy can't control her voice or the tears that escape and flow down her cheeks.

'Oh, Mum, I don't want to fly away from my life, from you. Yeah, OK, maybe from going back to hospital.'

Jesse leans towards her mum and wipes away her tears with her fingers so she can see to drive, loving the choking giggle Mandy can't control.

'I wasn't sure what to tell you about my time with Alex, because I didn't want to upset you by telling you I had an amazing experience which you, Dad and Sam weren't part of.'

'You won't upset me! Quite the opposite, I am so happy that Alex was able to do something for you, give you something that we couldn't.'

'And there is no way Dad would have let me go,' Jesse says quietly.

Mandy reaches over and squeezes Jesse's hand. 'He's trying, darling. He really is.'

'I know, Mum.' They sit in silence for a while, the hot air balloon hanging in the sky ahead of them. 'Do you want to hear about it?' Jesse finally says.

The look of love on Mandy's face is all Jesse needs to see before she starts sharing with her mother her flight in a hot air balloon.

Jesse is still telling the story when they arrive home and the two stay in the car until Jesse has finished. They hug each other over the middle console.

'We better get inside; Sam can't wait to see you and I'm sure he's driven Judith crazy with questions about when you're coming.'

The front door is barely open before Sam throws himself at Jesse.

'You have to let us come in, Sammy,' Jesse says as she propels the two of them, arms entwined, away from the front door so Mandy can come in. Their neighbour Judith appears and she and Mandy hug.

'Where's Dean?' Judith whispers.

'He stayed behind to pack up Jesse's things, he'll be here shortly. How was Sam, no trouble?'

'Sam, trouble? No, we chatted, and I watched him drawing. He just kept asking how much longer you'd be.'

'I'm sorry, we were as quick as we could be.'

'Mandy, I'm just next door and there is nothing Greg or I wouldn't do for your family.' Judith gives Jesse a kiss and a hug. 'See you later, Sam, make sure you show Jesse the drawings you did.'

'Thanks, Mrs Newman,' Jesse says. Judith looks at Mandy, at Sam then at Jesse. Mandy reads her mind – it's an expression she's seen so often since Jesse became ill. There but for the grace of God.

The sound of a car beeping its horn breaks the moment.

'Dad's here,' Sam says with excitement.

Dean, carrying Jesse's bag, passes Judith as he enters the

house. They exchange a genuine quick kiss and hug. This family might be broken right now but no blame is being apportioned.

'You looking after yourself?' the older woman asks Dean, twinkling up her eyes as they embrace.

'Getting there, Judith, getting there.'

'Well, you just make sure you do,' she says, before leaving the family.

Sam gives his dad a hug before taking Jesse's hand. Together, they slowly climb the stairs to Jesse's bedroom.

Jesse stands inside her room and looks around at her life displayed in front of her. Memories flash before her as she regards each object, each brimming with meaning: posters of pop stars and athletes; precious mementos on her dressing table; photo frames covered in shells she has collected that mean as much as the photo inside; necklaces hanging from the mirror remind her of the person who gave them to her, or a fun time wearing them. She smiles as she glimpses the lipstick she bought with her own money against her father's wishes. She hears his voice *You're too young to be wearing that,* and remembers wearing it smeared on nice and thick to dinner each night for a week, until he finally relented: *Can I borrow some?* he had teased. *Do you think it's my colour?* Sam stands silently beside her, watching her go through her returning home ritual.

Climbing onto her bed she hugs one of the soft toys leaning against her pillows as Sam joins her, snuggling up to his big sister. They both turn to the door as they hear the soft knock.

'Who is it?' Jesse and Sam chorus.

Dean peers around the door. 'Is it OK if I come in?'

'What's the password?' Jesse teases him.

Dean rolls his eyes. 'I've got your suitcase. I thought you might like it.'

'Correct. Thanks, Dad, yeah, I'll go through it later.'

Dean puts it beside her chest of drawers. He looks big and awkward in this space. He clears his throat. 'Ah, your mum has asked me if I want to stay for dinner.'

'Yay!' says Sam, jumping up and spilling the soft toys from the bed.

Dean and Jesse laugh at Sam's antics – he's jumping around the room with a big grin on his face.

'That's great, Dad,' Jesse says.

'I'll, um, I'll just help your mum with dinner,' he says. 'I'll see you down there in a bit.'

With the door closed, Jesse turns to Sam. 'Can I tell you something, something that happened to me, but you can't tell Dad?'

'Why not?' Sam asks.

'Because he won't like it. It's about Alex.'

'Then I promise I won't tell him.'

'Shall I tell you about the time I floated up in the air?'

Sam gasps and puts both his hands to his mouth. Jesse lets him snuggle into her side and then tells him all about the magical, wonderful balloon ride, how she was whisked away from the hospital to a flying balloon just for her, his eyes widening like saucers.

*

It's late, and Jesse's tired. Happy, but tired. It was possibly the best night they had had as a family since before she got ill. No, she thinks, it definitely was the best night, one for the record books. Mum didn't worry about the dishes that evening, she'd left them on the kitchen counter, instead making huge ice cream sundaes for everyone for dessert, Sam sneaking all the maraschino cherries from everyone's dishes and everyone pretending not to notice. Afterwards, they played board games, Jesse trying to outsmart her father and let Sam win at the same time. Her sides had ached from laughing.

Sam had to be carried up to bed, and Jessie followed not long later, exhausted. Her bed, her own bed, was soft and comfortable, the sheets cool and fresh and fragranced with the laundry powder her mother liked to use. She could hear the murmur of her parents' voices downstairs, a sound she remembered from before she got sick, a sound that made her feel secure and cosy.

She's just about to fall asleep when she senses her parents are at her door, looking in on her.

Neither parent moves, and Jesse finally falls asleep under their gaze, feeling happy, feeling safe, feeling loved.

CHAPTER 27

In her apartment, curled up in a blanket for comfort, with an empty coffee cup and box of tissues competing for space on the small table beside her, Kelly watches another black and white movie. A lamp in the corner of the room provides a sliver of light, the half-moon shining through a window she hasn't bothered to draw the blinds on adding to the eerie mood in the room. Realising she has not followed the movie playing out in front of her, that she's missed something, what's being said is not making sense to her, she hits the mute button and the room goes quiet.

She's stumbled on an old movie she's never seen before, *Rebecca of Sunnybrook Farm* which is playing on silently. She looks at the farm scenes and becomes Rebecca, a young girl in trapped a world she feels she doesn't belong in. Kelly is flooded with memories of hiding under her bed or disappearing onto the farm when one of her parents called out to her and her siblings to come and help. Every day, twice a day, came the call to collect the eggs from the chicken run, move the cows to the overnight paddock, feed the pigs: a million chores needing to be done. Night after night she sat at the dinner table, questioned by her parents about where she'd been all day, ridiculed by her siblings for not wanting to get her hands dirty, did she think she was better than they were?

'No,' she screams at the television. 'I didn't think I was better than them, I just wanted no part in that life, I couldn't allow myself to engage with it when I knew I was going to leave as soon as I could. I wanted to find a way to work with people, to make a difference.'

Grabbing the remote she switches the television off and puts herself in the foetal position on the sofa, burying her head under a cushion. Not even chocolates will help tonight.

Back in her own room, her own bed, Amy sleeps fitfully. She misses having a bed on the other side of the room and the company of a friend tossing and turning like her.

Mandy and Dean tiptoe from Sam's room and slowly open the door into Jesse's bedroom. They stand for several moments watching their daughter sleeping peacefully.

'I'd better be off,' Dean whispers.

Mandy nods yes and doesn't look back as he leaves. She remains leaning against the door frame. Only when she hears him close the front door does she allow herself to weep silently.

CHAPTER 28

'What am I going to do, Max?'

Alex studies Max's face, hoping he can read an answer to his question, his dilemma. Max tilts his head to show he's listening, and that he cares.

Sitting at his kitchen table, a cup of coffee half drunk, a piece of toast on a plate pushed away, Alex continues to stare at Max. He gets an answer when Max puts a front paw on his leg and whimpers softly.

'I'm meant to go to her house today to get more videos and photos from her mum. I've spent all weekend trying to work out how to do this for her, you know, buddy, make her wish come true. But I can't do it with what I've got, I need the studio and there's no way Ian will let me use it for this project with no money coming in. He wanted me to do this thing free of charge somehow, and I can tell he now thinks I've spent long enough. I can feel him trying to work out how to call it off without annoying his daddy-in-law. And then he'd like to get rid of me also.'

Max continues to whimper.

'Yeah, you're right, you're always right. I've got to tell Ian it can't be done then find a way to tell Jesse, and Kelly – and Luke and Ryan. And Mandy and Sam. The dad will be delighted, so there's a plus. Oh God, what have I got myself into? I've given it a good go, haven't I? I won't feel regret at not having finished it if I know I really tried?'

A low growl from Max suggests this mightn't be the solution, but he takes his paw away as if he knows it's time for Alex to stand up and leave. Sitting staring into space won't make it any better. He walks to the front door and waits for Alex to put his jacket on, grab his helmet and pat him goodbye.

Alex arrives late at the office. Again. He yanks off his helmet and pulls a hand through his hair, making it worse. Scuffed trainers. Crumpled shirt. He looks like he slept on a park bench.

'There he is,' Ian says, his voice unnaturally bright.

Alex stops. Ian is standing with a TV film crew – camera, boom mic, clipboard, all of it. A few colleagues peek over cubicle walls. No one's pretending to work.

'What is this?' Alex says.

'You're late,' Ian replies. 'And you look like something the dog dragged in.'

'Ian . . .'

'Alex, meet the crew. They're going to grab a quick shot of you at your desk before heading to the hospital to meet the girl.'

Alex blinks. The camera turns to face him.

He places his helmet and jacket on a colleague's desk, then grabs Ian by the elbow and steers him towards the reception desk nearby. The receptionist takes one look and wisely vanishes.

'Get rid of them,' Alex snaps.

'What the hell are you doing?' Ian hisses.

'There's no filming. No hospital visit. Get them out.'

'I don't care if you haven't finished the wish—'

'There is no wish. I can't do it.'

Ian waves a hand dismissively. 'Doesn't matter. I want footage of the girl. You. A thank you moment. A nice slow pan to the TriOptics logo. You might want to wash your face first – you look like hell.'

'She's not there anymore,' Alex says, voice flat. 'She's gone home. The treatment failed. She's spending her last weeks in peace and privacy. I tried, Ian. But we're not disturbing her now – not with a camera crew.'

Ian's face flushes red. 'All you had to do was build a simple game for a dying kid. I thought you had it in you.'

'Her name is Jesse. And it's not a game. It's . . .' He falters. 'It's something more.'

They push through the office door. The film crew is already packing up. Ian tries to salvage things, offering an interview, suggesting they *might* still get access. But it's clear the crew heard everything. This is a no-go. They bail.

'Alex! You're fired!' Ian shouts after they've left.

'No, I'm not.'

'You are! You've wasted weeks of company time moping around that hospital – what do you even have to show for it? Fuck all.'

Alex's voice stays calm. 'Only Frank can fire me.'

For once, Ian has no comeback, just a red face and shaking fists. 'Get out of my sight!'

Alex watches him storm off, then returns to his cubicle. One by one, colleagues approach – quiet handshakes, pats on the back. A hug. Steve is waiting.

'You OK, mate?'

'I . . . don't know.'

'We heard everything. So, Jesse's gone home. That means she's better?'

'No. It means the opposite.' Alex slumps into his chair. 'Shit, Steve. I'm supposed to be at her house right now.'

'Then go,' Steve says. 'Forget Ian. What's stopping you?'

'There's too much I don't know. Too much I can't fix.'

Steve gestures to the screens. 'How much can you access from here?'

'All of it. I've linked the home system.'

'Then boot it up. Let's see what we've got.'

Alex does. Videos, music, drawings – all flicker to life across his monitors. Sarah wanders over, eyes on the visuals.

'Slow down. What exactly are you trying to do?'

'I've been wrestling with this all week,' Alex says. 'The animations keep going out of sync. The conversations start OK, but after a minute they're all talking to the walls.'

Sarah studies the screens. 'What version of the cinematic manager are you using?'

'Version 4. The only one Frank lets me use.'

She winces. 'That was just a maze of bugs.'

She wheels Steve's chair beside Alex, grabs his mouse, and starts clicking through menus.

'Mmm,' she mutters.

'Mmm what?'

'We rebuilt this entire workflow when we upgraded to version 5 of the renderer. Way cleaner.'

'Too bad I'm not allowed to use version 5.'

'You're not. But I could backport the fix. Technically still version 4 just with a few, shall we say, tweaks.'

'How long would that take?'

'Dunno, maybe an hour to merge the code, another hour or two to run the automated system tests, shouldn't break anything. We were pretty careful when we built it.'

'You can do that?'

Sarah stands and returns Steve's chair to his cubicle. 'Yeah, easy, what source repository are you saving to?

Alex scrambles down one screen reading his reference documentation.

'Ahh, vol 2 slash Alex slash Phoenix.'

'Got it. Give me remote access to your machine.'

'Just fixes only, OK? No product updates or Ian will have my neck.'

'Can do. I mean, there may be some dependencies, but I'll work through that. How long did you say you'd been having these problems?'

'Since I started,' Alex tells her, feeling like the most incompetent member of the team, not the wunderkind.

'You've got some nice close shots of the lady who is just the social worker but nothing more, I see,' Sarah says, walking back to her cubicle, winking at Steve.

'Kelly,' Alex blurts out. 'Her name is Kelly.'

He grabs his jacket and helmet, just as Ian sticks his head around the door.

'GET BACK TO BLOODY WORK!'

He's met with half a dozen pairs of angry, cold eyes. No one moves. Flustered, he hastily retreats.

Kelly looks up from her desk at a gentle knock on her door. She smiles at Alex, expecting the usual silence and hurried departure.

'How long have I got?' he says.

'For what?' Kelly asks, concerned at his tone and his appearance. He's always quite dishevelled, but today he looks as though he's been in a fight.

'Sorry, I mean how long does Jesse have?'

'Alex . . .'

'Just tell me.'

'I can't. You know that.'

'No. You asked me to come here to make a wish come true for Jesse. Now I don't want any of your confidentiality crap. Just tell me how long's she got!'

Kelly stands behind her desk, weighing what she can say. Then, finally: 'Three, maybe four weeks. Not long.'

Alex slumps against the wall, clutching his helmet. Kelly comes around the desk, reaching for his arm. He pulls away, too upset. 'I've got to go,' he says, and pushes past her, making his way down the corridor and beyond the receptionist. He stops at the lift. One sign stands out: 6 EAST.

Ignoring the lifts and the dozens of people waiting, he sees the door indicating the stairwell and runs to it. Level 1.

Level 2. Level 3. He continues up, bursting through the door onto Level 6.

Slowing his breathing he walks through the automatic doors and to the nurses' station. 'Is Sandy available?'

'Hi, Alex, she's in her office. I'll call her and see if she's free.'

Moments later, he's ushered inside.

'Sit down, Alex, how can I help?' Sandy asks him as he closes the door behind him.

'I need to do something.'

'If this is about Jesse, I can't—'

'How do I get tested? For bone marrow compatibility?'

'You want to be tested?'

'I have the right blood group. Just . . . tell me how.'

Sandy pauses and looks at him. He can see her making a decision. What have they got to lose?

'OK. You need a mouth swab and a blood test.'

'Yes, I know that, but how do I do that?'

Sandy regards Alex thoughtfully. Then, reaching into a drawer, she places a pad on her desk.

'If you're serious . . .'

'I'm serious.'

'OK. I can write a request, and you can take it down to pathology on the ground floor. I'll have the result sent to me. Oh dear, this is highly unusual. I'm meant to do this for patients. You're not a patient.'

'I don't want to get you into trouble.'

Sandy writes on the pad. Tearing the page out she hands it to Alex.

'I've marked it urgent; I should get the results in a couple of hours. Give me your phone number and I'll call you. That's all I can do.'

'Thank you, Sandy, thank you so much. Ground floor, huh?'

'Pathology, plenty of signs.'

Alex takes the pathology form and hurries from the room, down the stairs to the ground floor, scanning the sign boards until he finds the Pathology Department. The wait is not long. No questions are asked. He thanks the technician and leaves the department.

Outside in the car park, he walks right past his bike. A car screeches to a stop as he steps into the road.

'Hey, are you OK?' a stranger asks.

Alex blinks, slowly coming back to himself. 'Yeah. I'm good.'

He doubles back, finds his motorbike, and sits on it. Cradles his helmet before slamming it against the engine. Once. Twice. Three times.

A couple in a nearby car stare. He ignores them.

He slides on the helmet, starts the engine and drives away.

CHAPTER 29

All eyes look up as Alex strides into the office. A few colleagues call out greetings, others offer a thumbs-up or quiet nods – small signals of solidarity.

He heads straight for Sarah's cubicle, where Charlie and Phil are already gathered. Charlie spots him and steps aside, revealing the screen: a scene of Jesse's family, talking and laughing together.

'That looks really good,' Alex says.

Sarah spins in her chair and grins. 'Yup, no more characters talking to walls, we are a family that is communicating.'

Alex leans in closer. 'No, that looks really good, better than it should . . . is that our new facial animation system in there?'

Sarah and Phil exchange conspiratorial looks.

'I said fixes only. If Ian sees this, he'll have me.'

'There was no choice,' Sarah shrugs. 'The patch depended on the Face-Tech module. Without it, none of the fixes would work.'

She pats Phil's shoulder. 'And I told him not to use it.'

'Hey, I just make it look good,' Phil says, hands up.

Alex exhales, not hiding his admiration. 'You did. Thanks. All of you. Send me everything – we'll keep pushing it from my end.'

He grabs his chair and wheels it over to Steve's desk.

'Man, where've you been?' Steve says. 'Ian's ready to fire your sorry arse, again.'

'I need your help. Tonight.'

Steve pauses. 'What about Ian?'

'Let him do what he wants. Are you in?'

Steve stands up, looking down at Alex, critically assessing him. This is someone he has not seen before, someone who is standing his ground, not rolling over to the demands, belittlement and humiliation thrown his way in the past. This is a young man on a mission – and that mission is to help a very sick teenage girl. He likes what he sees.

'Yeah,' Steve says. 'What do you need?'

'My place. Tonight. Tell your family I'm sorry.'

Steve glances at a photo on his desk – his wife and two kids, crammed onto a swing, all beaming at the camera.

'They'll understand. You staying here?'

'No. Heading home. See you later.'

He's halfway to the car park when his phone rings.

'Sandy?'

'I got the results. You were right about the blood type, but there aren't enough markers. You're not a match for Jesse. I'm sorry, Alex.'

Alex closes his eyes. 'Thanks for letting me know, for trying. Really.'

'You're already doing more than most. Just – know that.'

'Let's keep this between us?'

'Of course. But the results are on the hospital system now. I can't erase those.'

'Understood. See you.'

At home, Alex kneels beside Max. 'We're heading out early. Sorry it's still hot – let's run under the trees. Steve's coming over later. He's helping. You in?'

Max wags his tail, delighted.

Later, Steve arrives with a bag.

'Sorry about being late. When I told Lydia where I was going, she insisted I bring something for us to eat.'

'I don't think I want to know what you've been telling her about me,' Alex says with a knowing smile. He has no doubt his colleagues have all reported home about the loner who is first in each morning and last to leave each night.

'Do you want to eat first?' Steve says, eyeing the bag as he follows Alex into the kitchen and placing it on the bench.

'Oh yeah, sure, why not, I'll get some plates. Do you know what she's sent?'

Steve starts opening the bag, pulling out plastic containers. 'It's what we were having for dinner tonight. Pasta, salad and I think there will be some garlic bread in there. Any chance you have parmesan?'

'Ah, don't think so.'

'I'll look in the fridge,' Steve says, walking towards the refrigerator.

'Don't bother, I don't have parmesan. Does it matter?'

Steve goes back to unpacking the food. 'Hey, what do you know, my wife thinks of everything.' He waves a small container. 'Cheese.'

'Great, let's eat then.'

'Well, can we heat it up? It's warm but will taste better if we heat it up some.'

Alex looks around his kitchen, opens a cupboard, peers in before closing it. 'Oh yeah, I know where the pots are, they're under the sink.'

'Thanks, if it's OK, I think I'd better take over the food. Any chance you've got a beer in your fridge?'

'Now that's something I can get for you.'

Alex hands Steve a bottle of beer before sitting at the kitchen table and watching him heat up the pasta, then scramble around in cupboards to find a bowl to empty the salad into from its plastic container. Inside the oven he finds a tray, turning the oven on he places the garlic bread on the tray and pops it into the oven to warm. Within minutes they are enjoying a wonderful home-cooked meal, washed down with a second beer. They both surreptitiously slip Max a piece of garlic bread. Steve clears the table, putting the dishes into the dishwasher, packing the empty containers back into the bag. From the remaining container he shows Alex the home-baked brownies and isn't surprised when one is immediately playfully snatched away. The gentle moaning is testament to his wife's baking ability. The crumbs are hoovered away by Max.

'You're one lucky bugger,' Alex tells him.

'Nothing you couldn't have if you put yourself out there.'

'Yeah, sure. Come on, we've got work to do.'

The last thing Alex wants to do is talk about himself.

Opening the door into his office, Alex flicks the overhead light on. Following him, Steve stops in the doorway.

'Wow, look at all this kit!'

Steve slowly walks towards the wall of monitors, screens, keyboards which come to life with a flick of a switch.

'I think the guys at work may have solved my biggest problem but there's still so much to do.'

Steve is still taking in the sophistication of the equipment in front of him. 'Why do you work for a jerk like Ian when you could run your own business right here? Hell, you could put a man on the moon with this stuff.'

'I guess you wouldn't believe me if I said it's for the camaraderie of the office and our colleagues.'

'Nope, not buying that.'

'Truth is, I love what we do there, it's so cutting edge – well, it was – and as a team we're the best in the business, you know that.'

'OK, but how the hell did you afford all this? I mean, I know the cost of some of this stuff, way outside my budget.'

'I basically live like a monk; I've worked since I was a kid and saved every penny. I only buy tech stuff, feed me and Max. I know everyone at TriOptics is producing cutting edge work but there's a lot you can do with what I've got here, outside of the big shoots in the studio. I probably shouldn't tell you this, but I've been working on software to make a version of what we do at the studio, affordable and accessible to the average fifteen-year-old. Why shouldn't others be able to produce the experiences we do? We should share the knowledge.'

'But you'd copyright and protect your intellectual property. Sell the product.'

'Well, yeah, but I'd make it affordable.'

'And then you'd walk away from TriOptics, Ian and all his bullshit?'

'That's a tricky one to answer. If I didn't come into the office, the only person who would register my existence is Max. I've been pretty much a solo unit, until I started hanging out at the hospital with Jesse, her family and the other kids there. And Kelly.'

Steve turns back to the screens, to the different photos of Jesse, Amy, her family.

Steve pauses by one screen. 'Who is she?' he asks.

'Ah, that's Kelly, Jesse's social worker.'

Steve studies the photo of Kelly. 'This is the social worker you've been having a hard time with?' He looks at Alex, shaking his head, a wry smile on his face. 'You've got to get out more, my friend.'

'It's not that simple. She's ah, complicated.'

'Really. Huh. A complicated woman. Who would have thought?'

'Forget her. If you're ready to start, I'll show you what I've got and where the different files are.'

Max settles into his bed as Alex and Steve dive into the job at hand.

'Just hang on a minute while I update everything with

what Sarah did today, should now make it easier for us to plan what we need to shoot at the studio.'

Videos and still photos slide between the monitors.

Throughout the night, Alex and Steve identify and compile files, at times struggling to determine timelines based on what they think Jesse's age is in photos. Regularly they stand and stretch, go to the kitchen for water, the bathroom, to eat the remaining brownies.

As the room starts to lighten, Steve glances at his watch. 'Oh Christ, I've got to go, I've just got time to go home, have a shower, kiss Lydia and the kids hello and goodbye and get to the office. In the mood Ian's in right now he's just as likely to fire me for being five minutes late. You, well as much as he'd love to get rid of you, he knows Frank would boot him out the door if he did, so I don't think you are fired just yet. And, given what you said about not having anyone but Max to miss you, it's just the tiniest bit possible that you need us as much as we need you.'

Max barks at this point – the man is right.

'Sorry, mate, didn't realise how late it was.'

'It's not late anymore, we've gone beyond late, we're now early.'

'OK, off you go and please, tell Lydia thanks for the dinner and brownies, and sorry for keeping you out all night. And thanks. I mean it. I think we just might do this.'

'Are you coming into the office?'

'Nah.'

'OK. I'll see myself out.'

'Thanks, I'll give you a call later.'

Stopping to rub Max's belly, Steve leaves, turning back and catching Alex staring at a photo of Kelly.

Hearing the front door shut Alex stands and stretches, looking over at Max.

'Why didn't you tell me it was so late? Maybe we should take a break. Come on, outside.'

Max follows Alex to the kitchen and out the back door where they walk around the garden, taking in the early morning, refreshing and soothing after a long night at the screens. Wandering back into his living room, Alex blinks as the first bright rays of the new day break through the window. Wincing, Alex closes the curtains, making the room dark. Staggering to the sofa, he lies down and falls asleep. Max sighs. Breakfast will be late. He curls up next to Alex and falls asleep too.

The sound of rain and Max slobbering on his face wakes Alex some hours later. Wiping his face with his T-shirt, he slowly rises and staggers to the kitchen. After a long look in the fridge reveals nothing for either him or Max to eat, he takes the dog crackers from the bench and pours a decent amount into Max's bowl. He contemplates eating one himself before adding it to the bowl. In a cupboard he finds a packet of potato crisps.

Screwing up his face at the taste, he continues to eat them, carrying the packet into the bathroom, where, placing it on the vanity he fills his mouth while stripping off and getting into the shower. He watches as Max joins him in the bathroom, reaches up to the vanity and knocks the packet onto the floor, manipulating it to empty the contents out, swiftly hoovering up the rest of Alex's breakfast.

Dressed, Alex looks at his razor, runs his hands over his stubble and decides no, not today. There are more important things to do, and he and Max go back to his office. For several hours he manipulates scenes, videos and photos. Glancing at the clock on his desk, he grabs his leather jacket, helmet and heads to the garage. Opening the garage door, he notices it is still raining. Sighing, he guns the engine and pulls out on to the street.

Having previously noticed staff at the hospital leaving through a back entrance to go to the staff car park, Alex positions his bike to observe the end of the day for non-shift workers. The rain falling makes it difficult for him to identify the staff members, as many of them immediately raise umbrellas, blocking his view of their faces. Finally, he sees her. Kelly. She has no umbrella and accepts the offer from a colleague to share hers. He watches as she breaks away from her colleague and runs to her car. As she drives out of the car park, he pulls in behind her and follows.

The rain and peak hour evening traffic make their journey slow. Alex worries that Kelly will become suspicious of his bike remaining on her tail, but she shows no sign of being aware he is there. Finally, she pulls into a small apartment building. Parking, she runs through the rain and inside. Stopping beside her car Alex is concerned her apartment might be on the other side of the building; then he won't know which is hers. His patience is rewarded when he sees a light come on in an apartment on the third floor and recognises Kelly closing the curtains to the weather outside.

Entering her bedroom Kelly throws her jacket onto the bed. With one hand she unbuttons her blouse, with the other a clip is pulled from her hair which drops around her shoulders. Shaking it free, she smooths the wayward bits down. Her blouse is replaced by a sweat top and before she can switch out her skirt, she hears the knock on her door. Pausing, she waits to see if a second knock comes, wondering if she's heard something that isn't there. The second knock follows.

Opening her door, Kelly is shocked to see an unshaven, dripping wet Alex.

'How did . . .'

'I followed you from the hospital.'

'You what?'

'I'm sorry, but I need to talk to you.'

'OK, but what is wrong with my office?'

'Can I come in?'

Kelly makes no move to let him in or move away from the small gap in the door her body is blocking.

'Alex, why are you here?' She fights to keep her tone neutral, professional.

Alex looks down at his wet clothes, boots, notices the puddle of water he is making on the floor. He suddenly has no idea why he is here. He was acting on an impulse. Exhaustion and hunger hit him like a sledgehammer, and he realises he's swaying on the spot. She might think he's been drinking. He fights to pull himself together.

'You said you would help me,' is all he can manage to stammer out.

'With what in particular?'

'Jesse,' is all he can say.

'Alex, you look terrible, now what's going on? You need help with what, Jesse's wish?'

'No, no, I've got a friend, he's helping, well, he's not really a friend, he's a colleague, well, he might be a friend, I'm not sure. It's, it's . . .'

'Alex, what do you want from me?'

Struggling to hold it together; frustration, anger at Jesse's situation bubble up as Alex continues to stammer.

'You said you'd help me get through this, make it easier for me, but you haven't done a damn thing. I'm busting my gut here, I've spent hours at the hospital, *your* hospital, because you needed me, or so I thought. I've met this amazing girl who is going to die, and I don't know how to deal with that, I don't know how to deal with you. I'm probably going to lose my job but that's OK, I don't care about that. But what do I do when she's gone? How do I make sense of what I've been through? I just want a bit of help, that's all.'

A neighbour appears at the top of the stairs and walks towards them, concerned with what he is seeing. 'Hi, Kelly, make it home before the rain set in?'

Kelly forces a smile to allay the worry she sees in her neighbour. 'Hi, Andy. No, I copped it, but it seems to be coming down even harder now.'

Andy turns to Alex. 'Sorry, didn't mean to interrupt. See you, Kelly.'

'See you, Andy,' Kelly says back.

Alex watches the neighbour disappear into a nearby door. Not looking at Kelly he walks away, leaving Kelly standing in her doorway, uncertain what to do.

Walking slowly back out into the car park through the rain, Alex sits on his bike, staring up at the lights in Kelly's apartment. Putting his helmet on, he slowly drives through the car park to the street. Something catches his eye in his side mirror. A wet, bedraggled Kelly is running towards him. Clicking his stand into place in one motion he steps off his bike, takes his helmet off, placing it on the seat. Swiftly he unzips and removes his jacket. As Kelly reaches him, he wraps her in his jacket, holding her close.

Kelly looks up at him.

'I'm sorry, I'm so sorry but I didn't know what to say, I wasn't expecting to see you. You have to understand, my home is where I get away from my work, where I can pretend Jesse and the others don't exist and I do that so well, the pretending. I have to, don't you see?'

Tears now mingle with the rain running down her face.

'But I should've helped you. I shouldn't have been so hostile at the beginning, and I should've prepared you better, told you that you would fall for Jesse, like we all have. I'm so sorry, Alex.'

Alex attempts to wipe her tears away, chuckling at the futility of it as the heavy rain runs down her face. Letting her go, he straddles his bike. Then, placing his helmet on Kelly's head, he encourages her to sit in front of him, nestled between his legs. Holding tight, he slowly drives to the front of her apartment building.

They walk up the stairs, his arm around her, her head resting on his shoulder. Walking her to her open door, he takes his jacket from her. Pushing her hair away from her face, wiping it with the back of his hand, he smiles.

'I know I've broken every rule in the book coming here tonight, but can I ask you a favour?'

'You can ask,' Kelly replies with a smile.

'I want your help with what I've done so far, I need you to see what I'm doing to make sure I'm doing the right thing.'

'Of course I'll help you.'

'Ah, it means going to my home where all my equipment is. I can't pack it up easily.'

'You're asking me to come to your place?'

'Yes.'

'Then you better give me your address. Let me clean up and I'll be there.'

Kelly opens her apartment door and takes a step inside. 'I'll see you soon,' she says.

She watches him walk away and disappear down the stairs. Closing her door she runs to the window, opening the curtains a crack to wait for him to appear and get on his bike. She feels genuine disappointment when he doesn't look up at her. As he pulls away, he raises his right arm in a wave, as if he knows she's watching him leave.

CHAPTER 30

Showered and shaved, in casual clothes and bare feet, Alex fills Max's bowl with the appropriate dog food he bought on his way home. No one paid him any attention when he entered the supermarket, everyone there looking equally wet and bedraggled. Max has had a lovely run to the park in the rain and is feeling pretty good. He's enjoying the amount of time Alex is spending at home. The doorbell rings and Max bounds towards it.

'That'll be Steve,' Alex tells him.

Catching up to Max who stands impatiently, his tail wagging furiously, he opens the door. In the poorly lit entrance stands Steve, along with Sarah, Charlie and Phil.

'Max, back inside, boy, go to the kitchen.'

Head down, tail down, Max slowly saunters away with several backward glances.

'Hey, Alex,' they all greet him.

'I didn't know you were all coming?' Alex says.

'Hope you don't mind. I spoke to them this afternoon, told them your plans, and they asked if they could come and help.'

'Of course not, are you sure you want to help, though? If Ian finds out there could be trouble.'

'Let him try and do his worst. We're here for you man,' Phil says, showing off the three large pizza boxes he holds in one hand, and a carton of six bottles of beer. 'Hungry?' he asks.

'Let me in, I'm getting wet out here while you all babble,' Sarah says, pushing past Steve, Phil and Charlie.

Charlie follows Steve and Phil into the house, wearing a biker's black leathers complete with a patch that makes Alex wonder if Charlie is part of a gang. He can only hope it's the friendly kind, the kind that dresses up as Santa at Christmas and delivers presents to disadvantaged kids. He's carrying a portable music machine. 'Hey, Alex, I hope you don't mind a bit of music while we work?' He hits a button and rap music blares out.

'No, come in,' Alex tells him.

He hears Sarah say to Charlie, 'I play my music on a different kind of keyboard: show me where to go.'

They all follow Max into the living room where Kelly is waiting.

'Everyone, this is Kelly,' Alex says shyly. He points at the others, naming them.

Steve extends his hand to Kelly.

'Hi, Kelly, I've seen your photo, um, on Alex's computer, last night,' he stumbles over the words.

'That doesn't sound good, I'm almost too afraid to ask,' she replies with a smile.

'We met before, right, you were with Alex at the café,'

Sarah says, smiling, winking at Alex.

'Yes, I thought I recognised you when you came in. Hello again,' Kelly says, shaking Sarah's hand.

'What's that in your bag?' Alex asks Sarah.

'Data tracking module. Thought we could load it directly at the studio later – skip a step.'

'You shouldn't have – if Ian notices . . .'

'Nah, I signed it out as going to the manufacturer for a software update, won't be missed for a week and I'll have it back by then.'

Sarah's taken a risk for him; Alex doesn't know what to say.

From the kitchen, Max barks.

'Oh no,' Alex says. 'He's not used to this many people . . .'

But when he gets there, Phil's already sitting on the floor, handing Max half a slice of pizza. Max sniffs it, then devours it.

'We broke bread. We're cool now,' Phil says, grinning.

Over the next few hours, Alex and his team of mismatched friends work together to make Jesse's wish come true. There is laughter, music and off-key singing – sounds never heard in Alex's home. They trip over each other, over cables plugged from one piece of equipment to another. Max finishes off all the half-eaten pizza left in boxes on the floor. At one point, Charlie finds an old virtual reality helmet and puts it on Max who blindly stumbles among them before Alex rescues him. Kelly's main role is coffee maker – but she's also quite helpful in giving them a rough timeline of the images of Jesse.

Half-empty cups placed on the floor are sampled by Max, who's having the best night of his life. Kelly and Sarah chat, clearly getting on, they perform a duet together, rolled-up computer magazines improvised as microphones. As they finally finish work, Steve raps his knuckles on the table, and everyone goes quiet.

'Last one, boys and girls. As soon as this section finishes compiling, we are done, well, this part anyway. The rest will have to be done at the studio, live.'

They all squash together, looking at the one remaining screen. Alex stands behind Kelly. Placing his arms around her waist, he rests his chin on her shoulder, his exhaustion obvious. Kelly leans back against him, surprised and amazed at how natural it feels. Charlie drops into a chair, his stretching cut short by Sarah plonking herself on his lap. Phil walks over to the window and pulls open a curtain a chink. Early rays of sunshine briefly fill the room, but the pained look from Steve tells him to drop the curtain again quickly. Phil joins the others as they all stare at the image of Jesse outside on the hospital balcony at night. They follow her gaze into the star-filled sky, and the screen goes black.

Kelly breaks the silence. 'What happens now?'

Everyone looks to her. She's the only one who doesn't yet know the full scope of Jesse's wish.

Alex steps forward. 'I'll explain everything. But first – thank you. Steve, Sarah, Charlie, Phil – I don't have the words. What this means to me . . . to *Jesse*,' Alex says, his voice breaking.

'We're happy to help, in fact we need to thank Steve and you for letting us be part of this. I'm never going to forget what we did tonight. What do you say, Charlie, Sarah?' Phil says, pumping Alex's hand before drawing him into a firm hug.

'Charlie? Sarah?'

They join the embrace.

'And screw Ian, right?' Phil grins.

'Screw Ian,' they echo.

Sarah glances at Kelly. 'She really is that sick?'

Kelly simply nods.

Slowly Phil, Charlie and Sarah gather up their things. Max leads the way to the front door and everyone hugs goodbye.

Alex walks into the kitchen where Kelly has already put the kettle on. She rinses two cups, adds teabags to them and waits for the water to boil. Alex sits at the kitchen table, head down, exhausted. Max puts his head on Alex's lap and is rewarded with a big hug.

The cups are placed on the table and Kelly sits opposite Alex.

'In some ways,' Alex says quietly, 'what we did tonight was the easy part. Now we've got to finish the props, prep the studio. And . . . I need your help buying a couple of things for Jesse.'

'I thought tonight *was* the wish,' Kelly says, puzzled. 'The videos, music, poems . . .'

'It's part of it. Now we bring it to life.'

He takes a breath.

'We have a studio – a large soundstage. One whole wall is a curved screen, fifteen metres wide, five metres high. 300 monitors synced into one. What we built tonight – those visuals, that audio – they'll play across that wall. And Jesse and her family will be in the middle of it, surrounded by real props, immersed. Like they're in the park again. Or at the beach.'

Kelly stares. 'That's . . . like a movie.'

'Exactly. But it's *theirs*. A home movie, sure. But one that looks like cinema.'

'Wow,' Kelly mutters.

'Here's another way of looking at it. Consider someone writes a movie, a screenplay. The producers then go and find the locations and create the sets to film the story. What we have done is combined the screenplay and the location and set designs; the actors now just walk around the stage, sit at a table, walk on a beach, all in the comfort of our studio as we transport them into the scenes.'

Alex pauses, looking at Kelly. He's lost her.

'OK, let me give you an example of what we need to do. Think about the scenes of the park with the rotunda.'

'OK, I remember; it is beautiful.'

'Right. Yes, it is. Well, Jesse told me she and her family used to go to that park to play and they would have a picnic in the rotunda. One day she overheard her mum saying to her dad that this would be the perfect place for a wedding.'

'A wedding?' Kelly's eyes widen. 'Who's getting married?'

Alex holds up a hand. 'It's symbolic. Something Jesse and I talked about. Our team's recreating the rotunda set from the images. We'll stage a picnic, just like they used to.'

'And the wedding?'

'She wants to slip into a simple white dress, hold flowers, and walk towards her family. They'll turn, see her there – just for a moment. A memory her mum can keep.'

His voice falters. He can't finish.

Kelly stares at him, tears brimming.

'You're really going to do that,' she whispers. 'You're giving them that moment.'

She stands so suddenly her chair topples. Then she's in his arms, hugging him tight.

He pulls her onto his lap, and they stay hugging for a long time, holding each other in silence.

CHAPTER 31

Helmet in hand, Alex knocks on Jesse's front door. Stepping back to wait for it to be answered, he admires the manicured front yard, the flower gardens that border both side fences, the quaint gnomes carefully placed amongst the flowers, and wonders if they were put there by Jesse or Sam. He can't help but smile. So, this is what a 'normal' home looks like. Realising it has been some time since he knocked, he knocks again. He is startled when someone speaks from behind.

'There's no one home,' a neighbour over the fence is telling the woman who is walking up the drive towards him. The confused look on his face has her repeat, 'They're not home.'

Realising it is his turn to say something Alex blurts out, 'Oh thanks, I guess I'll come back later.'

He smiles as he walks back to his bike parked at the bottom of the drive, pausing by the woman.

'Excuse me. Are you a friend of the Morgans?' she asks.

'Yeah, kind of, I'm a friend of Jesse.'

'Are you Alex?'

Alex stops walking and faces the woman.

'Yes, how did you know my name?'

'I help look after Sam; he told me about you. Alex, Mandy has taken Jesse back to the hospital.'

'What? No, Kelly would've called me—'

'They only just left. Anyway, I've got to pick Sam up from a play date.'

Without another word, Alex jumps on his bike, slams on his helmet, and takes off – missing the neighbour's call: 'Drive carefully.'

Alex runs from the lift into the ward and heads towards Jesse's room. Sandy is walking in the opposite direction, sees him and raises her hand for him to stop. Taking him by the hand she attempts to lead him away as his eyes remain glued to the closed door into Jesse and Amy's room. Sandy tries again to coax him away gently, by pulling on his arm in a 'follow me' motion. Shrugging free Alex freezes, still staring at the door. Neither sees Dean approaching from behind.

'What the hell are you doing here?' he demands of Alex.

Dean grabs Alex by the jacket, propelling him into a nearby wall. Visitors observing the showdown gasp and pull small children close to them. Sandy hears a nurse call out to get security here now. Sandy calls back to the nurse, 'No, we can deal with this.'

Turning around, she sees Dean still has hold of Alex's jacket with one hand, his other arm forced up under his chin.

'I asked you, what the hell are you doing here?'

Alex tries to shrug himself free, but he's holding his helmet in one hand which hinders his struggle – and he's also trying very hard not to get angry and use force.

'I have to see Jesse; I've got to tell her . . .' Alex tries to stay calm and steady.

'I've told you to stay away from my daughter.'

Dean looks around at the commotion he has caused, at the concerned looks from nearby staff, visitors and children who cling close to their parents. Sandy gently places her hand on Dean's shoulder, noticing he is tightening his grip on Alex.

'It's all right, Dean; I'll take care of Alex.'

Dean slowly releases his grip on Alex but doesn't step away. He brings his face closer to Alex's, whispering in a threatening voice.

'Do you know what it's like to be told you're going to lose the single greatest joy in your life? Can you possibly have any idea?'

Alex looks down. He can't tell Dean he does know what it's like to lose the most important person in his life, the pain of being told his mother had died stabs at his heart. He can no longer look Dean in the eye, his shoulders drop. Defeated. Sandy indicates to a nearby nurse to take Dean away. Face red with a mixture of shame and rage, Dean allows himself to be led off.

Sandy takes Alex gently by the arm, and he allows her to lead him down the corridor.

'I've got to see her, you don't understand,' he mutters.

As Sandy guides him past the nurses' station, she asks the receptionist to find Kelly and send her to her office.

In her office, typing up a report on her computer, Kelly answers the ringing phone. The person on the other end is still talking when Kelly hangs up and runs from the room.

It takes all her effort to not run through the hospital, aware that a running person can signify an emergency and cause panic in others. Kelly pauses briefly by the bank of lifts. None are open, waiting for her, so she hurries to the stairwell and runs up the six flights, bursting through the door onto level 6, unaware of the looks she receives from people around as she continues hurrying to the doors that enter the ward. Forcing herself to slow down, trying to catch her breath, she walks quickly through the public area of the ward, barely acknowledging the staff who greet her. She pauses outside Sandy's office, slowing her breathing before turning the door handle and walking in.

Alex stops his pacing as the door opens and Kelly enters, shutting the door behind her. They each take a tentative step forward, unsure of their boundaries, aware of the growing feelings between them, fed by the long night spent with Steve and his friends working to make Jesse's wish come true.

'Why is she back here?' Alex blurts.

'I don't know, I've only just found out myself.'

'I need to see her; she doesn't know that we've finished the first part of her wish.'

'I know, and I want you to be the one to tell her, but you have to be patient. She needs to be with her family right now.'

'But how can she come to the studio and finish what we've done if she's here and can't leave? And how can we convince Dean to take part when he's just told me to stay away? Did I take too long to get this far?'

'Nobody could have done what you did in the time you had Alex. Nobody. Jesse knows that, we all do.'

'But how can we finish the project, make the wish, if there's . . .' Alex can't finish the sentence. He can't bear to say that there is no time. It's too much.

Kelly shrugs. 'I don't know. I'm really sorry, but I don't know the answers right now. We just have to wait.'

They are disturbed by a gentle knock. Sandy pokes her head around the door, takes in the scene, then enters, placing a glass of water on her desk.

'She's OK. Mandy panicked when she couldn't get the pain medication right for Jesse.'

The relief at hearing this has both Kelly and Alex take a step closer to each other before both looking back at Sandy: the chemistry between them obvious to the older woman.

'Mandy and Dean are settled, Jesse's feeling good now, and I overheard Mandy telling Sam on the phone they'd both be home soon. Jesse is going to stay the night but should be able to go home tomorrow.'

'Can I see her?' Alex blurts out.

'Well, we'll see. I'll have to clear it with Mandy.'

Alex nods. He's suddenly overcome by a wave of exhaustion. Kelly touches him on the arm, and he stares down into her vivid blue eyes.

'I have a few things I need to do. But why don't you wait in the café, and I'll text you when – and if – it's OK to see Jesse?' she says.

Alex nods. He's so tired, so upset, that he doesn't trust himself to speak. He mutters thanks to Sandy and leaves her office, making his way down to the café.

*

Sitting with a coffee and a muffin he has no intention of eating, Alex stares out the window into the garden where he and Jesse first sat together. Around him, doctors and nurses, some in differently coloured scrubs indicating their work in the hospital, others in civilian clothes. There are children and babies here, teenagers, some with attached IV poles and tubes leading into their arms. He focuses on a young boy playing a board game with a couple Alex assumes are his parents, and an older sibling. He looks like any normal boy of nine or ten, dressed in a Spider-Man T-shirt and board shorts. A baseball cap sits on the table beside him: the boy has not one hair on his head. He laughs and slaps his hands on the table. 'I win!' he shouts with glee.

A text from Kelly brings Alex back to time and place. He can go to see Jesse. He races out of the café.

Entering the ward, Alex sees Kelly talking to a nurse. He reads her face carefully and notes that she looks calm, is smiling and talking normally. His shoulders relax just a little. He waits to catch her eye, his gaze darting from her to Jesse's room. When Kelly sees him, she hurries over and pulls him to the side of the corridor. She appears normal. 'It's OK to go in. Dean's not here and Mandy has said it's OK. Just . . . she might be a little quieter than usual, OK?'

Alex nods. He gets it.

Jesse is the only one in the room, the bed beside hers neat and unslept in. 'Knock knock,' he says at the doorway.

Jesse looks up. 'Alex!' she says happily. She has a beanie on her head and is connected to an IV. Her eyes seem very bright, and she looks both paler and more fragile than at any other time he's seen her. Her appearance worries him, but he tries to keep his face neutral as he sits on the end of her bed.

'Hey, kiddo,' he says.

'Kiddo?' she says, teasingly. 'You've never said that word in your life, have you?'

Alex shrugs and laughs gently.

'So, what've you been doing the last few days?' Jesse asks playfully.

Alex fiddles with the blanket he's sitting on. 'Not much, how about you?'

'Just hanging out.'

They look at each other for a long moment. Alex doesn't know what to say next.

'Kelly told me you tried to visit me earlier,' Jesse says, rescuing him. 'I'm sorry I couldn't see you then.'

'Hey, you don't owe me an apology. Never. OK?'

She clears her throat and looks at him, forcing him to meet her eye.

'Alex, you know I'm not going to get better this time, there will be no remission for me, I can't take any more chemo, and the bone marrow transplant I had from Sam didn't work. Seems I've got funny blood, and donors don't grow on trees, apparently.'

Alex can't find his voice so simply nods, but he holds her gaze. She's so brave it takes his breath away.

'I want you to know something, Alex. These past few weeks, since you became my friend, with trying to make my wish, with us fighting, our balloon ride – oh my God, that was the best – well, it's all been wonderful. I've never had a friend like you before. I want to thank you, I know it's been tough on you, particularly with my dad and everything.'

Alex nods again. He's not sure anyone has spoken to him like this before – like he matters. Like he's made a difference. Like he's a true friend.

'I need you to do something else for me,' Jesse says.

'Anything.'

'Make it work out with Kelly, you two need each other,' she says, grinning.

Alex is stunned by her audacity and finally finds his voice. 'I don't know what you're talking about.'

'Alex, please, I may only be fifteen, but we've all seen what's going on between you two, or what you're both trying so hard to ignore. You could be soulmates if you just let it happen.'

Jesse pauses, looking at Alex, watching his reaction.

'You'll have to go after her though, she's a tough cookie, or so she thinks.'

Alex shakes his head, marvelling at the wisdom and maturity of the teenager in front of him.

'Can you keep a secret?' he asks.

'No.'

'OK, appreciate your honesty. I'll tell you anyway. You're right, the more I fight and argue with her, the more I want to see her. And, she hasn't said it, but I think she might feel the same way.'

Jesse bounces on her bed. 'I knew it, I knew it.'

'And it's all because of you,' Alex says beaming.

'Aw shucks, me, cupid?'

'Yes, you, cupid, well maybe, let's see. Do you want to know something else?'

Jesse struggles to sit up more, leaning towards Alex.

'We've done it. We've finished the main part of your wish. We just need you, your family and friends to come into the studio to bring it all together. Oh, Jesse, I gotta tell you . . .'

It's suddenly all too much for Alex. He abruptly stands, turns his back on Jesse and walks to the window, looking out at the night sky. Jesse watches his back, sees his hand rise and wipe at his face. With his back to her he hears her whisper, 'I knew you could do it. When can we finish it?'

Regaining his composure Alex returns to Jesse's bed and sits.

'As soon as you, your mum and Kelly can make it happen. But are you going to be able to leave here and come to the studio? And what about your dad? It isn't your wish if he isn't in it.'

'Leave my dad to me, I can bring him around. He loves me, he's told me many times there's nothing he wouldn't do for me, so it's time for him to listen and act on those words. I'll be well enough. Alex, we can do this, *I* can do this, I believe in you. You just deal with Kelly. Deal?'

'OK, it's a deal. Is there anything else I can do for you?' Alex asks staring intently at Jesse. He wants her to know that there is nothing he won't try to do for her.

Jesse looks away. 'There's a place I'd like to go one more time. With you – I'd like to show you before it's too late. Will you take me?'

Alex knows he was lucky to get away with it last time. But

he also knows he'd do anything for Jesse, anything he can. 'When?' he asks.

'Tomorrow morning. Mum is taking Sam to a movie, they planned it ages ago and I've told her she has to do it, and Dad said he has to clear some things up at his work so he can take some time off, and we both know why he needs to do that. I'm being discharged tomorrow afternoon, now they have my pain nearly under control. I could probably go home today but Christine wants me to stay.'

'Yeah. OK. But we'll have to tell Kelly and Sandy and a doctor or something.'

He looks at the IV connected to her arm, and she sees him looking at it.

'Oh, don't worry about this, it's easily removed. Ten o'clock, will you be here?'

'This is going to get me in all kinds of trouble, isn't it?'

'Yep.'

'Your dad's going kill me, isn't he?'

'Probably.'

They both laugh and are interrupted by Sandy knocking gently on the open door.

'Break it up, you two. Sorry, Alex, but it's late, Jesse needs her rest.'

'That's fine, Sandy, because me and Jesse have a plan,' he says, standing up.

'Shall I pretend I didn't hear that?' Sandy asks.

Jesse giggles. 'Maybe,' she answers.

Alex winks at Sandy and leaves the room. They have a plan, and he's going to do everything he can to see it through.

CHAPTER 32

Kelly is sitting in her office, typing up her notes from her last meeting, when she hears a commotion outside her door. 'I don't care if she's busy, I need to speak to her, *now*.' Dean.

She stands up, but there is no time to prepare herself when Dean barges into her office, the receptionist hovering behind him, concern written all over her face. 'Call yourself a social worker?' Dean yells, pointing his finger in her space.

'It's OK, Rose,' Kelly says to the receptionist. 'I can handle this from here.'

'*Handle this?*' Dean yells. 'I should be getting you fired! Where is she, Kelly, where's my daughter?'

'Maybe if you just take a seat, we can talk this through.'

Dean explodes, striding closer to Kelly. 'Don't tell me what to do, just tell me where she is and don't give me the run around, I know something is going on here.'

'She's with Alex. She wanted to go somewhere with him.'

'What? You just let her go out with that man?' Dean looks incredulous. 'Does her mother know?'

'Yes, of course. She gave her OK. Jesse wanted to go.'

'She's a minor, Kelly, or have you all forgotten that? Jesus, I feel like I'm the only one with any sense round here!' He rakes his fingers through his hair, exasperated. 'Now, where have they gone?'

'He's finished the main part of her wish, Dean. He did it.'

'What?' Dean stands stock still.

'Jesse's wish, it's well on its way to coming true.'

'Is that what all this is about? Her stupid wish?'

'The wish is for you, Dean, and Mandy and Sam,' Kelly tells him, desperate for him to understand how important the wish is to his daughter.

Dean slumps into a chair opposite Kelly. He holds his head in his hands, fighting back tears. Kelly gently sits beside him. She hears him quietly mumble, 'But where is she, where have they gone?'

'I honestly don't know. Sandy might know but she's not on the ward. Is there some place that is special to Jesse?'

'He made her wish?' Dean whispers.

'Yeah, the main part, apparently it now requires you and your family to complete it.'

'What do you mean it needs us?'

'Alex hasn't slept for days. He's been working on how to create Jesse's wish. He's probably going to lose his job and some of his colleagues are at risk too. They are a motley crew of brilliant special effects creators who have given up their time for Jesse. Heck, they even got me involved, though I'm not sure how helpful I was other than bringing them coffee to get through the night. They stayed up literally all night, Dean, working to try to create Jesse's wish.'

'What were they doing exactly?' Dean asks, perplexed.

Kelly registers that he's listening not shouting. She presses on, aware that she too could lose her job over this.

'I've never seen anything like it, it's utterly joyful. Jesse hasn't seen it either. Alex wants it to be as much a surprise for her as your family. It really is an amazing record of your daughter's life; but to fulfil Jesse's wish and fully create the experience it requires the involvement of you, your family and Jesse's friends. You'll all be filmed in a high-tech studio so that you will all exist in the virtual world Alex has created alongside Jesse, part of a record of her life. Jesse knows this and knows it can't happen without your participation and blessing.'

There's a long silence.

'What have I done, Kelly? What kind of fool have I been?'

'You're a father who is losing his daughter. There's no manual, no rule book on how you're supposed to handle this.'

'I love her so much. You do know that, don't you, Kelly?'

'I know that, and Jesse knows that. That's why her wish is so important to her.'

Finally, he looks up.

'Will you come with me?' he asks, holding his hand out to Kelly. She takes it.

Alex carries Jesse down the side of the house to the back garden, through the gate separating the lawn from the sand, and down the short path. Stepping onto the beach, he immediately recognises the outcrop of rocks a short distance away that jut out into the ocean. Carefully stepping onto the rocks, he carries Jesse to the edge and gently places her onto the wide flat rock she'd pointed to, with her legs dangling over the edge. He can tell immediately that this is her place, that she's sat here many times before. He feels her thin, frail body relax as she breathes in the sea spray floating in the air around them. Sitting beside Jesse, he places a protective arm around her, and she rests her head on his shoulder. He tucks a rug he'd grabbed from the back of the car around her shoulders. It's Max's travel rug, so it's a bit hairy, but he figures she won't mind. Small waves slap on the rocks and spray reaches their legs, making them laugh with pleasure.

Dean and Kelly run onto the beach and stop. Kelly follows Dean's gaze to the rocks a short distance away. The special place Jesse has told her about. She sees Alex and Jesse looking out to the ocean.

Dean starts to run, then slows to a walk, tears streaming down his face. Kelly follows a step or two behind, not knowing how this is going to play out.

Glancing down the beach, Alex sees Dean and Kelly coming their way just as Dean clambers onto the rocks. His shoes slip on the smooth stone, and he quickly pulls them off, dropping them on the sand.

Kelly kicks her sandals off and climbs onto the rocks.

Alex slowly stands and tenses. He feels this man's pain, and he'll take whatever he wants to dish out. Only he wishes he wouldn't spoil this moment for his daughter.

Jesse sits up now and puts her hand out to Alex, who carefully helps her to her feet. Dean stops a few feet away from them. It is painfully obvious to Alex and Jesse that he is distressed.

'DADDY!' Jesse cries out and attempts to run to her father. Dean steps forward, catches her and sweeps her into his arms. Kelly stays standing behind them, looking at Alex who is balanced precariously on the edge of the rocks.

Still holding Jesse, her head resting on his shoulder, Dean walks carefully towards Alex, who braces himself. Face to face, the two men look deeply at each other before Dean places his other hand on Alex's shoulder.

'Thank you,' is all Dean can get out.

Jesse smiles, giggles, so happy the two men in her life have made peace.

'Dad, let's not go back to the hospital. Call Christine and tell her you've busted me out of there? Let's just go and lie on the sofa and wait for Mum and Sammy to get home.'

'You've got it, my darling,' Dean answers.

As Dean walks away, still carrying Jesse, she looks over his shoulder and blows Alex a kiss.

Kelly walks up beside Alex and together they watch Dean, his beloved daughter in his arms. Alex turns around and sits back down on the edge of the rocks. Without being asked, Kelly sits beside him in Jesse's spot. Alex puts his arm around her shoulders and together they stare out at the ocean.

CHAPTER 33

B ack at the ward, Luke and Ryan stand looking into the
empty room of Jesse and Amy. Sandy has just told them
Jesse won't be back in today, she's home now and will stay
there for the time being – her dad has phoned to let the team
know. The boys know all too well what this means.

'Do you think she's going to get her wish?' Luke asks
Ryan.

'Dunno. She'd better,' Ryan tells him.

'If only there was something we could do to make sure it
happens,' Luke says wistfully.

Ryan taps his foot, staring off into nothing.

'Have you got your phone with you?'

'Nope, it's by my bed.'

'Let's go, we need to make a phone call.'

With both boys sitting on Luke's bed, Ryan scrolls
through the recent calls looking for one without a name.
Finding it, he hits dial, the phone on speaker.

'Hello, is that TriOptic Studios?' he asks, trying to sound
as grown-up as possible, before the person on the other end
can speak. Luke stifles a giggle.

'Good. Can I speak to the person in charge, please, I think his name is Steve, I've spoken to him before.'

'No, Steve's not really in charge, he covers for Ian, the manager, when he's not here,' the voice on the end of the line tells him.

'Well, if Ian is in charge, can I speak to him, please?'

'Well, Ian's the manager but he's out. However, the owner is Frank and he's in the building today, would you like to speak to him?'

'Yes, please.'

The boys look at each other in a mixture of fear and hilarity.

A few moments later a gruff voice comes on the line.

'Who is this?'

'Are you Frank? Are you the owner of TriOptic Studios?' Ryan stammers.

'And who are you, young man?' the voice answers.

'Hi, Frank, my name is Ryan. I'm a friend of Alex who works for you, I'm in hospital with Jesse.'

'Ah, OK. Well then, how can I help you, Ryan?'

The gruff voice sounds more friendly now.

'Can you come to the hospital and see me and Luke? We need to talk to you about Alex and Jesse.'

'Who's Luke?'

'He's my friend, we're both friends of Jesse.'

'And you want me to come to the hospital to see you?'

'Yes, please, and it needs to be soon, now, if you can? We can't come to you as we're receiving treatment.'

Ryan gets all of this out in a rush. Luke has his hand clapped over his mouth as he listens in amazement. There is a long pause. Clearly the gruff voice is giving the proposal some thought. After a long pause:

'Well, young man, I like your nerve, guess you'd better tell me where I find you. You're at the children's hospital, right?'

Ryan gives slightly garbled and breathless instructions.

There's another long pause.

'I'll see you in about an hour,' the voice says, warm now. He ends the call.

Luke and Ryan sit on the bed in silence for a long time.

'What are we going to say to him?' Luke asks finally.

'Dunno. Guess we just have to ask him to tell Alex to make Jesse's wish.'

'OK. You can do all the talking.'

'Think we better go and tell Sandy what we've done and that Frank's coming here.'

'You can do all the talking to her too,' Luke says, sliding off the bed.

Briefed by the boys, Sandy keeps an eye on the door, looking for a stranger. She's given up worrying about what is and isn't appropriate for the time being. Frank is easy to spot when he walks in, stops just inside the ward, and looks around at the vibrant chaos. She smiles to herself at the reactions flitting across Frank's face. Worried, scared, upset, lost, he looks at the activity of patients, families, staff bustling around him. She decides to rescue him.

'Hello, you must be Frank. I'm Sandy, charge nurse on this ward.'

Frank looks at Sandy and the outstretched hand.

'Hello, that's right. Not sure what I'm doing here but a young man asked me to come and see him.'

'That was Ryan. He and Luke are waiting to see you. I've given them my office to use, follow me.'

Sandy leads Frank into her office, where Ryan and Luke are standing in front of her desk.

'I'm sorry Mr . . . I don't know your surname?'

'It's Wallace, but please call me Frank.'

'Thank you. Frank, this is Ryan and Luke, they are patients on my ward, and unbeknown to any of us they asked you to come here. I hope you don't mind but I will need to stay with you, as they are minors. Precocious ones but minors all the same.'

Frank's face is amused.

'Of course not. Well, gentlemen, how can I help you?'

'Let's just grab some chairs and sit down, we may as well be comfortable,' Sandy says, noticing that Ryan and Luke are uncharacteristically tongue-tied. She brings chairs from the side of her office together with the two in front of her desk and forms a circle.

'OK Ryan, I believe you are going to be doing the talking, over to you.'

Ryan shuffles in his chair before looking directly at Frank. He clears his throat.

'Firstly, thank you for coming here so quickly, as this is urgent.'

'It's about Alex, right?'

'Yeah, we know Alex because he's making Jesse's wish . . .'

'And we've been helping him,' Luke jumps in.

'Yeah, we've been helping him. Anyway, we know he's been having some problems with it, something about his boss giving him a hard time, and not being able to do what he wants with your technology . . .'

'And don't forget the problems he's having with Jesse's dad,' Luke again chimes in.

'He's having trouble with the girl's father?' Frank asks, concerned.

Sandy decides it's time for her to say something.

'It's difficult for parents when their children are as sick as Jesse and yes, her father has not been helpful, but I believe they've sorted that out. I had a call from Jesse's father only this morning, and he was full of praise for Alex.'

'Well, that's good. So how can I help?' Frank asks.

'Is that right, has Jesse's dad decided he's OK with her wish now?' Ryan asks Sandy.

'I believe so, yes, they're sorting it out. You better tell Mr Wallace, Frank, what you want him for, I'm sure he's a busy man,' Sandy tells the boys.

'We want you to talk to Alex and tell him he has to keep going and finish the wish, he's so close. And you have to tell him that you will let him have whatever he needs from your company to make it happen, we – well, Jesse – don't have much time,' Ryan blurts out.

Frank leans back in his chair and studies Ryan and Luke. 'You really care for Jesse, I can tell.'

'She's the best, Frank, the absolute best,' Ryan says, looking Frank squarely in the eyes.

'We love her,' Luke adds.

'Well, I guess I'd better go and have a chat with Alex then.'

'You mean you will let him finish Jesse's wish?' Ryan asks. He needs to be sure that's what Frank is saying.

'I'll tell him he has my blessing, and that he can use TriOptic Studios, the staff and facilities – whatever he needs to make it happen. How does that sound?'

The boys impulsively stand, staring at Frank. 'You really mean it?' Luke says.

Frank stands and extends his hand to Ryan and Luke. They both shake it vigorously.

'Thank you, thank you,' is all Ryan can mutter.

'No, thank you for getting me here and telling me about your friend Jesse. I'll go and see Alex now, I think he's at home, I didn't see him in the office this morning.'

'This is so kind of you, Frank. I'll see you out,' Sandy says.

'Bye, boys, I hope to see you again.'

As the door shuts behind Frank and Sandy, Ryan and Luke slump back in their chairs. They can only look at each other and grin.

Max's barking alerts Alex to a visitor. He opens the door as Frank is raising his hand to knock. Frank is the type of guy who always looks dishevelled, his stubble unkempt, his hair in need of a comb. He's always given Alex the impression that he's too busy to look after the little stuff, like himself. He's got bigger things on his plate.

'Frank, what are you doing here?' he says utterly surprised. He hasn't seen him for weeks.

'Can I come in?'

'Yeah, sure, come in. It's OK, Max, he's a friend.'

Max leads the way into the kitchen, having decided that's where the two men should be, in case they'd like to offer him a treat.

'Can I get you something, coffee? Oh, I don't have any milk, it will have to be black.'

'Water will be fine,' Frank says, sitting down at the kitchen table.

Alex gets Frank a glass of water and sits opposite him. He runs his hands through his hair, making it stand out completely around his head in a mad halo.

'Look, Frank, I know Ian's pissed off with me for spending too much time out of the office, but . . .'

'It's OK, we'll get to Ian. I've just come from the hospital where I met two young men, I believe you know them: Ryan and Luke.'

'What! Yes, I know them, what were you doing with them?'

'I had a call from Ryan this morning, he asked me to come to the hospital to talk to him and Luke about you.'

Not knowing where this is going, Alex involuntarily stands.

'Sit down, Alex, you're not in trouble. Somebody else in the office might be, but not you. Now tell me what you're doing and how I can help.'

Gathering his thoughts, Alex is quiet for a while.

'You'd better come into my office, it's confession time.'

Frank follows Alex and Max into his office. As he walks in, he stops, surveying the equipment in front of him, half the monitors are black, others are lit up with images of Jesse.

'What the hell have you got here?' Frank asks.

'Sit down, I'll show you what we've done.'

They both pull chairs up to the monitors and Alex runs the program he and the others have created. It requires no explanation from Alex, this is also Frank's domain as creator of TriOptic Studios. As the last video finishes and the music fades out, he turns to Alex.

'And now you need the studio to create the wish.'

'Yeah, what we've got is great, but it needs everyone in the studio to complete it.'

'Well then, lucky for you we have some time between projects.'

'You mean it? We can go ahead with your knowledge, not behind your back?'

Frank laughs. 'You could have come to me, you know?'

'I'm sorry, I should have, it's just you gave me a brief to make a game for Jesse, but I've gone a bit beyond that.'

'A bit! You've got a bloody feature film here.'

'Can I show you something I've been working on?'

'Go ahead.'

'In my own time I've been developing a product we could market to the public. It could be made affordable for budding filmmakers and game creators, allowing them to take their projects to the next level.'

'Let's see it.'

Alex shows Frank a film he has created using Max. He has him under water in a submersible, flying a light aircraft, running through a forest and emerging in a desert. Real-life Max looks on proudly.

Frank whistles. 'This could be just what TriOptics needs to keep the wolves from our door. It could subsidise the company in between the big projects. How much do you want for the IP? I can help with marketing and the contacts to get this worldwide.'

'Make me an offer.' Alex forces himself to sound more confident than he's feeling. Half an hour ago, he was waiting for Frank to give him the sack.

'Seventy-five, twenty-five. You keep seventy-five. I demote that useless son-in-law, and you take over.'

Alex waits for a moment. 'What do you think, Max?'

Max thumps his tail enthusiastically.

'You're asking your dog?' Frank says.

'Yeah, he's never steered me wrong yet.'

'So, what did he say?'

'You've got a deal with one change.'

'Name it.'

'Put Steve in charge. He's better with people, and everyone listens to him and respects him.'

'And what do you want?'

'Call me his deputy if you want to give me a title, he knows I won't interfere and will accept his leadership.'

Frank extends his hand.

'I knew my instincts were right when I hired you. Partner.'

CHAPTER 34

It's early morning, and Alex, in his beaten-up old car, drives into an industrial park on the fringes of town, driving inside a warehouse through large heavy-duty doors.

'Is this your studio?' Kelly asks, sitting next to him. She feels strangely nervous, or maybe it's just anticipation – Jesse's wish has come together and tomorrow will be the big reveal. She wants to ask Alex if he feels nervous too – he must do, because of all the work he's put into it – but feels strangely shy.

'One of them, this is where we film. I'll explain more inside. I want to double check everything is ready for tomorrow.' He grins. 'And I want to show you how it will play out.'

Alex pulls up at the far wall and he and Kelly get out. From the backseat Kelly retrieves a large white box.

'Trust you to drive straight into the building,' Steve says to Alex, shaking his head. Then, turning his attention to Kelly, says, 'What have you got there?'

'It's THE dress,' Kelly says. 'Well, it's just a beautiful white dress I found. I think Jesse will look amazing in it. I'll also pick up some fresh flowers tomorrow before I come here.'

'Let's start with the dressing rooms,' Alex says, lightly taking her by the elbow. 'I want to show you around.'

Through a gap in large black drapes that fall from the twenty-metre-high ceiling to the ground, Kelly gets a peek at a screen stretching from the floor to the ceiling. She recognises some of the footage.

'No, no, I want you to see the other part of the studio before you see how we make magic,' Alex says, steering her away.

'I'll see you on the other side of the curtain,' Steve says with a wink, walking away.

Alex takes Kelly into a dressing room. It's the size of a small living room, with a sofa, coffee table, a sideboard and an ensuite. 'There will be snacks and drinks here tomorrow,' he says awkwardly, stuffing his hands into the back pockets of his jeans. Kelly knows she doesn't need to ask, he is nervous.

'Close your eyes,' she says.

'Why?' He closes them anyway, and she takes the dress out of the box and hangs it in the wardrobe, closing the door. It's going to be a surprise for him, too.

'This one's for Jesse. Mandy can be in here as well to help her out, plus you; just make sure Mandy doesn't open the wardrobe, you'll have to do that.'

'Can I see it now?' Kelly asks, her excitement mounting.

'Are you sure you don't want to check out all the other rooms?' Alex jokes with her.

'Seen one dressing room seen them all. Come on, Alex, I want to see what's behind the curtain.'

By the time they come back from the dressing rooms,

Steve has fully closed the curtains. Alex walks Kelly up to the join in the middle.

'Close your eyes, take my hand and when I say take a step, do so.'

'Stop teasing,' Kelly says.

'Then do as you're told.'

Holding her hand out for Alex, Kelly closes her eyes.

'Take a step,' he instructs gently.

Kelly takes a deep breath then steps forward.

'Open your eyes,' he tells her.

Nothing could have prepared Kelly for what she sees. Alex hears the gasp: her breath is taken away. Slowly she scans the scene in front of her. The vast screen is showing videos of Jesse and her family playing in a park, filmed by a grandparent, Mandy told Alex. Turning her head, she sees ten pairs of eyes all smiling back at her. Several people have elaborate headphones hanging around their necks. She looks at the cameras sliding across the room on wire cables above her, stretching from one side of the room to the other, the microphones moving up and down, side to side. To the left she sees a large console area, similar to what Alex has in his home, only this one is at least twice the size, the monitors much bigger. Steve is standing behind the console and appears to be controlling the moving cameras and microphones with a series of joysticks. In front of him, off to the side, she sees a large rotunda, a replica of the one in the video before her. Steve toggles a stick and the virtual rotunda glides silently into the front of the screen. It becomes all too much for Kelly as she recognises other props, play equipment, a table holding the picnic gear which will be placed in the rotunda. She puts her hand out to Alex, and he steadies her.

'Step towards the screen and you will experience what Jesse and the others will tomorrow.'

Hand in hand, Alex and Kelly walk towards the screen and Kelly gasps as she finds herself standing in the park, surrounded by trees, manicured lawns, a sparkling sky. A silent tear tracks down her cheek.

Alex gives her a few minutes, looking around at his colleagues, many of whom are fighting back tears, overcome by Kelly's reaction.

'Come on, say hello again to the magic makers,' he whispers.

Sarah runs into her arms, headphones and cables jangling around them. Charlie and Phil join in the hug. Dragging her away, Alex introduces Kelly to several other crew members who will be here tomorrow. He explains their roles. She nods in understanding even when she doesn't. It doesn't matter, she knows she will witness Alex make the impossible possible.

That evening Steve, Phil, Charlie, Sarah and Kelly come over to Alex and Max's house. Pizza and beers are shared as the new friends relive the night they spent creating Jesse's wish. Kelly tells Phil, Charlie and Sarah that Jesse wants to meet them, and they should be prepared to be hugged endlessly. At a reasonable hour, Steve suggests it is time for them to leave, they all have a big day ahead of them. As Alex walks them to the door, he wonders if he should ask Kelly to stay. She joins the others hugging Alex goodbye but adds a quick kiss on his lips. Max barks them his goodbye.

CHAPTER 35

I t's the day they have been waiting for. Alex arrives at the studio to find Steve, Sarah, Charlie, Phil and the full studio staff already there. They walk through the stage, everyone telling Alex they are good to go, everything is ready. He feels his phone ringing in his pocket and ignores it. Today is a special day; he wants nothing to interfere with his plans.

A few minutes later the phone rings again. He doesn't recognise the number, but something tells him to answer it. Excusing himself he walks away from the others.

'Hello.'

'Alex, thank goodness you answered. It's Sandy.'

'Sandy, what's wrong, Jesse . . .'

'No, no, it's not about Jesse, it's you.'

'What about me?'

'A senior technician in pathology called me a short while ago. He was going over bone marrow tests and saw yours. He's asked if I could find you and see if you would be prepared to take the next test, a biopsy. He thinks there may be enough markers to do the biopsy.'

'But I don't understand. I was told I wasn't a match.'

'Not a perfect match, very few donors are, but the technician feels it's worth going to the next step and doing a biopsy so that they can determine for sure if the markers are there. What do you think?'

'What do I think? Sandy, make this happen, of course I'll do whatever you say, just make it happen.'

'I know you're busy, but could you be here at six o'clock tonight?'

'That soon?'

'The sooner the better, Alex.'

'OK, yeah, that should be fine, we should wrap up here by mid-afternoon at the latest, I'll be there at six. What if someone sees me, what do I say?'

'Don't worry, you'll be on the day ward, ground floor, away from everywhere else. Can I tell them you'll be here?'

'Six o'clock. I'll be there. Thank you, Sandy, I didn't think this day could get any better.'

Ending the call Alex goes to the bathroom. He needs to get his emotions under control, he needs to splash water on the tears that threaten.

Kelly is the first to arrive at the studio an hour before Alex had told her to be there. She admits she has barely slept as she shows Alex the small posy of flowers she has picked up. One of the crew take them from her, promising to find a vase and hide them in an office where no one will go.

The curtains are closed, and Alex explains how Jesse and her family will be taken to two dressing rooms on one side of the building. They won't know that Amy, Ryan and Luke are also coming, along with their parents. They will be kept as a surprise, as will the wedding dress, and one more surprise that Alex insists he won't even share with Kelly. He asks her to play along and do as she's told.

It soon becomes obvious no one has listened to the times Alex gave them. Jesse and her family arrive early too. Alex watches her closely as she gets out of the car. It is clear she is using all her reserves of energy to make the wish she wants for her family. Dean takes a wheelchair out of the boot of the car, but she refuses to get in. Dean wheels it into the studio behind his family. Sam runs ahead and is stopped by Steve as he tries to peek behind the big black curtain. Alex has them meet the crew, one of whom takes the wheelchair from Dean and puts it to the side of the room. Sarah, Charlie and Phil are identified as having worked on the wish and, as predicted, Jesse hugs them all long and hard. They give a layman's explanation of what their roles are and what is going to happen. The Morgans understand that Alex and Steve will be co-directing what they are filming, and Jesse and Sam giggle with excitement when they are told they will be using the words 'action' and 'cut' to indicate when filming is beginning and ending. Dean asks where their scripts are.

'Families don't need scripts,' Alex tells him. 'You're playing yourselves, remember.'

'Can I get my money back if Sam says the wrong thing?' Dean jokes, ruffling Sam's hair.

'Course you can, see me after,' Alex replies.

'Ooh,' Mandy whispers to Kelly, 'he has a sense of humour, who would have known?'

'There's a lot about him we don't know,' Kelly whispers back.

'I hope you're working on finding out all his secrets,' Mandy says, giving Kelly a meaningful look.

'Mandy, really, our relationship is strictly professional.'

'Of course it is, how silly of me.'

Shown their dressing rooms – one for the boys and one for the girls – Sam immediately raids the chocolate bars on the sideboard along with fruit, cookies and cheese, a selection of healthy and unhealthy drinks. He insists on seeing Jesse's room in case she has something he doesn't. Kelly tells them Alex wants them dressed for a casual day in the park and leaves them to get ready. They've brought along various outfits. She tells them she will be back shortly to take them behind the curtain.

She returns to find the family dressed in summer clothes for a day at the park. Sam is hopping up and down with excitement. He's insisted on putting on suncream – method acting, he tells them. He's been doing some research. Kelly walks them to the curtain where Alex is waiting for them. He tells them to hold hands and close their eyes. When he says take a step, they can step forward a pace or two.

After a lot of coaxing, Sam promises to keep his eyes closed as he and Jesse stand between their parents. Finally, they're ready. Alex and Kelly pull back the curtains.

'Step forward,' Alex says.

They step forward and instantly Sam screams out 'WOW'.

In front of them, a still photo of Jesse covers the vast screen. She looms over them. Dean is immediately drawn to the screen and walks forward, as Jesse's beaming smile envelops him. Dean's eyes fill with tears. For the first time he understands the enormity of what Alex has achieved and created for his family, free of charge, without demands or drama – well, maybe a little drama. Once more, he fights down the feelings of shame and remorse at his behaviour. He and Mandy look at each other over the heads of their children. They both know that their daughter has made this happen – with Alex's help. She's built a legacy for them, a world they can enter when Jesse is no longer with them. It's astonishing, and humbling. They begin to cry, but their tears turn to joy as Jesse and Sam whoop with excitement and laughter. They nod at each other: tacitly acknowledging that they're allowed to enjoy this moment for what it is, revel in it, with no thought of what lies just ahead for them all.

Alex slowly explains to them what they are seeing. Steve runs some video footage for them to see the park they know so well, they recognise the trees, roundabouts and swings. Alex explains that by walking around the stage in front of the screen, multiple cameras will capture them from all angles, all cameras immersing them into the scenes. The footage Steve and Alex filmed of the park, the beach, Jesse's balloon flight, have been put into simulated software. What they re-enact today will be captured on film which will be edited together with the existing footage to create their story. Music has been embedded but can be adjusted, and Mandy has recorded her poems which will be used at some points, alongside shots of some of Sam's drawings.

'Where are the camera operators?' Dean asks.

'Over there,' Alex says, pointing at Steve sitting behind the large console. 'Everything is computer controlled; we've already set them to film, close up, move around, kind of like the Daleks from *Doctor Who*. Steve controls them and can take over if he feels he wants a different angle or wide screen shot.'

'I get the picture, I think. This is incredible, Alex.'

Dean sees Sam sitting on Steve's lap being shown the monitors he will watch and control. 'I think you might have a new crew member.'

'Happy to have him here anytime, never too young to learn,' Alex tells him gruffly. He's still a little wary of Dean.

Alex's attention is diverted as the curtains open. They weren't expecting anyone else.

Frank and Ian step inside the curtained area and look on. Alex walks quickly over to them, anxiety and concern written on his face. He's primed for trouble.

'Hi, Alex, do you mind if we watch? I promise we won't interfere,' Frank says.

'Of course, come and meet everyone, then grab a couple of chairs and make yourselves comfortable. Good to see you Ian,' Alex says.

Ian shuffles his feet. 'You don't mind me being here? I mean . . .'

'You're fine, I'm glad you came. You get to see what you told me to do, make Jesse's wish.'

'Thanks, Alex, I mean it. Thanks.'

The crew watch the interaction, not knowing what is

being said or what will happen next. They all breathe a sigh of relief when Frank and Ian are introduced to Jesse and her family. Dean thanks them both profusely for their part in making Jesse's wish. The crew roll their eyes as they hear this conversation, register Ian nodding and taking the credit.

Over the next hour, the family are filmed having fun in the park. They sit underneath trees and listen to a poem, the rotunda on the stage replaces the one filmed, and Sam and Jesse run to it and step inside. Dean takes Mandy's hand, and they slowly walk to join their children.

The family is sent back to their dressing rooms to change into beach clothing. On set, they play on the beach and when Sam runs into the water a crew member to the side splashes real water onto him. Alex calls cut so they can set up another scene on the rocks and, while they position themselves, he tells Kelly the others have arrived.

On the other side of the curtain Kelly approaches Amy, Ryan, Luke and their parents, her finger held to her mouth indicating that they are to remain silent. Shown to their dressing rooms, they are asked to wait until someone comes to get them and explains what they are to do. The parents will be shown where to stand off-camera to watch the filming.

Jesse and her family are asked to change into other casual clothes. Next, they are going to be filmed visiting Jesse in hospital. Back on set they see the video of the room Jesse and Amy shared at the hospital. They are asked to walk over to Jesse's pinboard and look at the photos. With the cameras rolling they look at the photos and cry out in surprise when one of Sam's drawings flies off the screen and around him. They don't hear the others enter the set, and the shock is obvious when Amy runs to join them.

'Hey, girl, hi, Sammy, Mr and Mrs Morgan.'

Jesse squeals with delight as she and Amy embrace and dance on the spot. Their room continues to revolve around them, transporting them back to the hospital. Sam, Mandy and Dean hug Amy and they all talk at once. The noise levels increase as Ryan and Luke walk onto the set.

'You two having a party without us?' Ryan jokes.

The four friends embrace and chatter. The boys greet Sam, Mandy and Dean before the three of them walk off the set and watch from behind the cameras the beauty of friendships forged from the most difficult of shared experiences.

As scenes are shot, reshot, played out in different ways, the parents stand together supporting each other, wiping each other's tears, hugging and wordlessly acknowledging the pain they all know so well. Sam has been taken to sit with Steve and see what the camera is capturing.

With the hospital scenes shot, Alex asks Amy and the boys to join their parents: they want Jesse and her family to change one last time for another family picnic scene at the park. While they are changing, picnic food, drinks and utensils are placed on a large red and white check tablecloth on the floor of the rotunda.

The family come back and once again walk through the park to the rotunda and sit around the food. Jesse nibbles on a sandwich, before asking if she can be excused, she wants to go to the bathroom. Kelly walks off with her and

Alex explains he is keeping the cameras rolling as it would be perfectly natural for one of them to leave the picnic and return.

Sam, Mandy and Dean are laughing, popping food into each other's mouths, relaxed. Mandy and Dean have their backs to where Jesse will re-enter the scene. Sam sees her first.

'Jesse, you look beautiful,' he breathes.

Mandy and Dean turn around to see Jesse walking towards them dressed in a long, soft cotton dress, gathered gently around her neck, pinched into her petite waist, delicate spring flowers dotted over it. A dress in the style of the sixties – it suits her perfectly. Kelly has chosen well. A shoulder-length wig, the colour of her natural dark hair, with soft curls, frames her face, in her hand she carries the small posy of daisies.

Mandy collapses sobbing into Dean, who gasps for air. Jesse sits beside her mother who can't speak.

'I heard you whisper to Dad one day that this would be a lovely place for a wedding. I can't give you a wedding, but will this do?'

The sobbing and whispers of amazement of the parents, crew, Amy, Ryan and Luke are picked up by the microphones, but Alex doesn't care. He pans a camera around to capture everyone in the room witnessing a moment that they know will never really happen. Amy runs into the scene and joins the family, and the crew look to Alex for direction. Amy wasn't meant to be in the family scenes at the park. He indicates to keep rolling, then motions for the others including the parents and any crew not operational to join the family in the rotunda.

It takes some time for everyone gathered in the rotunda to calm down enough for Alex to join them. He has one more scene to film. He asks that everyone except Jesse, Mandy, Dean and Sam leave the rotunda, telling them Steve will now direct them in how the final scene is to be shot. As Steve starts talking, no one notices Alex disappear.

With Steve behind the console directing the cameras, he calls action. Jesse and her family follow the directions he gave and slowly walk from the rotunda towards the middle of the stage. Behind them videos of the park play out, placing them in the scene, in the park. Several people are seen walking and running past them, many of whom have dogs running around them. Alex comes onto the stage from the far side and places a small puppy, a golden retriever – a miniature Max – on the floor and pushes the pup gently towards the family. Mandy, who is in on the surprise, sees the puppy first and takes out a packet of doggy treats. It is enough to get the puppy to run towards them.

'Sammy, turn around,' Mandy says softly. Jesse, Dean and Sam all turn as the puppy bounds towards them. Jesse grabs Dean's arm as Mandy places a treat on the ground and steps back with Dean and Jesse, leaving Sam standing frozen, as the puppy gobbles up the treat and comes to him.

'Somebody's lost their dog,' Sam says, bending down to pat and play with the puppy.

'I wonder who he belongs to?' Mandy says as she kneels beside her son and the puppy.

Twisting the collar around she reads the small disc on the collar. 'It says, "I belong to Sam Morgan."'

Sam looks at his mother. 'No, it doesn't. Does it, Mummy? Is he really mine?'

'No, my darling, he is not yours, *she* is, she's a girl.'

Jesse and Dean kneel with them as Sam clutches the puppy to his chest sobbing uncontrollably.

'How did you do this?' Dean whispers to Mandy.

'It was Alex's idea, he got her for Sam, I just agreed, I hope you don't mind.'

Dean hugs Mandy tightly and they topple over and now sit on the floor with Sam and the puppy, who jumps all over them, licking faces, barking with his small puppy voice.

'I love you with all my heart,' Dean whispers to his wife.

Jesse has remained standing, watching her family make a fuss over the new puppy. Her heart breaks with joy at the sight of her little brother with a puppy; hearing the words her father whispered to her mother. She looks at the faces of the crew, Kelly, Amy, Ryan and Luke and their parents, all of whom are crying and hugging each other. Finally, her eyes rest on Alex, standing to the side wearing the biggest smile she has ever seen on his face. With her last ounce of energy, she hurries to him, falling into his arms, exhausted, overwhelmed, grateful beyond words for what he has given her. It is her turn to sob with joy.

Kelly clings to Steve watching Alex and Jesse. He has stopped filming and allows himself to be caught up in the emotion of the day.

'She isn't looking good, Kelly, is she OK?' Steve asks.

'Yes, and no, it's been a huge day for her, I think it might be time for her to go home.'

Dean looks up and sees Alex holding his daughter. He hurries over to Alex, who places Jesse in her father's arms, where she belongs.

Dean holds his daughter close.

'I think it's time we took you home, honey.'

'I think so too, Daddy, I'm so tired.'

'I'll get your wheelchair,' Alex says.

Kelly has beaten him to it and pushes it over to Dean, who places Jesse in the chair as Mandy and Sam – clutching the puppy close to his chest – join them. Sam places the puppy on Jesse's lap. It licks her face several times before settling down and falling asleep.

Amy, Ryan and Luke join them and gush over the puppy. Dean takes the opportunity to turn back to Alex.

'What can I say to you? There are no words. Thank you doesn't seem enough but I do thank you. For today, for all the yesterdays you spent with Jesse when I was too blind to see what she needed, what she wanted. I thank you and I apologise, from the bottom of my heart. You are one in a million. And as for the puppy, I should have made it happen, it took you to do it, for you to do a lot of things I should have done . . . thank you, Alex. I hope you can forgive me.'

Alex can only nod; he doesn't trust his voice. He is surprised when Dean pulls him into a long, hard hug. Alex stands motionless, arms by his side. But Dean isn't letting go any time soon and, finally, Alex feels himself give in to the warmth and affection being offered to him. Gradually, he relaxes and finds himself hugging Dean back. Kelly and Mandy look on, clinging to each other, laughing and crying.

As everyone chats, praising Jesse for what she has done in bringing them all together, Alex notices for the first time Sarah, Phil and Charlie standing on the far side of the stage in the shadows. He beckons them over. Sarah is struggling to keep it together, and it becomes obvious that Phil and Charlie have been greatly affected by what they have witnessed too: both men have red watery eyes and clear their throats several times.

Jesse sees Sarah, Phil and Charlie standing near Alex. Mandy takes the puppy from her lap, handing him to Sam, then wheels the chair over to them. Jesse struggles to stand up. Charlie gently pushes her back down.

'I have to thank you properly and I should do that standing up,' she says choking on her words.

'No, Jesse, please stay sitting, it is us who want to thank you. We can't tell you how much it meant to us to be part of your wish; it is our privilege so, thank you,' Charlie says.

Sarah bends down and hugs Jesse, still crying. Phil gently pulls her away.

'My turn,' he says as he envelops Jesse. Charlie waits his turn and is rewarded with a kiss on his cheek. Dean joins them, both parents shaking the team's hands and hugging them; they thank the unlikely trio for their part in making Jesse's wish.

'Frank, Ian, come and join us,' Alex calls out.

The two men saunter uncomfortably over, both clearly overcome by what they have witnessed as well. Hands are vigorously shaken by the men; Mandy insists on a hug, as does Jesse.

The puppy lets out a bark.

'I think she might need a trip outside,' Alex says, 'I'll take her.'

'I'm sorry to be the one to say we need to leave, but I think we need to get Jesse home for a rest,' Mandy says.

It still takes a while for everyone to say goodbye to the Morgan family. Kelly tells them to go home, she will gather up their things in the dressing rooms and bring them over. Slowly everyone makes their way out of the studio. Phil, Sarah and Charlie remain behind to see from the technical side what they have filmed.

Alex helps Kelly gather up the Morgans' things and take them to her car.

'Mandy has asked me to stay and chat with them when I get there, are you coming over? I'm sure they would love to have you there.'

'No, I can't, I have an appointment,' Alex tells her.

'More important than being with Jesse and her family?' Kelly asks, surprised and more than a tiny bit put out.

'Yeah, I'm afraid so. I'll call you,' Alex replies, not meeting her eye as he holds the car door open for her to get in.

Surprised and upset by his response, at the end of such an amazing day, and with so little time left, Kelly gets in her car and drives off.

CHAPTER 36

B ack at the hospital but in a different ward this time, Alex follows a nurse into a small cubicle. She hands him a clip-board and pen and indicates the gown he is to change into.

'After you're changed, bring the papers back to the desk and a technician will be with you shortly. This is marked urgent, so we'll get it done and analysed quickly.'

As the nurse closes the curtain Alex sits on the chair and reads the heading on the two-page document: CONSENT FOR BONE MARROW DONATION. He immediately turns to the second page and signs; he's not interested in reading the details – nothing could deter him from helping.

Changed into the gown, Alex hands over the consent form. A nurse dressed in scrubs introduces herself and asks him to follow her. Taken into a small room, Alex does as he is told and lies on the bed as two other staff join them.

'Remember this is just a biopsy to type your marrow for a possible transplant if a suitable recipient is found. We thank you for being part of the bone marrow registry, your results will go worldwide. I see you have a rare blood group, so that will be very helpful,' one of the technicians says.

'Yeah, I had a bike accident a few years back and discovered it. I've been a blood donor a few times, probably not enough but I'll do better.'

'I understand you know someone who might be able to benefit from your donation. I hope we can make it work for both of you,' she says.

'I hope so too.'

'We need to take a small amount of bone marrow from your hip. We'll have you lie on your right side; we'll give you a local anaesthetic injection into both the skin and bone to numb the area. You will feel a sharp sting when the numbing medicine is injected.'

The nurse holds up a large needle. Very large. Alex thinks of young Sam going through this to help his sister.

'As you can see this needle is quite wide; there is a needle inside the needle, so to speak. We will insert the larger needle into the bone of your hip, then remove it, leaving the smaller, hollowed-out needle, which will be moved deeper into the bone. We will attach a syringe to the thin needle and remove a small sample of bone marrow. This won't take long. When we remove the needle we will apply a pressure bandage to the area, give you a cup of tea or coffee, and ask you to wait around for about half an hour. Do you have any questions?'

'No, thank you for explaining it. I'm ready.'

'OK then, if you're ready, will you roll onto your right side?'

When Alex returns to his clothes, he checks his phone to see several missed calls from Kelly. Dressing, saying goodbye to the staff, he waits until he is sitting in his car before returning her call.

'Hey, it's me.'

'Where have you been?' Kelly asks him.

'Ah, just sorting out a few things.'

A pause. Kelly waits for Alex to say more but he remains silent. He hates that he is keeping from her where he is and what he has done but he has to, no one can know anything until the results are in.

'OK, well.' Kelly takes a deep breath. 'I thought you'd want to know that Jesse was very weak when they got her home this evening. She was asleep when they took her out of the car. Mandy and Dean couldn't rouse her or get her to eat anything. They put her to bed, but they were so concerned that they rang Christine. She's suggested that they take her back to hospital for a while.'

'Hospital?' Alex realises what this means. 'So, this might be . . .'

'We can't know, Alex,' Kelly tells him. 'She might recover after proper rest and fluids, if she's not eating. It's just one day at a time at this stage. She'll sleep at home tonight and return to the hospital in the morning for assessment.'

Alex stares out the window of his car, letting her words sink in. He can't think of anything to say.

'Dean has raced out to buy things for the puppy – they're grateful for the bed and toys you supplied, but they need more food. And other things. I thought they could use the support right now. I'm not Jesse's doctor but I think they might feel able to relax a little if I'm here.'

Again, Alex is silent. All he wants to ask is how long Jesse has, but he knows there's no answer to that question – at least not until she's back at hospital in the morning.

Kelly tries again. 'So, I wondered if you'd like to join me here? I thought we could have pizza, find a movie for us all to watch, and take turns checking on Jesse. Alex . . . are you still there?'

Alex clears his throat. 'Sorry, I'm just shattered after the past few days working to get Jesse's wish made. I'm going to have to crash tonight. Good luck, I hope it all goes OK.'

Kelly is puzzled by Alex's tone. They're all shattered. He's been so amazing these past weeks. What has suddenly changed?

'OK, fine. Well, you get some rest.'

'And Kelly—'

It's too late, she has ended the call.

Late that evening, curled up on the sofa with Max, music playing but not heard, Alex is staring into space, more asleep than awake. He pretends he doesn't hear his phone ring. Max watches him ignore the ringing phone. Max places his large paw on Alex's hand and nudges him. Alex stirs and looks at the missed call: not Kelly or Jesse or Mandy. An unknown number. Dropping the phone back on the sofa beside him he closes his eyes. He is about to nod off when he jerks up, grabs the phone and hits return call. It answers on the second ring.

'Hello, Alex, this is Christine, Jesse's doctor.'

Alex says nothing.

'Are you there, Alex?' Christine asks.

'Yes. I'm here.'

'We have your bone marrow results back.'

'Uh huh.'

'I can't say you're a perfect match, but Alex, you have enough markers for me to go and speak to Mandy and Dean.'

'What are you saying?'

'That, if you're willing, and Mandy and Dean agree to what is a risky procedure given how sick Jesse is, we would be prepared to undertake a transplant.'

'What do you mean, markers?'

'Well, it's quite complicated but we can only consider a transplant if there are a certain number of matching markers between the donor and the recipient. I'm saying you have enough markers for us to do so.'

'You're saying you could give Jesse a transplant from me, and it might work?'

'Yes, if you are prepared to donate and Mandy and Dean say yes to the procedure.'

'OK.'

'What does that mean? I need to hear you say yes.'

'Yes! I mean yes!'

CHAPTER 37

Sandy checks the IV running into Jesse's arm. Dean, Mandy and Sam sit on her bed. Jesse tries to keep her eyes open, she wants to talk to her family, but she can't stay awake. Dean looks over at Amy's bed, stripped bare, her pinboard empty. Once again, he is overwhelmed by conflicting emotions – the sight of the empty bed reminds him that Amy is at home with her family, getting stronger. *Soon, Jesse's bed will be empty, but . . .* He can't finish the thought.

There is movement at the door and Amy, Ryan and Luke appear. Dean nudges Mandy who sees them and smiles, indicating for them to come in. Looking at Dean, she nods at Sam and signals to the door. Dean picks Sam up and the three of them leave the room and join the parents of the three friends.

Watching Jesse's parents and brother leave, Amy, Ryan and Luke climb on the bed with Jesse. Amy strokes her friend's hair and Jesse opens her eyes and immediately her face lights up. She tries to sit up, but can't. Luke snuggles up to Jesse and kisses her on the cheek before climbing off the bed and walking away. Ryan gets off the bed and stands leaning over her face. For several moments they smile at each other before Ryan tenderly kisses her on the lips. A tear falls onto Jesse's face. With nothing more to be said, Ryan squeezes Jesse's hand then slowly walks out of the room without looking back.

Amy lies beside Jesse, cuddling into her as she falls back into a deep sleep. A short while later, Amy is gently coaxed off the bed by her parents. Kelly has come into the room and sits on Amy's bed watching the two girls. Mandy joins Amy and her parents, and she and Amy embrace for a long time. Picking up a beanie from Jesse's bedside table Mandy places it on Amy's head. She watches as Amy's mother helps her daughter from the room.

Kelly is startled when Christine taps her on the shoulder, whispering something urgently to her. Kelly's face registers amazement. Nodding her understanding, Kelly approaches Mandy and Dean.

'Can you join me outside, please?' she whispers. 'Sam can stay here with Jesse; we won't be long.'

Kelly, Dean and Mandy follow Christine and Sandy into a nearby office.

They sit in silence for a moment. Mandy reaches out and takes Dean's hand as they steel themselves for whatever news they are about to hear.

Christine takes the lead. 'I'm sorry to take you away from Jesse but there's something I need to discuss with you.'

'What is it?' Dean asks, annoyed at not being with his daughter, and wanting to hear whatever awful news this is quickly.

'The donor register, I mean, the bone marrow register, a new donor has come on it—'

'What are you saying?' Mandy interrupts.

'It's not a great match, it's probably not even a good match, but—'

'Christine, what are you saying?' Mandy again interrupts. This is almost too much to bear. Are they about to get a reprieve?

'Ordinarily I wouldn't suggest this. Do you remember that we didn't attempt the transplant from Sam until Jesse was strong enough to take it, and she's far from that right now...'

'Doctor, are you saying there's a possible donor out there? Someone who matches Jesse?' Dean asks, his voice rising.

'Yes, but...'

'No buts, there are no buts, please, I beg you to do it. Oh God, Dean, our little girl, our Jesse...' Mandy blurts, close to hysteria.

'Mandy, please slow down and listen to what I'm saying to you, this is very important. It's not a great match but the markers are there, and the donor is willing, but I must tell you of the risks—'

'We don't care about that, what choice do we have?' Dean asks.

'You're right. I agree with you. There's no other option but to give this a try. But you have to be aware that if it doesn't work then it might hasten the end for Jesse,' Christine tells them.

Sandy interjects. 'If we're all in agreement, shall I start prepping Jesse?'

'Yes, straight away. What can I do, what can we do?' Mandy asks.

'Say goodbye to Jesse. I'm so sorry to have to say that to you, but you need to be aware of the possibility that this is the last time you'll see her alive. Her chances of survival, and the transplant taking, are slim,' Christine tells them.

'How long have we got?' Dean asks.

'I have a theatre waiting and the donor is prepped. Fifteen minutes,' Christine says sympathetically.

Mandy throws herself into Christine's arms and Dean hugs Kelly who has been standing with them listening to the conversation, numb with hope. She fights back tears. Breaking free from Dean, Kelly tells him to go and be with Jesse and Sam.

Dean grabs Mandy in a strong embrace, they each wipe the other's tears before rushing back into Jesse's room. Christine and Sandy walk off, planning the upcoming procedure. Kelly stands alone, looking lost. Shaking herself, she takes her phone from her pocket and punches in numbers. Pacing up and down she stares at the phone.

'Come on, Alex, pick up, pick up.'

The line disconnects, she redials, it rings on and goes to voicemail.

'Alex, where are you, please phone me straight away, it's about Jesse. I have news for you, ring me, ring me. Oh, it's Kelly, by the way.'

It's late. Kelly is curled up on her sofa, wrapped in a blanket, her companion, the television, is off, its black screen adding to her sense of despair, a box of tissues beside her. She jumps when her phone rings.

'Hello,' she says.

'It's Alex. You were trying to get hold of me?'

His voice is strangely muffled.

Sitting up, knocking the tissues flying, Kelly yells into the phone. 'Where have you been? I've been calling for hours!'

'I've been busy, what is it?'

Kelly pauses at his abrupt tone.

'Alex, it's Jesse. A donor, we found a donor and she had a transplant this afternoon.'

'How is she, tell me, how's she doing?'

'She made it through, but she's not waking up. We . . . we don't know yet, it's too soon. Oh, Alex, she was so weak, I think it might be too late.'

Alex doesn't respond.

'Are you there, Alex, did you hear me?'

'Yeah, I heard you. What does it mean that she's not waking up?'

'Not good, she should've come around straight away, the procedure isn't that complicated for the recipient. Look, can I come over? I don't want to be on my own tonight.'

Alex tries to roll over on the bed where he lies propped up by pillows.

'I'm not home. I'm sorry, I can't see you tonight. Call me tomorrow and let me know how she's doing?'

Stunned by his response, Kelly hurls the phone across the room.

Shutting his phone off, Alex places it on the hospital bedside table. Rolling onto his side, he winces in pain.

It's still early, but the sun burns brightly when Alex walks out of the hospital and goes to his car. Phoning Steve, he thanks him for taking care of Max and asks if he can stay with him another day, as he's not up to taking care of him just yet.

Knowing he has little to eat at home and suddenly hungry, he drives to a local café. He finds the last vacant table outside and eases himself into a chair. A waitress approaches, handing him a menu. Changing his mind about eating he waves away the menu and asks for a coffee. Leaning back in the chair he watches the passing traffic, oblivious to the noise. The waitress reappears and places a cup of coffee in front of him as his phone rings: it's Kelly.

'Hello,' he says.

There is nothing said in response.

'Hello?' he says again.

He listens for a few seconds before disconnecting the call. He slumps in the chair, staring into nothing, seeing nothing, hearing nothing.

The diners at the table beside him leave, are replaced by other diners who eat and drink and leave. His phone rests on the table beside the untouched coffee. The waitress approaches him, tearing the check from her pad, her signal that this punter needs to order more or move on. Alex slowly stands, using the back of the chair to drag himself to his feet, and walks away. The waitress watches him go. He's forgotten to pay. Screwing up the check, placing it in her pocket, she takes away the untouched coffee.

Alex pauses outside the doors which have opened for him to enter. He looks at the sign he's seen so often: 6 East.

Nudged by others coming and entering the ward he takes a step in. Walking past the nurses' station he looks at the staff there who give him their usual warm smile, nothing else to be read from their faces.

He stops at the entrance to Jesse's room, suddenly overwhelmed with fear. He can only see the backs of Mandy and Dean standing over the bed, Sam sitting carefully at the foot. His heart is racing. Then Mandy laughs softly and moves enough for him to see Jesse sitting up, eyes open, smiling. She sees him.

'ALEX!' she cries out.

As he steps into the room, Sam jumps from the bed. Dean turns and walks towards him, but Sam beats him to Alex, throwing himself at him, hugging him, knocking against his hip. Alex winces and moves Sam away.

'Easy there, Sam,' he says, with a pained voice.

'Sorry, Alex, have you got a hurt? I had a hurt once on my side, it was when I gave some stuff out of my body to make Jesse better, but it didn't work,' he says with the innocence of a child.

Dean walks towards Alex and hears this exchange. He stops in front of Alex and propels him out into the corridor as Sam runs back to Jesse. He places his hand over his mouth to stifle a sob. He stares at Alex.

'Alex . . . it was you . . . Oh my God, I didn't know . . .'

Alex reaches out and grabs Dean's arm.

'There's nothing to say, Dean. Really.'

'Oh yes there is, for now it will have to be the sincerest thank you a father has ever given to another human being. Thank you.'

'Between you and me, Dean, let's keep it that way, OK? Jesse: how's she doing?'

'Early days, early days, but hopeful.'

'Good news. She's just returned the favour.'

'What favour? What are you talking about?'

'I made her wish come true, now she's made mine.'

'Alex, get back in here,' Jesse calls out, her arms outstretched.

CHAPTER 38

One week later

Alex runs from the lifts waving his arms at the doors in front of him for them to open. He's in a hurry. Dodging patients, staff and visitors he signals to the nurse standing behind the nurses' station he's heading her way.

'Is Sandy here?' he asks, looking around.

'She's in her office; do you want me to tell her you're here?'

'Yes, please, ask her to come to Jesse's room, I'll be in there.'

'Her family are all with her,' the nurse calls out as Alex hurries on.

'Jesse,' he calls out, bursting into her room. An empty room. Shocked, Alex walks slowly towards her bed, quickly glances at the noticeboard, breathes a sigh of relief seeing the posters, photos, drawings all where they were when he was here earlier in the day.

Turning to leave the room he hears Sam laughing and sees the door open onto the balcony. Standing in the doorway he watches the family. Jesse in a wheelchair, her parents either side of her, Sam pacing.

'Can we go soon, Mum? Jesse, you don't mind if we don't stay long?' Sam asks.

Before Jesse can respond, Mandy kneels and takes Sam's hands in hers. 'Honey, we will go when it's time. Right now this is where we are meant to be.'

'But Bea, Mum, what about Bea?'

'Bea is just fine. Judith is with her, spoiling her no doubt and letting her sit on the sofa.'

'So where did you get the name Bea from again, Sammy?' Dean asks.

'It's short for Beatrice, Dad.'

'OK, I get that, and?'

'The day before we went to Alex's studio, I was reading a book and the girl in it was called Beatrice. She helped people. Alex helps people and I couldn't name her after him.'

'Excuse me,' Alex says, gently tapping on the glass door.

The family turn around as Alex steps towards them, Sam running and wrapping his arms around his waist.

'I didn't know you were coming back today,' Jesse says, wriggling in her wheelchair to face him.

'Hi, Mandy, Dean, I'm sorry for interrupting your family time,' Alex says, shaking Dean's hand, hugging Mandy, looking into the star-filled night sky.

'We came out here to watch the sunset and it's such a beautiful night, we thought we'd stay out. It's so peaceful out here,' Mandy tells him.

'Alex, hello, is everything all right?' Sandy says, bursting out onto the balcony. 'I'm sorry I took so long; I was on a call and just got your message to come here.'

'Can you leave the ward for a little while?' Alex asks her.

'Yes, if I must. My shift has ended. I'm just finishing up paperwork, I hate leaving it for another day.'

'What's going on?' Jesse yells at her friend.

'I want you all to come with me, just downstairs.'

'What for?' Jesse beats everyone asking.

'It's a surprise, do you trust me? Will you all come with me. Do you think you can stay away from Bea a little longer, Sam?'

'Where are we going, where are we going?' Sam is jumping up and down.

'Will you come with me?' Alex asks, looking at each of them.

'I'm game,' Mandy says, taking a step forward.

'Right, let's go,' Dean adds.

Alex leads the way back into the room ushering everyone out. Sandy walks beside him whispering, 'Is everything OK?'

'Better than OK, Sandy. Follow me.'

Alex leads his troop through the ward to the lifts. When they are all inside, he pushes the button for the ground floor. No one says a word.

When they reach the ground floor Alex leads them through the main reception and down a corridor, where he stops outside a set of double doors and gently knocks. Voices and scuffling are heard behind the door before Kelly steps out to join them.

'What's going on, Alex? Kelly?' Dean asks.

Alex kneels in front of Jesse. 'It's time to make your wish.'

Kelly opens the doors and Alex wheels Jesse into the

room with the others following. They are greeted with loud cheers, clapping and weeping from Amy, Ryan, Luke and their families. Steve with his wife, Sarah with hers, Charlie and Phil, Frank and Ian continue clapping and cheering as Alex wheels Jesse to the front of the room, in the style of a theatre with raised seating. Jesse kicks the foot plates on the wheelchair away and triumphantly stands, laughing and smiling at her friends. Mandy, Dean and Sam join her, soaking up the reception. Finally, Dean lowers his arms several times, indicating the others to sit.

As the room goes quiet, Dean turns to Alex who is standing off to the side. 'Well, Alex, care to tell us what we're doing here?'

Kelly gives Alex a nudge and he steps forward.

'Ah, thank you all for being here. Jesse, I hope you don't mind but Kelly invited everyone to be with you and your family while you watch your wish. Are you OK with that?'

Jesse wraps her arms around Alex's neck. 'Of course I am, oh Alex, is this for real?'

'Yes, all you have to do is sit down with your family and watch. Though before you do, some of Kelly's colleagues are handing out popcorn to anyone who wants it, there will be drinks and nibbles after in the foyer.'

Kelly shows Jesse and her family where to sit. 'Will you sit with us?' Mandy asks Alex.

'Thanks, Kelly and I will watch from the back, if it's all right with you?'

Mandy glances at Kelly, attempting to control a giggle. 'Of course it is, you guys go up the back.'

Charlie dims the lights. The sound of Taylor Swift singing 'You Belong with Me' fills the room as a photo montage of Jesse with her family appears on the large screen. Before long everyone finds themselves soaring with Jesse in the hot air balloon, laughing and running on a beach. The music changes, as Mandy's voice is heard reading one of her poems over a video of Jesse in her room with Amy, out on the balcony looking at the night sky. Sam's drawings come to life, the childish illustration of a dog in so many of his sketches is replaced with Bea, playing with Sam, the family looking on. To the sound of cheers, tears and sobs, whooping and clapping. An hour disappears all too quickly.

Slowly Charlie raises the lights. Alex and Kelly sit holding their breath, waiting for the reaction to die down. Moments drag on before Jesse stands and turns around to face her friends. Her smile tells them how she is feeling, and they jump to their feet, applauding again. Amy runs to Jesse followed by Ryan and Luke and the four teenagers dance together. Mandy and Dean step back, brushing away tears, revelling in seeing their daughter happy with her friends.

Alex puts his arms around Kelly, pulling her into him as they watch the scene playing out in front of them. All the adults are talking excitedly, the teenagers gabbling incoherently.

'Excuse me, can I have your attention for a moment?' Frank says standing at the back of the room. Everyone goes quiet and turns to Frank. Alex stands and looks at his boss, perplexed.

'I know we only met briefly at the studio, I'm Frank

Wallace, owner of TriOptics and, now, Alex's business partner. I just want to say thank you to Jesse.'

Frank pauses, choking back tears, with his voice breaking.

'You are the bravest person I have ever met. You inspire me to be a better person. And Alex, I knew you could do it. I wasn't quite sure what it was you were doing, but my goodness, this is incredible. So, Jesse, thanks to you, TriOptics will be making available a similar wish to any child or teenager going through something comparable. I'll make sure everyone here and at Inspire a Wish knows that.'

Kelly looks at Alex wondering if he wants to say something. She sees how ill at ease he feels, how uncomfortable he is in this environment.

'We have drinks and nibbles in the foyer, why don't we all go out and we can keep on chatting there?'

Slowly everyone moves out of the room into the foyer where drinks and plates of food wait. Jesse sees Frank go to Alex and the men shake hands. She excuses herself from Amy and her parents and approaches the men.

'Oh, Mr Wallace . . .'

'Please, call me Frank.'

'OK, Frank it is. Can I have a hug?' Jesse asks.

Before he can answer she wraps her arms around his neck and kisses him on the cheek.

'There's one more thing I wanted to say to you. I'm feeling strong enough to speak to reporters if you want to arrange an interview, I know that's why you agreed for Alex to meet me.'

Frank pulls away, shaken. 'No, no, that will not happen,

I would never subject you to that, I'm so sorry that I even considered it. Not happening.'

'Thank you. I didn't really want to do it, but I would have for you, for Alex.'

Alex looks down at his friend, astonished yet again by her maturity and generosity.

He puts his arm loosely around her shoulders.

'Well, Jesse. I guess it's a wrap.'

CHAPTER 39

Three months later

'Alex, there's someone here to see you.'

Alex responds to the tap on his shoulder more than the words barely heard through the headphones and the screens in front of him which consume him completely.

TriOptics' receptionist stands behind him with a huge smile on her face. Other heads pop up and look towards Alex, they've all heard her talking in a loud voice to get Alex's attention.

'What?' he asks her.

'There's someone in reception to see you.'

She pauses before continuing.

'A woman, a beautiful woman; she said her name is Kelly.'

'Kelly, Kelly's here?' Alex asks standing, glancing at Steve who grins at him before throwing him a wink.

'Yes, she's asked if she can see you.'

'OK, I'm coming.'

Pushing past the receptionist, trying to ignore the smiles and winks coming at him from everyone in the room,

Alex rushes outside, the receptionist following quickly behind because she doesn't want to miss anything.

Opening the door into the reception area Alex sees Kelly standing, looking at the door she presumes he is coming through. The receptionist nudges him.

'I told her to take a seat,' she says watching as Alex walks towards Kelly.

Unsure what to say or do, Alex returns the warm, loving smile coming from Kelly. He knows the receptionist is watching but doesn't care and gently kisses her on the lips.

'Hi,' he finally says.

'I hope you don't mind me coming to your office, I was wondering if you would be able to have lunch with me,' Kelly says softly.

'Sure, absolutely, is it lunchtime?' he asks, oblivious to what the time could be.

'Yes, kind of, as long as I'm not interrupting.'

'You can interrupt me any time, this is a wonderful surprise.' Alex turns to the receptionist. 'Would you tell Steve I'm going out for a bit?'

The receptionist nods and hurries back into the studio, eager to spread the gossip of Alex kissing a girl, oh and he's taking her to lunch, who knows when he'll be back?

Alex and Kelly walk a short distance to a nearby café, take a seat outside and quickly look at the menus waiting on the table.

'How can you be here, aren't you meant to be at work?' Alex asks Kelly as he reaches for her hand across the table.

'Yes, no, my boss told me to take a half day, I'm apparently spending too much time at work.'

'She's not wrong, is she?'

'Well, these last few months, since you and I, well, I've gotten better, haven't I?'

'Yeah, you have and I'm very happy about that.'

A waitress interrupts and they both order an iced coffee and the same salad sandwich.

Kelly watches the waitress walk away. Alex sees a change sweep over her face. He registers how tightly she is squeezing his hand.

'Kelly, what is it, what are you not telling me?'

'It's Jesse . . .'

'What about Jesse, we saw her what, three days ago, she was fine.'

'No, she's not, Alex, she's not.'

'What are you saying? Kelly, please, what's happened to Jesse?'

'That's the thing about Jesse, she's very good at pretending everything is fine, she wants everyone around her to have a good time, but the bloods don't lie.'

'What are you saying?'

'For the past four weeks Jesse's tests have shown a decline in her acceptance of the transplant, the transplant from you. I'm sorry, Alex, her body has rejected your bone marrow.'

'What does it mean? Does she need more? I'll do it again, I'll do it right now, Kelly we should go to the hospital and do this now.'

'Alex, listen to me,' Kelly says gently. 'Her body has

rejected the transplant, if we did it again, it would be rejected again and we're not going to put her through that. You gave Jesse and her family the gift of more time together, which they never thought possible. You have to understand just how great a gift that was.'

'Where is she?'

'Mandy and Dean brought her back to the ward this morning.'

'Amy, does Amy know?'

'Jesse spoke to Amy, Ryan and Luke last night, they are coming to see her this afternoon.'

'Why didn't you say something sooner? I would have been there for her.'

'You were there for her, you've been with her more than anyone; she didn't want you to know any earlier, she didn't know how to tell you that what you did, going through all the pain of donating, hadn't worked.'

'She knew it was me? I thought only Dean and you knew.'

'Alex, really, Jesse worked it out on day one when Sam told her you had an ouchy on your hip, just like he had.'

'She never said anything.'

'It's not a conversation she wanted to have with you. She loves you more than she can say and didn't want your friendship to be affected by you knowing that she knew.'

'Can I see her?'

'You know you are listed on her admission as family to be admitted any time of the day or night.'

'Is she ...' Alex can't finish the sentence.

'Dying? Remember what I told you when you asked me

that question once before. It only takes a moment to die, the rest of the time we are living. Is her time short? Yes.'

'How short?'

'Days.'

'Here you are, two iced coffees and two salad sandwiches,' the cheery waitress says, placing the drinks and food on the table between them. Looking from Kelly to Alex she realises something is up and silently backs away.

Kelly pushes back her chair, takes the two steps to Alex, and sitting on his knee she cradles his head into her chest, stroking his hair, letting her own tears fall.

'Take me to her, please.'

The door to Jesse's room is closed. Sandy sees Kelly and Alex stop outside, clearly hesitant to knock, to open the door.

'You two can go on in. Amy, Luke and Ryan left a little while ago. There's just Mandy, Dean and Sam with her but I know she would want to see you.'

'Thanks, Sandy,' Kelly says, quietly knocking on the door and opening it.

Dean, Mandy and Sam are all sitting on the bed and look up as Kelly and Alex slowly walk to the bedside. Alex stands at the foot of the bed. Jesse is so frail, so vulnerable, so perfect.

Sensing he is there she opens her eyes and smiles. 'You came, I'm so glad you came,' she says, her voice barely above a whisper.

'Had to see my favourite girl,' Alex replies, forcing a smile.

Jesse weakly turns her head towards Kelly. 'Hi.'

'Hi, Jesse, I found this one loitering around a café and we thought we'd come and see you,' Kelly says.

'Thank you. Would you all mind giving me a few minutes with Alex? There's something I want to talk to him about,' Jesse says, looking between her parents, brother and Kelly.

Alex sees the reluctance in Mandy's face at leaving her daughter. Dean gently takes Mandy's arm. 'It's OK, honey,' he says to his wife. 'We'll be right outside. We can give her a few moments with Alex.'

Not trusting her voice, Mandy lets Dean guide her and Sam out the door, followed by Kelly.

'Can you come close? Please sit here,' Jesse says, patting the bed in front of her.

Alex sits, taking her hand in his, looking into the eyes of the wisest person he's ever known.

'I loved seeing you come with Kelly, that means you were together.'

'Yes, we were having lunch when your name came up, as it does every time we're together, so we thought we'd come and see you.'

'Thank you for not asking me how I am. You know people still ask me that when, duh, it's obvious.'

'Yeah, people can be funny like that. So, how you doing?' Alex says playfully.

'Better for seeing you with Kelly. I think you've finally learnt the lesson of life, the meaning of life.'

'Oh, have I, wise one? Why don't you tell me what it is just in case I haven't fully understood.'

'That letting people into your life, letting them love you

like I do, and loving them back like I know you love me, is the whole point of living, of life, and my final wish for you has been realised. Now you take this lesson you learnt with me and share it with another. I think you know who I'm referring to.'

'I think I do.'

'So, Alex, if you want to be with her and I think you do, then do something about it.'

'I will. I promise.'

'Do you?'

'I do.'

EPILOGUE

One Year Later

Alex, Kelly and Max step onto the beach and look at the scene ahead. A large marquee with a table holding buckets of ice and drinks and huge platters of food, covered to keep the insects off, wait for those gathered. A volleyball net is embedded in the sand: Amy, on one side, is taking on Ryan and Luke on the other. School friends, cousins, grandparents and friends of the Morgans laugh and chatter, watching, and cheering their children who are engaged in various games on the sand. Alex spots Steve with his wife and children building sandcastles, laughing at Ian and Frank taking on a group of teenagers in a game of football and looking ridiculous. They watch Sam and Bea splashing at the water's edge. Max pulls on his lead and Alex bends down and releases him. He runs across the sand to join Sam and his best canine friend. Seeing Max, everyone turns and shouts out to Alex and Kelly who quickly join them, hugs and kisses all round, the volleyball game paused as Amy, Ryan and Luke greet Kelly and Alex.

Mandy watches and waits until Amy, Ryan and Luke return to their game before walking towards Alex and Kelly, they meet her halfway and long hugs follow. Dean joins them.

Alex looks around at the fun and laughter, the joy he sees on everyone's face, everyone who was touched by Jesse.

'This is perfect,' he tells Mandy and Dean.

'It is, isn't it?' Dean says, his arm still around Kelly. 'You know you two are going to be roped into a game of volleyball or football at some stage.'

'I'm up for it,' Alex tells him as the four of them join the other parents and accept a glass of sparkling water.

'You'll stay and watch Jesse's wish with us after, won't you?' Mandy says.

'Absolutely we will, this day of celebration doesn't end on the beach,' Kelly replies.

'I'm starving, when are we going to eat?' Dean asks, taking a step towards the marquee and the food waiting to be uncovered.

'Soon, my impatient husband, soon,' Mandy tells him.

'Ah, before we do, Mandy, can I have a word?' Alex says, drawing looks from Dean and Kelly.

'Take me away, sir,' she says with a wink at Dean, looping her arm in Alex's.

Slowly, unspeaking, they walk away, towards the rocks. Behind them they hear Dean ask Kelly if she knows what's going on, only to be told no, she has no idea.

'Can we climb up onto the rocks?' Alex asks Mandy.

'You sound like Jesse,' she says, kicking her sandals off and

301

stepping up on to the rocks and walking towards the end, to the point where she had watched Jesse so many times sit and talk to the waves.

As Alex joins her, they both sit and dangle their legs over the edge, looking at the retreating tide, their backs to everyone below.

They sit in silence for a while, comfortable in each other's company, staring at the waves beyond, feeling the warmth of the sun on their faces.

'Can I show you something?' Alex blurts out, suddenly overwhelmed with nerves.

'Of course, you can,' Mandy tells him.

From his pocket Alex produces a small box. Opening it, he shows it to Mandy.

'What do you think Jesse would say? I mean, if she was here I think I would probably ask her permission to marry Kelly. After all, it was she who brought us together. Our love for each other is a tribute to her, and spending the rest of my life with Kelly is Jesse granting me a wish I never knew I needed or wanted. And I do, I need and want to be with her.'

Mandy chokes back tears. 'This is the happiest moment I've had since Jesse died. Alex, we all love you so much, and Kelly too. Jesse knew you would become part of our family. You honour her with your love for Kelly, and you honour me by showing me this beautiful ring and making me part of your proposal. Thank you so much.'

'I'm going to ask her tonight. Do you think she'll say yes?'

Mandy touches the ring; the small diamond comes alive with the colours the sun is throwing on it. She looks into his eyes, she feels the love she knows he has for Jesse, knowing right now she is Jesse's proxy. She sees the love he has for Kelly.

'Yes.'

AUTHOR'S NOTE

Hello, and I want to say first a big thank you for reading *The Wish*. This is a story very close to my heart, one that comes from my experience working in hospitals, and one that I hope has touched your heart too. I wanted to tell you how I came to write this story, and what it means to pass it on to you.

In the past I've written historical fiction based on real events; I've had the privilege of being asked to work with men, women and families to recount their stories. *The Wish* is my first contemporary story. I'm told that one of the first lessons at writing classes is to write about what you know. That is what I've chosen to do with *The Wish*.

For over twenty years I worked in the social work department of a large metropolitan hospital. Every day, the women, men and children who came into my life were only there because something tragic or traumatic had happened to them or a loved one. Many of these people I met briefly, their stay in hospital not very long for a variety of reasons. Then there were the others.

The words 'chronic illness' often meant I would get

to know a patient, their family and friends over many months and years.

And then there were the words 'terminal illness'.

In every community, there sadly exists teenagers who are diagnosed with cancer. I have seen the impact a sick child or teenager can have on their family, friends, neighbours, whole communities. It is profound and long lasting. These young people exhibit a maturity and wisdom beyond their years as they comfort, support and uplift those around them. *The Wish* is the story of one such girl and the emotionally isolated computer game designer who comes into her life. Through their story of courage and resilience, I hope to show that it is never too late to reach out, to ask for help.

The Wish is not a story about a particular patient who passed through my life over those twenty years, it is inspired by many patients, their families and friends who I was honoured to meet, get to know, laugh with, cry with. Every one of you inspired me to be a better person. Your bravery and resilience and sheer determination to never give up hope lives with me.

It was one of you who said these words to me: there is no such thing as false hope, there is only hope. That word, hope, is a word I never use lightly but reverently, remembering the many ways it was said to me: *I hope I can live long enough to walk my daughter down the aisle. I hope I can live long enough to hold my first grandchild, I hope my darling child lives long enough to see their tenth, sixteenth birthday.* So many hopes, dreams and wishes were muttered to me. And thanks to the wonderful organisations that exist in many countries, I have seen some of the thousands of wishes by toddlers, children and teenagers come true.

Inspire a Wish Foundation is a fictitious organisation. If you have been moved by Jesse and Alex's story and want to learn more about the various foundations and organisations that 'make a wish' for infants, children and teenagers, please see more information at the end of this author's note.

You might think it is strange I have included infants here. How can an infant possibly verbalise a wish? When infants face a terminal diagnosis, it is their parents or perhaps a sibling who request a wish on their behalf. This could be going to a theme park where the family will take photos of videos of their sick child and remember their time together. It could be something as simple as wanting to return to a homeland that the infant would not otherwise visit to meet extended family, walk on a beach or through a forest, a place that has special memories for their parents.

I remember a grandfather asking for a wish for his baby granddaughter. He wished to walk through a forest to a stream where he grew up, played, swam, taught himself how to skip stones over a stream. He wanted to explain the sights and sounds and his memories of the place to his grandchild, and to video that experience for his family to view later. He wanted to describe to his tiny granddaughter the sound of walking on leaves and twigs, the texture of different trees and flowers, identify the bird songs. With two camera people, one in front, one behind, a sound technician walking beside him holding a boom microphone above him and a nurse, just in case she was needed, his wish was made reality. Tears run down my cheeks as I write this, remembering the wish, remembering that grandfather coming to tell me it was the most loving thing he had ever done and what an incredible experience it was for him and for his baby granddaughter who had reached out to touch the leaves, giggled at his narration.

Memories, that's what making a wish under the most tragic of circumstances is all about. Memories for the living.

My commitment to telling this story is simple. These extraordinary young people and their families can teach us all so much about the importance of family and connection to others, and that it takes but moments to die, the rest or the time we are living – so live. If you can take away only one thing from Jesse and Alex's story, let it be a commitment to pause, think about what you are doing with your family and friends, find something in every outing, event, interaction, to make a memory.

This story is dedicated to Toni, a dear friend, and my brother Ian, both of whom are teaching those of us who are privileged to know and love them the meaning of never giving up as they fight a cancer diagnosis. And to social workers everywhere, in hospitals, in schools, in the community, in the services. Know that you make a difference.

I very much hope you have enjoyed the story I have written in their honour.

– Heather Morris, June 2025

These organisations provide support for children with cancer and their families:

Make a Wish: www.make-a-wish.org.uk

Great Ormond Street: www.gosh.org

Teenage Cancer Trust: www.teenagecancertrust.org

Children with Cancer UK: www.childrenwithcancer.org.uk

Macmillan Cancer Support: www.macmillan.org.uk

ACKNOWLEDGEMENTS

Since 2018 when *The Tattooist of Auschwitz* was released, I have spoken often to my publishing family about a story I had written over twenty years ago. It has been a passion project of mine all these years. A passion project listened to and supported by my friend, my travelling partner, my publishing editor Margaret (Mav) Stead – fellow Kiwi. Its time will come, she repeatedly told me, and I believed her. Its time has come. Margaret, you know how much I love and adore you and I once again write the words: *Ngā mihi nui ki a koe i tō awhina, me tō arahi. Nāu i kawe mai a Hehe rāua ko Alex ki te tūranga pūmau o te ao mārama.* (Thank you for your inspiration, support and guidance. You have brought Jesse and Alex into the light where they belong.)

2024 was an enormous year for me. I had a new book out, my first book was being released globally as a six-part miniseries, I was travelling continuously. I was struggling to settle down long enough anywhere to write this story. Kate Parkin and Bill Hamilton came to my rescue, providing me with the perfect writing location. In a small town in

Normandy, France, the first draft came to life. You are two very special people in my life for many reasons, but I thank you here for the sanctuary of your home.

Thank you, Sarah Benton, for reading my screenplay of this story and encouraging me to write this novel that you now publish.

Tēnā rawa atu koe (Thank you very much) Juliet Rogers, Managing Director and Publisher, Echo Publishing, for your love and support throughout my short publishing career in Australia. Like Sarah, you read the screenplay, loved it and told me to get on and write it.

Benny, Benny, Benny (Agius). To paraphrase *The Sound of Music* – how do you solve a problem like Benny? How do you catch her and pin her down? I'm not going to try. You put your friend hat on when needed, your brilliant publishing hat when needed, your assistant hat all the time, your counsellor hat every now and then. That's a lot of hats for one person but you wear them all with love, support and advice when needed, even if not asked for. Thank you.

Thank you, Justine Taylor, for embracing this story with your editorial eye. Your commitment and passion to making this the best it could be I am most grateful for.

When it came to the final touches, Sarah Bauer stepped in and stepped up. Knowing there are brilliant copyeditors like you out there to fix the myriads of errors from the missed comma to the repeated sentences, makes my life a lot easier. Thank you.

Stella Giatrakou, Rights Director, Bonnier Books UK and her amazing team – Ilaria Tarasconi, Amy Smith and

Tamara Coulthard – who send my manuscripts far and wide and do the deals that produce millions of readers.

I write the words, many of you read the words, and a lot of you listen to the words via audio book. Two outstanding women arrange for this for you: Laura Makela and Chelsea Graham. They find the perfect voice for you and I am so grateful to them.

Clare Kelly, Publicity Director, Bonnier Books UK and her amazing team, Lucy Richardson and Florence Philip, for guiding me through the maze that is promoting this novel, introducing me to incredible people who will review the story, and sending me to wonderful places to meet and engage with readers.

The folks at Bonnier Books UK for their brilliant work: Nick Stearn in the Art Department, Natalia Cacciatore, Holly Milnes, Enisha Samra in Marketing, in Sales – Stuart Finglass, Vincent Kelleher, Evie Kettlewell, Stacey Hamilton and Kim Evans – can never forget the sales team. Thank you all very much.

Emily Banyard, Publicity Director, Echo Publishing, thank you for sending me far and wide across the vast countries of Australia and my homeland New Zealand. You make travelling, speaking and meeting people so easy with your incredible organisational skills. I love travelling and being with you.

While writing this story in the beauty and comfort of Normandy, I was cared for, cooked for, entertained by my wonderful sister-in-law Peggi Shea and my brother Ian Williamson. Thank you so much from the bottom of my heart for being there with me, for me. All your interruptions were welcomed as we enjoyed our environment, ate and drank and laughed our way around the region. No greater companions could I have.

For over twenty years I worked in the Social Work Department of Monash Medical Centre in Melbourne, Australia. Many social workers, experienced and straight out of university passed through the department. My time with each one of you was valued and remembered. If any of you are wondering if Kelly is based on me? She's a little bit of all of you.

Glenda Bawden (boss) you made coming to work every day a joy. Your support not just to me, but everyone who worked in the department, the wider areas of Allied Health, the staff, patients and families, I acknowledge on their behalf and thank you. You are a special human being.

To the patients and families who passed briefly or for extended periods during my time at Monash, I say thank you for touching my heart and it is for you this book has been written. Your courage inspired me every day. Here you were the ones asking for help, not knowing the difference and impact you were having on me, and I dare say, all my colleagues.

I always leave them to last, what is it they say about the last scene of a movie, or the last chapter of a novel – it is what is remembered! Well, my family I leave you to last because it is you I want remembered. You go through every part of the development, writing, publicising of my books. Always encouraging, never doubting I can and will do it – finish what I start. Individually and collectively, you support me to keep going with this incredible 'third act' of my life. Ahren and

Bronwyn. Jared and Bec. Dea and Evan. You are the most important adults in my life.

Some of you are not so little anymore but you remain the reason I get home-sick and can't wait to return home. My darling grandchildren – Henry, Nathan, Jack, Rachel and adorable Ashton. What joy you bring me.

HEATHER
MORRIS

If you would like to hear more from me, why not join the
Heather Morris Readers' Club?

I'll keep you up to date on all upcoming
projects, with early exclusives like extracts, videos and
behind-the-book details; as well as more on all my published
titles including real-life research, deleted scenes and
giveaways.

You can join anytime at
www.heathermorrisauthor.com/heathers-readers-club